The Highlander's Warrior Bride

Book Four: The Stolen Bride Series

By
Eliza Knight

The Highlander's Warrior Bride

Their greatest opponent won't be battled with a sword…
But with their hearts…

Ronan Sutherland is a fierce warrior. Swearing off all else, he thrives on his powerful position within William Wallace's army. Freedom for the Scots is his mission—until he meets fair Julianna. She captivates him, intoxicates him…makes him want more out of life than what harsh dangers he's accustomed to.

Lady Julianna is no meek maiden. She's trained in the art of war, sister to one of Scotland's most powerful men, and tasked with keeping the future king safe. Until she's kidnapped by a rivaling clan. Now her only hope is for the one man she trusts—and desires—to save her.

Together, they'll have to face down one of Scotland's most treacherous foes… And keep from falling victim to the one thing they've both eluded thus far—love.

****

FIRST EDITION
March 2013

Copyright 2013 © Eliza Knight

Cover Design by Kimberly Killion @ Hot Damn Designs

ISBN-13: 978-1482531893
ISBN-10: 1482531895

****

Also Available by Eliza Knight

The Highlander's Reward – Book One, The Stolen Bride Series
The Highlander's Conquest – Book Two, The Stolen Bride Series
The Highlander's Lady – Book Three, The Stolen Bride Series
Behind the Plaid (Highland Bound Trilogy, Book One)
A Lady's Charade (Book 1: The Rules of Chivalry)
A Knight's Victory (Book 2: The Rules of Chivalry)
A Gentleman's Kiss
<u>*Men of the Sea Series:*</u> *Her Captain Returns, Her Captain Surrenders, Her Captain Dares All*
<u>*The Highland Jewel Series:*</u> *Warrior in a Box, Lady in a Box, Love in a Box*
Lady Seductress's Ball
Take it Off, Warrior
Highland Steam
A Pirate's Bounty
Highland Tryst (Something Wicked This Way Comes Volume 1)
Highlander Brawn (Sequel to Highland Steam)

Coming soon…
The Highlander's Triumph – Book Five, The Stolen Bride Series
Bared to the Highlander (Highland Bound Trilogy, Book Two)

Writing under the name Annabelle Weston

Wicked Woman (Desert Heat)
Scandalous Woman (Desert Heat)
Notorious Woman (Desert Heat)
Mr. Temptation
Hunting Tucker

****

Visit Eliza Knight at <u>www.elizaknight.com</u> or
<u>www.historyundressed.com</u>

The Highlander's Warrior Bride

Dedication

To Andrea — Thank you for being my travel companion! Visiting Scotland, and the castles of my tales in particular, was amazing and magical! I'll never forget our adventures! You're a dear friend, and I thank you so much for all your support!

Acknowledgements

Once again, special thanks to Vonda, Andrea and all of my loyal and new readers. These books would not be possible without you!

Chapter One

The tent was dark. Cold. If Lady Julianna had a candle, she'd surely see her breath upon the night air. Puffs of white spilling from her mouth in angry bursts.

Damn the Ross and his ill-fated decisions. Damn the English and their desire to crush the Scots.

If she could go back a few days prior, she would do everything the same way—save maybe tucking more weapons on her person.

At least she wasn't shackled. Although having free reign of a prison cell made of fabric and surrounded by guards wasn't really any better. Her numerous attempts at escape had been quickly thwarted. She rubbed her arms furiously against the winter chill. Her cloak was thick and well made, but after a while, layers did not keep a body warm. Oh, what she wouldn't do for a nice, blazing fire and a dram of Cook's spiced whisky.

Three days ago, she'd been intent on speaking with Lady Myra at Eilean Donan Castle—an act that landed her here within the camp of her enemy.

Even still, she wouldn't change a thing. It wasn't Myra's fault they were kidnapped. She and Myra had gotten off on the wrong foot, and Julianna wanted to make up for it by helping her escape. Although she wasn't sure why Myra would want to leave when she obviously loved Laird Murray, but who was Julianna to judge?

She shrugged in the darkness. Truly, she had no right to pass judgment on anyone. Hadn't she eschewed her own feelings of desire, of passion—of dare she say it—something emotionally deeper? Not that it mattered. Julianna couldn't marry until her brother deemed it so, and for the foreseeable future, that didn't seem to be the case.

She was glad. Marriage would only bind her. Wrap her up in a neat little package and put her on the shelf. That was not the life Julianna wanted. She was a warrior.

Trained in the arts of war. Trained to protect the King of Scotland. Little good that did her now, seeing as how she sat prisoner in this Godforsaken tent, by the devil Laird Ross.

"Humph." She crossed her arms over her chest. Still, she'd not change a thing.

When she slipped into the passageway leading to Myra's room and saw her being carried away—gagged and trussed up—she had to save her. That's what she was trained to do. She had no other choice. Myra had traveled a long way, risked death, all to give Robert the Bruce a message. A message that saved his life.

Following the brutes who dared harm a lady, Julianna thought little of her own safety, only of saving Myra. No one else witnessed her being abducted. As a warrior, Julianna felt it was her duty to see to everyone's safety.

She'd jumped in front of the men, stopping them in their path and demanded they unhand Myra. They'd laughed at her. Right in her face, their breath foul, spittle flying. Julianna ignored their laughter and offered to take Myra's place. That made them laugh harder. And harder. They knew who she was, and she recognized them too. Colin and Alisdair. Two relatively new retainers in Robert the Bruce's army. They knew Julianna was important. But she was sure they didn't know *how* significant. She was a kitchen servant, or at least that's what they thought her to be. It did not go unnoticed that she had the ear of Robert. No one, however, knew just what her role was. They'd kept that a secret. They'd had to. It was the only way to protect themselves.

After all, theirs was an illusion created to distract, to confuse.

Colin and Alisdair took her up on the offer—but then double-crossed her by refusing to release Myra. The bastards. But in the end, that didn't matter, they hadn't succeeded because she'd helped Myra escape. Unfortunately, they could not both escape, there wasn't enough time and Julianna had to distract the guards while Myra ran. Now Julianna only needed to bide her time.

The Bruce would be fine for a day or two without her— albeit by now he was probably in a mighty temper.

As soon as Myra came too, Julianna forced her out of the tent and toward the woods, to freedom. Myra meant nothing to Ross. He'd kill her without giving it a second thought. Julianna, however, was another story. Another story indeed. He wouldn't dare harm her. Not if he valued his life. By killing her, Ross would be signing his own death warrant. And she was pretty sure he knew it.

Though she still wasn't sure if he knew exactly who she was and what role she played, it was evident he wasn't going to take any chances. The fact that she'd sworn on her life and that of the future king's, then declared that she was valuable enough for a ransom only made him double the guards around the tent—and then triple them after Myra escaped. Now, she was trapped by a wall of guards. Escape seemed impossible. *Seemed.*

In truth, she'd already devised a plan.

Reaching up, she touched the two pins that held her hair in a tight knot.

She'd bide her time.

Besides, hadn't she asked Myra to give Ronan Sutherland her regards?

Ronan. Forbidden.

And so much more.

Could they ever have more than witty conversations? She was foolish to think so. It could never happen for them. *Never.* Oh, but how he made her heart flutter… Julianna lay back on the chilly cot and stared into the blackness. , imagining him riding headlong into the camp of their enemy. But, she had a right to her dreams, even if one day they might break her heart. She imagined him riding headlong into their enemy's camp. He'd swipe his sword in one arc after another, cutting them all down. And then he'd spot her. Their eyes would meet, and he'd whisk her up onto his horse and ride away with her.

That was only a fantasy.

No man in their right mind would step into the Ross camp alone. And she'd never ride away with him.

Her duty was to Scotland.

No man besides the Bruce would ever have her loyalty.

Julianna flopped an arm over her face. She was drained. But sleep did not come. She'd barely closed her eyes in the three days since she'd been captured. But she wasn't tired of mind. Her thoughts raced constantly, though her body was beginning to show signs of exhaustion. She often kept herself up days at a stretch, training or fasting to prepare herself for times such as this. The first two days had been easy. This last day was taking its toll.

She was starving. Ross barely fed her. What food he gave her in the beginning she'd given to Myra to aid in her escape. And what food she had now, was barely enough to sustain life. She licked her parched lips. This too she'd overcome.

Perhaps if she just allowed herself to rest a little... On the morrow she'd attempt an escape.

"Get up, bitch!"

Julianna had barely dozed off when she was jolted awake. Sunlight streamed through the opening of the tent where one of Ross' men stood holding a mug and a bowl. His hair was greasy and his clothes equally foul. These men had been too long away from civilization — if the Ross' holding could be called that.

"Your breakfast. Eat up. Ye'll need your strength today. Ross has something special planned for ye."

The way he wiggled his brows gave her cause to shudder, but she kept it hidden and smiled at him, throwing him off balance.

"I certainly do enjoy special things," she answered, proud that her voice came out so clear.

He glowered and slammed the mug and bowl onto the small table in the middle of the room.

"Ye willna enjoy this, I promise."

Julianna laughed and sat up. "I enjoy all things, ye rat."

The man left the tent grumbling about a mad wench.

Good. If they thought her mad, she might gain the upper hand. But panic was also setting in. What sort of *special* things did Ross have planned for her? Being a woman held by a ruthless, cruel man did not bode well. Whatever Ross had planned would be painful, scarring.

"Dammit." Julianna rose from the bed, walked on shaky legs to the table and gripped the mug. It was filled with a yellowish liquid, and one sniff told her it wasn't watered ale.

She flung the mug across the tent and gritted her teeth. Her mouth was parched. Tongue felt swollen. When was the last time she had a drink? She didn't know. Was that vomit? Gazing at the plate didn't improve her mood at all. Where the hell was Ronan? She planned on waiting for him to arrive with reinforcements. Robert would want to take the Ross down. Especially after this injustice. Wasn't that his plan after all? To stamp out Ross and all who served him? Being saved by Ronan was her reward, and she deserved to be rewarded because she had planned to join them in the fight.

But she was too weak and dizzy. Her fingers tingled, and she was certain by the end of the day she would collapse. Her plans had to be altered.

To stay alive she had to escape. There was no other option. As much as she wanted to wait for Ronan, to fall into his arms while he played the hero, *her hero*, she couldn't wait. She had to act now. Crawling toward the back of the tent where she'd cut a slit for Myra to escape—which had been promptly sewn up— she glanced under the hem to see how many men stood on the other side.

They were nearly feet to feet.

She closed her eyes, pressed her forehead to the cool ground and said a prayer for patience, for perseverance, for strength. Pushing herself to her feet, Julianna took a deep breath, and with all her might, shoved her hands against the tent and into one of the retainer's backs.

Anger did not begin to describe the burning feeling that surged through Ronan's veins.

No, anger was an understatement. He was mad with fury. Not even rage did his reaction justice. His very skin was afire with the need to slice, dice and maul ever last Ross warrior.

How dare they infiltrate his camp and steal one of the most fascinating women he'd ever met—not to mention they'd kidnapped and beaten his cousin Murray's wife, Myra. They would pay. Every last devil-worshiping one of them.

And worst of all, how had he not known they had enemies walking amongst them? Ronan was a trained warrior. A man of honor. He was second in command to William Wallace and in charge of training the future King of Scotland's own army. They needed the men, the funds, the training, in order to beat the English. Their bastard king was hell bent on destroying the Scots and taking their country away from them.

He even raped brides on their wedding nights hoping to breed the Scots from their own lands. Well, Ronan was not about to let that happen. He would fight to the death—and be victorious—every last English bastard and any Scot who betrayed their country would fall on his sword. The English could not be allowed to rule here. He wouldn't allow his brothers' and cousins' wives to be raped by the English. No matter what it took, blood, sweat, tears, whatever he had to do, he wouldn't allow his country to be shattered.

Even if it took him the rest of his life. He would fight every Ross wannabe from the east to the west, from the north to the south, and see to it that Robert the Bruce remained in control and that the Scots stayed Scots. William Wallace was an inspiration. A warrior with heart, courage and a set of ballocks Ronan had only seen the likes of in his eldest brother Magnus. Ronan would like to believe that he too had ballocks of iron, his sword certainly was.

But seething about the war wouldn't help anything at the moment. Right now he needed to concentrate on this battle, this mission.

Crouched in the woods, sans his horse, but with two dozen warriors from Robert the Bruce's camp, Ronan had the element of surprise on his hands.

He watched as one particularly vile man entered a tent surrounded by a wall of warriors. In his hands was a mug and bowl. A meal for himself or someone within. Judging from the fence of men, it had to be Ross' tent, no one else needed that much protection. The bastard most likely expected an attack, which meant he was on alert. Male laughter sounded from within the tent, and then the man left, spitting on the ground.

Ronan looked to the side, making eye contact with one of his men and nodded. They retreated back to their horses.

"The tent surrounded by warriors has to be Ross' tent," he said. His men nodded in agreement. "I counted a dozen men lining the tent. Plus another two dozen milling about the camp. There are at least another half dozen scouts."

"Aye, and dinna forget those that sleep within the erected tents." Graham was Ronan's second and he trusted him with his life.

Ronan nodded. He'd spotted tents surrounding a cooking fire. Not a large army of men, but enough to do damage. "I know we are far superior in skill, and we have the element of surprise on our side. Think ye can take on at least four to one?"

All of his men smiled wide in response. They loved a challenge just as much as he did. Ronan could take on half a dozen men at once; he was that confident. His men practiced daily in fighting several men at a time. In a battle situation, one never knew how many men would be on the opposing side. The more men a warrior could fight off, the better chances he had of surviving, especially since the English swarmed the country like ants on a discarded meal. Ronan imagined that all the English did was breed, feed and fight.

Ronan tied his hair back with a leather thong. "I say we make the Ross pay for attacking us. For stealing our women. For siding with the fucking English."

Two dozen men raised their fists in a silent cheer.

"Mount up. We'll surround the camp. But I want three of ye with me to attack Ross' tent. If he's got a dozen guards on the outside, there are probably more on the inside."

They approached the camp on horseback with such stealth that his men were able to surprise the scouts perched in the trees and those upon the ground. No one to warn the Ross of their impending attack. Five down.

A light wind whistled through the trees skimming over his heated flesh, cooling him, and then leaving him with the sense of calm he needed to attack methodically, not emotionally. Julianna was most likely fine. She had to be. Hadn't she attacked dough with a vengeance and faced down the Bruce as though he were a child in need of scolding? The woman had guts. There was no doubt about it. She was safe. He had to keep telling himself that. Julianna would fight with everything she had. She wouldn't let anyone harm her.

But if they had…

Ronan growled, and spurred his mount forward. As they neared the edge of the woods, his men fanned out to encircle the clearing where Ross and his minions had made camp. Why in blazes would they set up camp here? Was it some sort of strategy? It made no sense, why would they choose a spot where they could be so easily surrounded? It was either a very stupid move, or a smart one.

But, Ronan couldn't think on that now.

He narrowed his eyes on the men who surrounded his enemy's tent. Did the tent just move? For a brief moment he thought it was his imagination, that his eyes were playing tricks on him, but they weren't. The tent wavered, sending a guard careening forward. Ronan pulled his horse to an abrupt stop, and stared. What the hell? Was the guard pushed? Did someone inside the tent do it? Julianna? Could it be her?

Was it possible?

Were the men surrounding a prisoner and not their leader?

Was that prisoner Julianna?

Ronan held up his hand for his men to stop. He needed to reevaluate the situation before all hell broke loose.

Chapter Two

Julianna lost her balance. The solid warrior was bigger than she expected—or she was more tired than she realized. She stumbled backward, trying to catch onto anything that would hold her steady, but only managed to grasp the wooden stake that held the tent up in the middle.

Splinters sank into the tender flesh of her palms and she bit her cheek to keep from crying out. Warriors didn't scream from splinters.

The entire structure wobbled. *God's bones*. The last thing she needed was for the tent to collapse. She'd be suffocated or pounced on by angry warriors. Neither option was even remotely appealing. There was nothing else she could do. No other choice. With a shocked cry, she let go of the pike and fell to her bottom on the hard, cold earth. All the air burst from her lungs in one painful, whoosh. She couldn't breathe. This wasn't good. Calm. She had to be calm. If she panicked, it could be bad. She closed her eyes and tried to take a few quick breaths. They burned. Oh God, what was she going to do? She had to get out of this tent.

Shouts sounded all around her and Julianna gaped as warriors began pouring into the tent. The sun beamed through the opening with a blinding glow. After letting her eyes adjust, Julianna ripped one of the long pins from her hair and sliced into the first man's chest. Her pins were specially coated with dried poison. A trick she'd learned from the herbalist in the castle she'd grown up in. The man dropped within seconds, foaming at the mouth.

'Twas potent—crushed poisonous mushrooms.

The next warrior who lunged at her got spiked in the neck, dying more from the perfect hit to his pumping vein than from poison.

Julianna whipped the sword the hilt at her second victim's hip and somehow managed to garner up enough strength to arc it in the air and end her next assailant. Normally, the task would have been easy, but she was feeling more and more depleted as the minutes ticked by.

The next warrior glanced at the downed men and charged, fury in his eyes. He made a fatal mistake. The most important rule of war, and the first one she learned—never allow your emotions to take over your actions. A lesson this warrior learned as she ran him through. Blood soaked her trembling fingers and she dropped the sword and stole a dirk from one of the men's sleeves. Her arms burned. There was no denying it, she was exhausted. She wasn't sure how much longer she could go on. Maybe the dirk would make defending herself less of a challenge.

When the next man entered, she reacted before thinking and flung the knife through the air. Her vision blurred. Something familiar.

The warrior ducked, then cursed when the weapon sank into his shoulder instead of his heart, where she'd aimed.

"Ye've wounded me!" The voice was familiar. But who was it? Her mind was hazy.

She swayed. Felt her body sinking. Her knees hit the ground and she stared at her bloody hands, then at the man who stood in front of her, gripping the hilt of the knife she'd driven into his shoulder. Blood poured from the wound turning his white *leine* shirt red. Chiseled face. Fierce green eyes that reminded her of spring. Lips that made her tremble, for they were made for kissing. No…

"Ronan?"

"Aye, woman. When did ye learn to throw like that?"

She smiled wanly, little black dots floating before her eyes. "At least it wasn't one of my pins."

"Pins?"

Laughter echoed in her head. Or had it come from her lips? "My pins have poison on them." She was delirious. Sharing secrets with a stranger. No, not a stranger. It was Ronan. Wasn't it? Her vision left her. She would die. Any thought to lick the poison from the pin and die before she could be tortured was stopped by Ronan's voice.

"Yet another way ye astonish me." His touch caressed her wrist and she realized she'd reached up to grab the second pin from her hair. "Ye'd kill yourself? After I've come to fetch ye? The Bruce will not be pleased."

She wanted to know if *he* would be displeased. Wished he'd tell her. She longed for him to pick her up and carry her away from here. Desired nothing more than for him to take her to a place where they could change who they were.

"I need ye," she murmured, her voice feeling exceptionally slow, muffled. Her tongue was dry, heavy.

"I'm here, lass," he said.

Julianna was suddenly weightless, and she realized it was because Ronan had lifted her into the air.

"Your shoulder," she whispered, feeling all her strength leave her. She was so tired. So thirsty.

"'Tis nothing."

He lied. She'd seen it buried deep in his flesh. Witnessed the blood. Julianna tried to shake her head, but it ended up flopping back and forth against his uninjured shoulder.

"Dinna fret, lass. Ye're safe."

Idiot. She fretted for his safety, not hers. He could die from blood loss or infection. The man shouldn't be carrying her. Not to mention they were surrounded by Ross warriors. Why the hell had he come alone? And why had she fantasized about it?

"Put me down," she said.

"Hmm?"

Well, she thought she said it. In actuality, she wasn't sure words were passing over her numb tongue.

"I need water," she croaked.

Her body swayed with the movement of his walking. Battle sounds faded in and out of the background. He'd brought more men. She knew he would. Why had she questioned that fact, even for a moment? Ronan was no fool. He was a seasoned warrior. He wouldn't charge in head first all emotional for anyone. Not even her.

Julianna felt herself being tossed over a horse. Her belly hit the leather, and she let out a whoosh of air. Was there a man alive who knew how to be gentle? *God's teeth*. He could have broken her ribs. Then again, she supposed she couldn't expect much gentleness from a man whose shoulder still held the dagger she'd put there. Thank the Gods it was not her own poisonous weapon. Or he'd be dead.

The saddle shifted as Ronan climbed up, cursing from the pain in his shoulder. He grabbed the dagger, yanking hard and then tossing the weapon. He pressed firmly to his wound, sucked in a breath before pulling her into his lap. Water dribbled over her cracked lips and onto her cheeks and chin, when he pressed something to her mouth.

"Open, lass, or the water will do ye no good."

Julianna concentrated on opening her mouth and felt the drops of cold liquid hit her parched tongue. Ronan tilted the skin and it poured down her throat. She choked, and sputtered. Was he *trying* to drown her?

"Easy, lass, easy," he crooned.

His voice was calm, and soothing. So, maybe he wasn't trying to drown her after all. She focused on his encouraging words, and figured out how to swallow as though she were a babe. The cool liquid branded a path down her throat and settled like ice in her belly. Her muscles constricted, and she forced herself not to vomit.

"When was the last time ye had food or drink?" An angry edge rimmed Ronan's words.

Julianna tried to shrug. She wasn't sure she could speak.

"Ye look half wasted away," he muttered. "Let us get ye back to Eilean Donan."

"Ross…" she choked out. She'd not been able to hear her voice before, but this time it was loud, somewhat raw, but intelligible.

"He ran. But we cleaved two-thirds of his army from his grip. The bastard canna run forever."

They'd failed. Ross would come after them again. A ruthless, vicious man, she doubted he would take his failure lightly.

She certainly didn't.

"Shh…" Ronan said, his grip on her tightening. "Dinna work yourself up over it, lass. I swear to ye, Ross will die by the blade of my sword…or yours."

The conviction in Ronan's voice was enough to calm her. She would concentrate on regaining her strength, making sure Ronan was healed, and then she would hatch a plan to dispatch of Ross herself.

For Robert the Bruce's sake, if nothing else.

Hell and damnation!

Ronan's shoulder hurt like the devil. He managed to pull the blade free, but with Julianna across his lap, wrapping the wound had been impossible. Signaling to his men, he spurred his mount on. They would follow when they finished with the camp. Their victory was already assured.

Except Ross had run again. Bastard! He was a cruel coward who felt no remorse inflicting pain on others, but never stuck around to accept the consequences. He was the worst type of evil. One who brutalized with pleasure but wasn't willing to pay the ultimate price.

Without a doubt, Ross would always run. Having sided with the English, the man thought himself invisible.

Ronan's men would hunt him down and bring him back a prisoner.

"*Mo creach.*" A spasm of pain overtook Ronan's shoulder and fresh blood oozed from the wound.

Julianna must have severed a vein. Weakness threatened his limbs, but he forged ahead. Eilean Donan was not too far from where Ross had made camp. When he arrived he'd be sure to send out more men to scour the woods.

Ross would not be allowed to run forever. He'd not make it back to the fortifications of his castle. Or to the vile English. He would pay—and suffer—sooner rather than later, and Ronan would see that it happened.

As soon as he got his shoulder taken care of.

He peeled back his woolen plaid that wrapped around his shoulders to keep him warm. The linen of his shirt had turned red across his chest and down the length of his arm. Blood loss. A lot of it.

He widened his eyes, forcing himself to remain strong. The pain subsided, now it felt numb around the edges…and on his fingers. That couldn't be good.

Good Lord, what a pair he and Julianna made.

The beauty in his arms, passed out—most likely from the onset of starvation. If she didn't ingest something within the hour she might not survive. And he was losing blood faster than his heart could replace it.

Ronan should be furious with her for injuring him, but he wasn't. He was in awe of the lady. Running around Eilean Donan like a drill sergeant dressed as a kitchen maid. He couldn't figure her out. She could knead bread and chop carrots like no other. Yet, when the Bruce spoke with her in private, he always came back to the men with sound advice. Sometimes better advice than even Ronan or William Wallace gave him regarding plans he had for fighting the English, training his men or fortifying the castle.

Julianna was an enigma.

He might not know who she was, but for certes she was no ordinary kitchen maid. No matter how decadent her rosemary garlic bread was smothered in melted butter.

His stomach growled. A welcome sensation. He wasn't dead yet. And though his shoulder and arm were numb he still had feeling in other areas.

Ronan groaned. Julianna shifted restlessly in his arms. Her body temperature had risen since he'd found her and heat seeped from her flesh into his. She was feverish. That had him worried. But he was also worried about how her fevered flesh and lush curves were affecting him. Blood rushed straight to his groin. Damn. He needed that blood!

He looked toward the heavens, taking in the sun as it beamed through a puff of white cloud, and willed his body to behave. Curse his body. Now was not the time. He needed to concentrate on getting them back to the castle without further injury.

A heavy trod of hoof beats echoed in the forest behind him. Ronan squeezed his mount, urging him spring forward. He didn't know who followed. While he'd fight to the death, it would come quick considering he was having a hard time staying upright on his horse.

Fear tried to find a place in his mind, but he wouldn't allow it.

"Hold tight, Lady Julianna," he muttered, not knowing whether she was lucid enough to comprehend him.

She must have understood some of it as she snuggled closer and whispered something unintelligible.

"Faster, Saint!" he growled to his horse.

Saint lowered his head and surged forward. With his good arm holding Julianna, Ronan wasn't able to use his sword to block low hanging branches. Several thin ones whipped into his face. Luckily, the larger ones he was able to see in time and duck.

"Ronan!"

He could have sworn someone just called his name. It seemed like his ears were stuffed full of sheep's wool. Everything was muffled and echoed at the same time.

"Slow down, man!"

Graham. Ronan slowed, and his second galloped up beside him.

"Jesus, ye look like hell. And ye're covered in blood. Yours—" Graham nodded his head toward the unconscious Julianna. "Or hers?"

"Mine," Ronan croaked. His mouth was dry and he was suddenly parched. So thirsty, he might cut off a man's hand in order to get to a drink.

"Let me wrap it." Graham's words held no room for argument.

Ronan slowed Saint to a stop. Graham ripped a strip of linen from his shirt and wrapped it tightly around Ronan's shoulder. Hissing from the pain, Ronan forced himself not to punch Graham in the nose.

"Ye've lost a lot of blood, man. I'm surprised ye're still sitting that horse."

"I've more important things to worry over than losing my seat."

"What about your life?" Graham frowned. "Give me the lass. Ye need all the strength ye can muster. And ye might want to block some of the branches. Ye look like your overlord took a whip to your face."

Ronan glowered and tightened his hold on Julianna. He didn't want to surrender her.

"Give her to me, Ronan."

"Ye do not issue me orders." He tried for overbearing, but instead his voice came out weak, and the effort he'd used made him dizzy.

"No, I dinna, ye're right about that. But I did take an oath to protect ye, and I intend to do it, even if 'tis from your own stubborn arse. Now give me the lass."

Reluctantly, Ronan attempted to lift Julianna from his lap. She moaned, her head rolling from side to side. He was loathe to admit that he couldn't lift her. When had he become so weak? What had he done to deserve such a demeaning feeling? He felt no better than a babe out of the womb.

Graham simply reached across his horse and plucked Julianna from Ronan's lap.

"I'll keep her safe, I promise."

Ronan narrowed his eyes at Graham, who avoided his gaze. *Graham promised?* Oh hell, that sounded like more than just a pledge to do his duty. Did Graham know he had an interest in the lass? Was it possible that others had seen Ronan's interest in her as well? No good at all. Ronan had absolutely no plans, whatsoever, *ever*, to settle down with a woman. No matter how much she captivated him.

He was ensconced in the war for Scottish independence. A warring man. No woman deserved to tie herself to a man who would make her a widow.

Julianna was worthy of more than that. And that was all he would think on the matter.

'Haps when he returned to the castle, had his shoulder stitched up and twenty drams of whisky in his system, he'd prove he wasn't interested in taking a wife by bedding down with three or four of the female servants. There were plenty who'd offer him services. The one toothless gal had been particularly good at...

Ronan's lip twitched with disgust. He was an arse. No women. Just whisky and sleep.

"Go," he ordered.

Graham took the lead and Ronan followed. He was finding it more and more difficult to keep his eyes open, if he hadn't grabbed a handful of his horse's mane he might now be laying on the ground. It felt like an eternity before they reached the bridge leading over Loch Duich. Eilean Donan sat on her island surrounded by mist. She was ethereal, but intimidating all the same. Shards of sunlight glinted off the weapons of the guards atop the tower. Arrows pointed at their hearts.

Graham raised his arm and sounded their call so the guards would know who they were. A return call split the midmorning air, and they took the cue to cross. Praise God. They made it. The clopping of horses' hooves on the bridge was a welcome sound. Soon he'd be sewn up, liquored up, and warm beneath a pile of blankets. His skin prickled with chill, his teeth chattered and his eyelids quivered. Damn. Only a few more feet.

"Cold," he said.

"What's that?" Graham called behind him.

"I'm…cold."

Just before the end of the bridge, Ronan felt himself slipping. He grappled ineffectively with the reins, with the saddle, with Saint's mane — anything that he could grab hold of, but everything slithered through his fingers. He clutched his thighs tighter, but it was like his legs were made of grass, no strength, no stability.

He was falling. *Ballocks*. This was not happening.

But it was. And the impact of his head hitting the bridge hurt like the devil. He was not a weak man. He did not feel pain like ordinary men. That's what he kept telling himself. He willed himself to get his lazy arse off the bridge. However, it was easier thought than done. Pain seared across his head, his shoulder. He felt like he'd been dunked in the frozen loch, attacked by wild animals.

"*Mo creach*," he mumbled before passing out.

Chapter Three

A savory scent wafted back and forth beneath Julianna's nose. She found herself following the smell, much like she'd seen her horse do when she offered him a treat.

What was it? She was starving. Thirsty. Dying to get her mouth on whatever that delicious smell was.

"Wake up. Come now, take a sip."

Heavens yes, she would!

Her eyelids were heavy, her limbs heavier. She could barely move, but she forced her eyelids open. The light was bright, searing a painful blindness. Julianna blinked, then focused on Lady Myra who sat beside her. The woman was beautiful and put together as always. Well, not always. When Julianna first saw her, Myra had been quite a mess. But having escaped death, it wasn't completely out of the question for Myra to have appeared the way she did. Now her skin looked like strawberries and cream, her raven hair glossy and neat.

Utterly feminine. Not like Julianna.

Julianna was propped up on pillows in her chamber. The scents of her soap and dried flowers a familiar comfort. One of only a few she allowed herself. A fire burned high in the hearth making her chamber warm and inviting.

"Ye're back." Myra's smile was genuine, pleased. "I feared I might have to force this broth down your gullet."

Julianna managed a weak smile. "I dinna have a gullet, I'm a lady. I sip."

Myra laughed. "Apologies." She held a wooden spoon to Julianna's mouth and she greedily drank.

The broth tasted better than anything she'd ever consumed before. Or 'haps that was the starvation talking, but the liquid was warm, tasty and bordering on hot, just the way she liked it.

"Careful, not too fast," Myra cautioned. "Ronan says he wasn't sure when ye ate last."

Julianna took another sip. Beef. It was definitely beef broth with a hint of onion and rosemary.

"I dinna know," she managed to say. How could she tell Myra that she'd given her everything, and eaten nothing since she left? Julianna didn't want her friend to feel like it was her fault that she lay here weak and helpless as a newborn calf.

"Did ye eat while being held in the Ross camp?"

Julianna bit her lip, not wanting to confess. "After ye left, they gave me piss to drink and vomit to eat."

Myra's eyes widened and she stilled. Julianna managed to reach up and guided the spoon to her mouth. The broth really was delicious.

"Ye jest," her friend said.

Julianna gave a feeble laugh, then lied, "Aye. They simply forgot to feed me. I was a prisoner, not a guest."

Anger flashed in Myra's eyes.

"Ye weren't a prisoner, but a victim."

Wrong words to utter. "I am never a victim." Julianna spoke with vehemence. She struggled to sit up, pushing up on her elbows, then managing to scoot her hips back. Every muscle, bone and joint ached. "I shall feed myself. Go and do whatever it is ye do."

Myra looked taken aback, her lips thinning somewhat. "I meant no offense. I was merely angry over how they treated ye."

Julianna swallowed back a retort. She would be the first to admit that her temper was short, that there was no middle ground. She could be sweet one moment and through the roof the next. Myra was a friend. Not her enemy. She'd brought broth to help her regain her strength. Snapping at her was not right. She owed Myra an apology.

Knowing all this, however, only embarrassed Julianna further. She just wanted to be left alone. Wanted to finish her broth in peace. Then she'd take a nap, and when she woke, it would be time to dress and search for Robert the Bruce. They had much to discuss, first and foremost her apology for allowing herself to be taken. Whether or not she'd confess that she went willingly was a matter she'd not yet figured out. "I would like some time alone. To rest."

Myra stood, rolled her eyes and thrust the warm bowl of broth at Julianna. "I thought we'd gotten over the impasse that seemed to be our relationship. That after what happened, we'd forged a bond. I suppose I was wrong."

Myra whirled and headed for the door. They had come a long way. Things had changed since Julianna spied on Myra and refused to speak to her. They were friends now.

Julianna bit her lip to keep choice words from flying out. "Wait."

Myra turned around, arms crossed over her chest. "Aye?"

"I'm...sorry. I'm verra tired."

"As expected, in fact, I didna even think ye'd wake. Ye look like hell and at least a stone lighter than when ye left."

Julianna frowned into the broth and took another sip. "I'm not used to having...friends."

And she wasn't. Friends had never been a luxury afforded her. Life had been all about her studies, her training, and when she was deemed fit, she was given her duty to Scotland. Whenever she'd attempted to play with other children, she'd been hauled back in for more preparations. At the time it had seemed cruel, but now she understood why. A person in her position couldn't have close, meaningful relationships. The loss was too strong. That much she understood and she respected her mentor for taking away her choice to have companions or friendships.

"Are we friends?" Myra looked hopeful.

With the arrival of Myra, Julianna had been given a rare gift. The chance to form a rapport with another female. It probably wasn't the best course to take, but heaven help her, she desperately wanted someone she could talk to... Not just any someone — another woman. Myra. Julianna longed to tell her about the feelings sweeping through her. Forbidden or not, she couldn't deny how they made her feel. How *he* made her feel. Maybe Myra could give her some advice. After all, Myra had already pledged her life to the man she loved, and that man, the one she'd married wasn't who she was promised to. Myra had to know something about forbidden love. Didn't she?

Oh, what was she thinking? It didn't matter anyway. In a few years Ronan would be married. And not to her. She shouldn't be thinking about him, let alone speaking about him. She could be friends with Myra, but she could never allow herself to open up.

Opening up was out of the question.

"Aye. We're friends."

"Good. Then as a friend, I want to thank ye for saving my life. Rest now. I've told everyone ye're not to be disturbed."

Julianna shook her head and set the bowl on the side table. "Nay. I must speak with Robert immediately."

Myra frowned. Oh hell. Julianna slipped and referred to the Bruce by his name. Being too at ease with Myra could be dangerous. She may have to rethink her need for friendship. Myra stepped back toward the bed.

"Ye might use more caution. I know not the nature of your relationship with the Bruce, but I do believe it may turn heads if anyone else were to hear ye address him so familiarly." Myra looked around like she expected someone to jump from within the walls. "I tell ye this as a friend."

"'Tis nothing like that!" Julianna's exasperation showed in her outstretched hands and widened eyes. "I told ye that I've his ear, that I protect him, but never in this lifetime or the next would he be my…lover." The thought of it brought bile to her throat. She could say no more. "I hope ye'll trust in what I say."

Myra chewed her lip. "There was a time that I would have said no, but I do trust ye. I canna say for certain that Daniel does."

Daniel Murray, Myra's husband, had been a questioning thorn in Julianna's arse since he arrived at the castle to help train the retainers. Not only was he Ronan's cousin, his cousin Andrew Moray, who had been Wallace's leader, was the reason Wallace welcomed him into the fold.

Ronan took Daniel aside the last time she'd seen him, and he hadn't bothered her since. Albeit, that was only a day or two before she went with the Ross traitors to save Myra's life.

"He still doesn't trust m, even after I returned ye to him?" Men were so damn stubborn. Even Ronan for all his handsomeness and bravado was a stubborn mule. She'd nearly forgotten… "How is Ronan? His shoulder?"

Heat crept into her cheeks and she resisted the urge to cover them with her hands.

A flash of fear crossed Myra's features, and Julianna watched with anxiety as her friend squared her shoulders and jutted out her chin. "He's resting."

"And...?" Julianna prompted.

"In his chamber." Myra fidgeted with the coverlet, pretending to straighten it. "Well, I'd best be going."

"Wait!" Julianna called as Myra rushed to the door. But the minx didn't stop. Didn't even turn around. She whipped open the door and flung herself into the corridor in her haste to get away.

This was not good. Something was wrong, else she would have told her more about Ronan.

Was he resting...with the Lord? Oh God. Had he died? She'd never be able to live with herself if she killed him. Mustering up her strength, Julianna tossed her covers aside and frowned down at the frilly nightgown she wore. Where had it come from? She didn't own a thing like this. In fact, Julianna slept in the nude. Normally hot blooded, if she wore clothes to bed, she would sweat. It had to be Myra's. Perhaps Myra had left her a robe to wear as well.

But she didn't see one. Julianna shifted her legs, uncomfortable with how heavy they felt, over the side of the bed. She was still weak. Roaming about the castle was not the best idea, but she had to know how Ronan fared.

She wiggled her toes, watching them curl in and out. Toes appeared to be functioning well. Nobody understood how important suitable working toes were for walking. Toes kept a body balanced and could easily grip the ground harder to keep one from wobbling.

Julianna stood. Her legs shook, knees knocking together, and her breaths quickened. Oh, God...She sucked in several breaths to keep from vomiting. Dizziness took her vision for a moment. She gripped the ground with her toes, hands searched for the post of the bed. She willed herself to stay upright, and finally her vision returned.

"Ye can do it," she chanted to herself.

She managed to make it to her wardrobe without passing out. At least that was progress. Chills raced along her limbs, so she reached inside the wardrobe pulling out her cloak and boots. She tucked the laces inside, not bothering to tie them. There was no time, and quite frankly she wasn't sure she'd be able to bend over without falling or losing consciousness. Standing was an effort in and of itself.

Julianna shuffled slowly to the door using whatever she could find to balance herself—the foot posts, the wall, a chair and finally the door. She leaned her head against the wood and took several deep breaths.

The more she moved, the better her balance. Her will to continue improved her equilibrium.

She opened the door and stepped into the corridor. Where was Ronan? He usually slept with his men in the barracks.

But Myra said he was resting in his chamber. Where in the hell was his chamber? Was it the one a few doors down from hers, or the empty one behind the great hall? She hoped it was the one a few doors down, because attempting the stairs was a bad idea. She wouldn't be the first person to die from a fall. Even though her strength appeared to be improving, she didn't want to push her luck.

Using the wall to steady herself, she made her way down the stone corridor. She stopped in front of the chamber door, and prayed Ronan was inside. The door was not barred and so she pushed it open. A dim light came from tallow candles ensconced in two different iron candelabras as well as a modest fire. The shutters were tightly closed, making the room cozy, and warm. Lying in the center of the bed with his eyes closed was Ronan, his massive size taking up a good portion of the mattress. Stubble covered his chin and his light-colored hair lay on the pillow, though a few strands had fallen onto his forehead. Full lips were parted, as though awaiting her kiss. He was shirtless, and except for the bandage at his shoulder, his torso was completely exposed. His chest rose and fell in even, steady breaths. She wanted to touch him. To run her hands up and down his broad, muscular, sun-kissed, chest. She imagined how it would feel to caress him, to let her hands travel downward, following the trail of hair that led too... Oh hell. Forbidden thoughts. She needed to clear her mind. This could only lead to trouble.

Julianna bit her lip. He was even more impressive than she'd imagined. Her belly twisted and she leaned against the door jamb to keep herself upright.

Candlelight made his hair shine golden-red, and beads of sweat slicked his locks to his skin. Fever. Nay. Please God. But it was obvious, his body was raging with fever.

A fever she'd caused.

What if he died? What would she do? She shook her head. That wouldn't happen. Couldn't happen. He was young, strong and had the will to live. More will than anyone she'd ever known. He would be fine. He had to be, because she couldn't live without him. Guilt riddled Julianna. It was true, she couldn't live without him — even if she had no other choice. She pushed into the room and moved toward the bed. Beads of perspiration lined Ronan's brow and upper lip, and his chest was slick with fever. He murmured, and his legs and arms shifted for a moment before he went still again. Too still. Julianna focused on his chest to make sure he breathed.

Wanting to ease his discomfort, she glanced around for something, anything. A basin of water and a linen square sat on his bedside table. She dipped the cloth in the cool water and pressed it to his forehead and then to his cheeks wiping away the droplets of sweat that beaded there. Rinsing the linen, she repeated the action, though this time pressed it to his parched lips, letting a few drops dip into his mouth.

"I'm sorry," she whispered. "If I'd the ability to see the future, I'd not have thrown the dagger."

Julianna continued to bathe him in cool water, pressing the cloth to his neck, his shoulders. She dared not go lower, although her eyes roved over the massive expanse of muscle displayed before her. Ronan was like one of the ancient Gods come to life. Power exuded from every inch. She found herself biting her lip, unable to pull her gaze away from the dips and ridges of his tight abdomen.

"Ye must be cold," she mumbled and pulled the coverlet up to his neck. Really an effort to hide his bare flesh from herself.

Ronan thrust the blanket back down—this time even further. The coverlet lay haphazardly against his hips. His chest hair tapered to a light crisp line that disappeared beneath the dreaded blanket—teasing her, tempting her to pull it further down and see if he was…

Oh, Saints! Was she really wondering if he was nude?

He couldn't be. Wouldn't be.

Save…a sick man never lay in bed with his plaid. Nay, someone would have seen that braies were at least put on to cover his parts.

Wouldn't they?

Julianna let out a grunt of disgust and tossed the linen square into the basin. Water splashed from the bowl, landing in droplets on the table and floor. She glared at them but didn't bother to wipe them up. Instead she stalked—well as much of a stalk as she could muster in her present state—to the window and pulled open a shutter to stare down at the bailey below. A cold gust of air stunned her for a moment.

Warriors trained, servants worked. All looked normal. But Ronan was laid up in bed with a fever. Wasn't anyone the least bit worried about him? Anger filled her. She wanted to hit something. Didn't anyone care? Tears stung her eyes. She wasn't mad at everyone else, what could they do? They had to keep the castle protected.

The English wouldn't stop coming at them because Ronan was injured. Laird Ross wouldn't cease his scheming. If she was mad at anyone it was herself. She shouldn't be here. In Ronan's room. It was off limits. He was alive. Good. That's what she wanted to know. She prayed the fever would dissipate. But, there was nothing more she could do. 'Twas time for her to get dressed and meet with Robert. They needed to devise a plan. She needed to apologize for her absence and for having injured one of his best men.

"Julianna…"

Julianna whirled around. There was no one else in the room besides her and Ronan.

Had he called her name? He seemed to be sleeping peacefully. Was he dreaming of her?

"Julianna…" he said again, and this time she watched his lips move to form her name. Never before had it sounded so sensual.

He shifted, then hissed when he jerked his injured arm.

"Dinna move," she said urgently, rushing to the bedside, and falling against it as a bout of dizziness took hold. She gripped the sheets and waited for the shakiness to subside. When it did, she stroked his arms, putting them back at his sides. "Ye dinna want to injure yourself further."

Ronan opened his eyes. Red-rimmed, glassy and bloodshot. Filled with fever. His gaze connected with hers.

"I willna let him harm ye, lass," he said. His voice was a harsh croak.

"Shh… We're safe now. Sleep."

He shook his head, then looked about the room as if demons were falling on him. "Nay. He'll be back. I must protect ye." Ronan gripped her arm tight and yanked her down so she draped over his chest, her face an inch away from his.

"We're safe, ye dolt, now let go of me." Julianna quelled the bit of haughtiness that edged her tone — the man was obviously not himself.

"I'll never let go," he whispered. Ronan slid his hand up her arm, giving her more goose flesh than she already had. He gripped the back of her neck and tugged, closing the distance between them. His lips tenderly brushed hers.

What in all of heaven was he doing? She tried to pull back but he only held her tighter. Decadent, foreign sensations stirred within her.

Julianna sighed and kissed him back. Her first kiss.

Ronan's lips were moist from the water she'd pressed there. Soft, full. Sparks of something wonderful fired inside her. She'd never dreamed that the touching of lips could be so wonderful.

But it was over all too quickly. Ronan gripped the sides of her face and forced her to look into his eyes. Were they more lucid than moments ago — or were hers more cloudy?

"Dinna go far, lass," Ronan said, then promptly fell asleep.

Chapter Four

"Glad to have ye back with us. Took your sweet time."

Ronan blinked to adjust his eyes to the light streaming through an open window. His head pounded, shoulder throbbed and he was in need of a good scrubbing, but otherwise, he felt strong.

Lifting up onto the elbow of his uninjured arm, he saw Robert the Bruce standing at the base of his bed.

"My lord," Ronan croaked, disturbed by the sound of his voice. "How long have I been in here?"

"A week."

Damn. Seven days? How had that much time passed without him even being aware of it?

The Bruce grinned. "Lazy arse."

Ronan chuckled. "I was due a break, nay?"

"Nay. But 'twas not your choosing."

"Julianna," Ronan said, the memory of her throwing the dagger coming back.

"Aye?"

"Where is she?"

Robert went to the window and looked out. "I've ordered a bath to be brought up. The healer doesna think ye should eat much food yet, so only a porridge and ale is set on the table for ye. Once ye've garnered your strength a hearty meal is in your future."

"And where is Julianna?" Ronan was irritated with how his future king avoided the question.

"She is not your concern." The man's voice was placid, giving away nothing.

Ronan sat up all the way, pleased when dizziness did not accompany the sudden move. "Ye didna punish her did ye?"

The Bruce whipped around, a fierce glower covering his features. "I said she was none of your concern. Ye brought her back; that was your task. Now ye must see to my army."

"What of Ross?"

"Still running."

"I will go after him."

"Ye have a duty here."

The man was stubborn as a mule. Not willing to budge no matter how hard his arse was pushed. How could he make him see reason? "Aye. But I also have a duty to ye, my lord. And the Ross is a danger to ye, to Scotland. I want to take him out of the equation."

Bruce grunted. "We'll discuss it later. Wallace needs ye down in the barracks. Ye've had an onslaught of new recruits. Seems the threat of the English coming this spring with a massive army has finally reached more ears. Despite it being winter, men are coming in droves."

"We had best make sure none of them are spies."

"Daniel and Wallace have been working on that. But they need your help. When ye've cleaned up and eaten, go see Wallace."

Ronan nodded. "Aye, my lord." He'd had a chance to recover from his fever, but this was war and harsh times, which did not allow lenience for a man of his importance.

Robert left the room.

With a deep sigh, Ronan tossed back the coverlet and stood, stretching his limbs and enjoying the chilled air on his nude body. Despite Ronan having lain abed for several days, his legs weren't as shaky as he'd thought they'd be.

A flash of Julianna's face, her lips, came to mind but he thrust them aside. Bruce was right, she was not his concern. The last thing he should be thinking about was her.

But the thought wouldn't leave. If anything, it only grew. Real. Raw. Potent. A soft brush of her plump lips. Her breath on his face. The crush of her plush breasts against his chest.

A dream, nothing more. He'd been in a fevered state for days, no doubt his imagination acted out every wicked desire he had—and Julianna was definitely one of them.

However much he desired her, Julianna was a guilty pleasure he'd never indulge in. Not only was marriage not in the cards, but Robert the Bruce held a special fondness for her. Not in a romantic sort of way, more like a protective...older brother? Come to think of it, Robert treated Julianna a lot like Ronan treated his younger sister Heather—except Ronan would never take advice from Heather. She was a free spirit, and still young. But even if she were older, Ronan doubted he'd take her guidance on strategy. Hell, she'd have him taking on the entire English army by himself.

Ronan rolled his eyes. Robert couldn't be Julianna's brother. Or could he? But if he was, wouldn't everyone know? It didn't make sense to keep something like that a secret. Wouldn't it put

Julianna in more danger? Would the Bruce put her at risk? And for his own personal gain?

Servants knocked on the door pulling him away from his thoughts. What did he care? It was none of his business anyway. His aching bones craved the warmth of the water, and he watched as the servants quickly placed the tub near the fire and filled it with buckets of steaming water. As much as Ronan wanted to sink into the tub's depths and linger for hours, he hurried through his ablutions, scrubbing every inch of sickness from his limbs. He climbed from the tub, forcing himself not to shiver, and dried off. On a chest he found his freshly cleaned plaid and a folded linen shirt.

Ronan hurried to dress, and gritted his teeth, as he struggled into his shirt. He strapped his claymore to his back, and choked down the cold porridge, trying not to gag at the cold, sloppy texture.

The throbbing in his shoulder subsided with a swig of whisky.

"Ugh," he growled and shoved the bowl aside. He loathed porridge. Always had.

Washing down the last of the ale, he stomped toward the door, hoping the rest of his day went better than the beginning.

Ronan hoped to see Julianna. But she was nowhere to be found. He hid his disappointment as he made his way out of the castle and into the barracks. He'd even made a detour through the kitchens hoping to catch her kneading bread—but she wasn't there. He had hoped to see her fingers sinking deep in the dough and maneuvering it with precision. Och, the vision of Julianna and the dough made his cock hard. God's teeth, had the fever addled his brain? He shouldn't be searching her out. She was off limits—and more trouble than he needed. So, why he was looking for her? He knew why, just didn't want to admit it.

The blast of cold air whipped against his face, and brought some sense back to his brain, taming the wild beast that threatened to run rampant around the castle grounds until he found her.

Something didn't feel right. It wasn't only the Bruce's refusal to tell him where Julianna was, but something in the air. He couldn't quite explain it, didn't really understand it, except to say something felt off.

"Ronan! Ye're awake!" William Wallace's roar from atop the gate tower rescued him from his thoughts.

He raised his hand and waved. "I was never asleep," he called back.

Wallace laughed. "Always a warrior."

"Never a bairn," Ronan answered with a chuckle. He sauntered across the courtyard nodding to other warriors as he went. Some wished him well, others jeered at him for having lost consciousness over such a trivial wound. But the results were the same, the people at Eilean Donan, the men within the Bruce's forces, respected him.

Respect was something Ronan had wanted for as long as he could remember. Not that his home life wasn't full of love, friendship—and respect. But it was a different kind. Ronan being the third son, no one expected him to grow up to be a leader. He was taught to fight with a sword, how to write his name and do arithmetic, but no one cared how he fared. Or at least that was how it appeared. His mother thought he might like to be a priest, and his father never told him otherwise. They'd died, a terrible tragedy, when he was just a boy.

From a young age, he'd looked up to his oldest brother Magnus. Not only as head of the clan, and as his leader, but as an example to follow. Magnus was a man others compared themselves too. A true hero if there ever was one. Ronan often emulated what his brother did—as did his brother Blane, who was a few years older than himself.

Ronan wanted more. He didn't want to be a priest. Didn't want to stand in the shadow of his brothers. He wanted to make a name for himself. And that's what he did. He pushed himself hard to excel as a warrior, and Magnus took notice. In return Magnus had heaped duties on him within their clan's army, and Ronan couldn't have been happier. But when William Wallace saw him in battle and offered him a place in the future King of Scotland's army, it was an opportunity Ronan could not pass up. And he was glad he took the proposition.

He was no longer in his older brothers' shadows. Here, he was a leader of men. The sky was the limit, and he was reaching for it.

Ronan climbed the stairs to the battlements where Wallace waited. A bit winded, and slightly dizzy, he leaned a hip against the stones and stared out over the loch and land, as he tried to hide the fact that he was catching his bearings. A sennight in bed with fever had left him slightly weak, but he didn't want the men to see that. And his shoulder hurt something fierce.

"See anything?" Ronan asked.

"I see a lot of things."

"Anything that raises alarm?" Ronan didn't bother to hide the sarcasm from his voice.

Wallace frowned. "Nay."

"Ross is still running."

"Aye."

He glared over the expanse of pure Highland wilderness. They were surrounded by beautiful waters—deceiving waters. The temperature was frigid, and if one were to slip a toe into its depths, that toe may not last long.

Snow dusted parts of the grounds, larger clumps in some areas, and only grass in others. The fields lay fallow and covered in white. He'd not seen the grounds in spring and summer, and actually looked forward to the beauty of nature coming alive.

If he were Ross, he'd probably go in search of warmth. They'd been camped out in the dead of winter for weeks.

But Ross' castle was days away. He wouldn't go all the way back there. Not if he planned to retaliate. Ross might be a bastard and a traitor, but he wasn't a full on idiot. The man had a plan. He would want his revenge. Ronan took out two-thirds of his army, and Julianna escaped. That was a huge blow to his ego. He had to be seeing red. So what in the devil was he up to? Where had he gone?

The closest stronghold was Urquhart. Lord Comyn wouldn't house Ross—would he? Nay, he was holding the castle for the Bruce. But did he know Ross was a traitor? Oh hell. There were several small villages before Urquhart that Ross could invade.

"Has the Bruce warned the earls that Ross defected to the English?" Ronan asked.

Wallace raked a hand through his hair and blew out a breath. "Nay."

"Why in the hell not?" Ronan had to rein in the next thing he wanted to say, else he be thrown in the stocks for a day or whipped until he was bloody. But for God's sake, 'twas downright stupid not to warn anyone. Suicide. Did the Bruce have a death wish?

"I've advised him to do so, and he's waffling with the missives. Wants to make sure he gets his words right."

"Why not just state the facts? 'Tis simple."

Wallace shook his head. "The Bruce doesna tell me everything, ye know, but I have a feeling the earls are starting to...fuss."

"Fuss?"

Wallace glanced at him with strained eyes. "Aye. The English King has put gold in front of them. Offered them titles and lands. 'Tis hard for a man to turn down such."

"In the face of losing freedom? One's own country?"

"Ye're preaching to the wrong man, Ronan. I'm with ye. But I canna make the Bruce see reason. There is only one person who is ever able to get through to him."

Silken, reddish-gold locks came to mind. "Julianna."

"Aye."

"Where is she?"

"Haven't seen her."

"Seen who?" Daniel Murray said from behind.

Ronan turned to see his cousin stepping onto the ramparts. He grasped Daniel's arm in a firm shake. Daniel was another man he looked up to. He exuded strength, and power, and reminded him of his brother Blane. They both had dark hair, and dark eyes. Daniel's mother was Ronan's aunt—the sister of his father.

"Julianna."

Daniel frowned. Ronan was full aware that his cousin did not approve of the woman. Had even caught Daniel questioning her. He had hoped that his cousin would get used to Julianna's place within the Bruce's camp. But he also understood how hard it was to trust someone new, especially if their worth couldn't be gauged.

Julianna was worth a hell of a lot more than most of them—if not all of them.

"Myra was attending her a few days ago, but said Julianna turned a different corner."

"What does that mean?"

"She'd been friendly and open, welcomed Myra, but then suddenly thrust her out. Hasn't opened the door for anyone in a couple days."

"Is she eating?" Ronan's gut twisted. Daniel's words weren't offering him any comfort. If anything they only confirmed what he'd thought earlier. That something was amiss. He would find out what was going on with Julianna later. Now he had more pressing issues to attend too.

Daniel shrugged. "I didna think much on it. I was mostly concerned for my wife. Had to comfort her." He grinned mischievously. "Had to distract her."

Ronan rolled his eyes. "I'm glad ye're happy in marriage, cousin, but I'd just as soon not hear about your rutting."

Daniel laughed heartily at that. "Ye're just jealous."

Ronan crossed his arms over his chest, wincing at the pain in his shoulder. "Jealous?" Ronan snorted. "I'm not jealous in the least."

Wallace guffawed. "Then ye must have a penchant for cock, because nearly every man at this castle is jealous of Daniel, including myself." His face turned dark and he returned his gaze to the landscape.

"I've no need for a wife." Ronan wasn't about to back down.

"Just a particular lass, then?" Daniel pushed.

"Nay. None."

"Och, man, will ye give it up? Even the stones know ye have a liking for the lass." Wallace snorted with disgust. "Dinna make us all out for fools by denying it."

"My desires have nothing to do with my wants."

"That doesna even make sense," Daniel muttered.

"It doesna have to make sense to ye." Anger built a small fire in Ronan's chest. He didn't have to explain himself to these louts. They didn't know anything about him. They didn't know what his plans for the future were, or what he could or couldn't handle. They could go jump in the frozen loch.

"Ye're right, Ronan. Apologies. I once thought the same way. Know this, if ye ever need anyone to talk to, I'm your man." Daniel clapped him on the back and changed the subject. "Did ye see the bastard when ye attacked?"

Ronan frowned and shook his head. "Nay. We watched for a short time to ascertain the layout of their camp. What we thought was Ross' tent turned out to be the one holding Julianna—most likely the same one that held Myra. She was surrounded by retainers." Ronan put his hands on his hips and glanced over the castle, wondering where Julianna was. "I dinna know what spooked her, or if the Lord looked down on us because when we attacked, Julianna had begun to fight." Ronan explained the falling warrior, what he saw when he entered, and how she'd thrown her dagger. "She's a fierce wench."

"How does she know how to fight like that?" Daniel asked, his brows furrowing. "Myra can defend herself, but I am not certain she'd be able to ward off several vengeful warriors."

Wallace cleared his throat. "Julianna has had some training."

"Some training?" Daniel and Ronan said at the same time.

"Aye." Wallace headed toward the stairs ending the conversation. "I've a need to speak with the Bruce."

"Wait," Ronan said. "Are we going to devise a plan regarding Ross?"

"Aye. But it will have to wait."

Frustration dug deep. Seemed like there were a lot of secrets Ronan wasn't privy too. As soon as Laird Ross was dealt with, he would get to the bottom of one particular question—just who in the hell Julianna was.

He stared after Wallace, then turned his attention to Daniel. "What news?"

"From the newcomers, we've learned to expect Longshanks in two to three months' time."

Ronan shook his head,, ignoring the dull ache in his temple. "I'll have to work with the new recruits right away."

Daniel nodded. "Aye. There are a good many of them. Half have had extensive training, and willna require too much of your time. The other half I'd be afeared for my life if I were to fight beside them in battle. They might get confused and start hacking at me." Daniel chuckled, crossed his arms over his chest. "But with your training, I wouldna be surprised if ye have them fully competent within a month's time."

"I thank ye for the confidence."

"No need. That's one thing ye've always been good at, cousin. No one ever need fear ye were not a good leader or warrior. I'd have ye at my back, even with your sad shoulder."

Ronan rolled his eyes. "I think the tip was poisoned." That jest reminded him of something Julianna had said. He frowned and pursed his lips. "I need to see about something."

She'd mentioned poisoning her weapons. What kind of a woman would need to do such a thing? Ronan intended to find out.

Chapter Five

Julianna waited outside the stables until the groomsmen left for the evening meal. Didn't these lads get hungry? Heavens. She leaned up against the wooden wall, counted to over a thousand, and watched her breath go from steam to frosty clouds. 'Twas cold.

Her stomach growled, reminding her that she'd not partaken in the morning meal and she'd missed nooning. She'd helped to prepare the bread, smelled its delicious, comforting scent as it baked, but then she'd slipped out before taking her usual chunk smothered in honey.

God's teeth! She couldn't go about this chore without food. Ever since she'd kissed Ronan, her mind wouldn't function properly. A ninny, that's what she was becoming.

Stifling a curse and kicking a frozen clump of snow, Julianna trudged back toward the castle. If she was not waylaid, she could pack a satchel and be back at the stables before the lads returned to tend to the horses.

Julianna picked up speed, lifting her thick wool skirt for a quicker pace. She would not be delayed. Not by anyone. She hadn't discussed her plans with Robert — he'd only see to it that she remained behind. But who was he to tell her anything? Well…he was the future king, never mind the answer to that question.

There was a mess that had to be cleaned up. By her. She was the only one who could take care of it, and she'd not let it go untended.

She crept around the back of the castle, and wrenched open the door that led into the store room. At least she had the tenacity to take the board off the door last night. So, maybe part of her brain was working.

When the door closed behind her, Julianna was pitched into blackness. Blazes! She hadn't thought to bring a flint and torch. Damn Ronan. She might just get herself killed if she didn't put him out of her mind.

But, that was easier said than done. The memory of his hand gripping the back of her head — so possessive and sensual at the same time — refused to leave her. Whether awake or asleep, she saw his face, felt his lips on hers. She could still feel the faint tickle of his warm breath on her cheek. Her flesh burned. Her body ached for his touch. She savored the memory before cursing herself again.

"Damn him!" He made her want things she'd never dreamt about before. Never dared to want.

They weren't in the stars for her. Love. Romance. Kisses. Those were things other lasses dreamed of. Not Julianna. Julianna dreamed of swords. Knives. Poisons. The best way to attack with the least injury to one's person and the most damage done to your opponent. Those were her dreams. Ronan was changing that, changing her. He was opening her eyes to things she'd been denied. Things she'd shunned. Laughed at. How could this be happening? She was strong, tough, resilient. No man could break through her defenses. Things like this didn't happen—not to her. But it was, and worst of all, she wanted to kiss him again. She wanted to feel her breasts crushed to the hardness of his torso, to delight in the rise and fall of his chest against her own.

Julianna made her way down the stairs to the store room, one hand holding up her skirts and the other sliding over the stone wall, keeping her balanced. The stairs were always damp. She didn't know why. But being damp and worn made them slick. And dangerous. Not being able to see didn't help matters. If she were to trip she could break her neck. She had to go slow and be extra careful. The task took twice as long as it would have if she had only brought a torch or candle. Damn her conflicted mind.

What had Ronan done to her? No matter how preoccupied she'd been in the past, she'd still been able to perform her duties. It had to be more than the kiss. It was like she'd suffered a poisoning. Not the lethal poison she rubbed onto her blades, but some other toxin. The kind that made one's heart soft. 'Twas changing her, and she didn't like it.

A thought started to brew deep in her mind. Had part of her chosen to be so haphazard because she hoped to fail? Julianna stopped and gazed into the darkness, the idea jolting her.

Nay. She'd never shirk her duties.

Continuing her descent, she refused to think about what tricks her subconscious was trying to play on her. Her duty was to Robert, to Scotland. She had to rid the country of one of its greatest foes.

And she needed to do it with a clear head.

Rounding the last step, Julianna searched the shelf to her right for the flint and torch she knew would be there. Moments later the storeroom came to life in a soft glow. Barrels of ale and wine. Jugs of whisky. Baskets of stored vegetables and fruits. Wheels of cheese and bundles of jerky. A stack of stale oatcakes was shoved onto a shelf. The scents were overwhelming, and Julianna had to take a moment to let them sink in. Anything off could have her gagging, but the smells in the storeroom were fairly pleasant.

Taking a deep breath, she stepped further into the room and grabbed a bundle of jerky and a few of the hardened oatcakes. The cakes were usually eaten within a day or two of baking. Those left over were stored for emergency use, until they grew moldy. Luckily, these were not yet rotten. She should have pilfered a few when she was in the kitchen.

A bag. She needed a bag. With a glance around, she found a small woolen bag that had been used to bring in grain. Julianna stuffed the food into the bag, took some carrots, then swiped a hunk of cheese. Only apples sat on the shelves and she had no interest in them. That ought to do it. She didn't need wine or ale, her wineskin was already filled with water.

With provisions in hand, she made her way up the stairs — fully lit this time, and sent a prayer up to the Heavens she hadn't slipped on the onion left idle on the middle stair. She tucked it into her sack and continued on.

Now all she had to do was sneak into the stables. Last eve she'd placed a bag with her weapons and an extra plaid in her horse Brave's stall. Hopefully none of the groomsmen had taken it upon themselves to give her warhorse a rub down. No one was allowed to touch her horse. She hoped she'd made that clear. He preferred her touch over anyone else's, so that was a comfort. 'Twas important. Her horse trusted no one else. In battle they were each other's protection.

Trying for nonchalant, Julianna traipsed across the courtyard, and headed to the back of the stables. She kept her head down so she didn't catch anyone's eye or bring attention to herself.

She slipped inside. All was quiet save the soft breathing of each horse and the occasional nicker. Even still, Julianna used cautious steps in approaching Brave. There were rows of horses on either side of the main walk. Double doors in the front and a smaller door at the back—although one could still fit a horse through it.

Dark as night and shiny in the coat, her horse was a beauty. His mane was wavy, long and sometimes made her jealous considering her own untamed locks.

"Hello, boy," she said softly, stroking over his muzzle. Brave lipped at her palm. "Ah, ye want a treat do ye?" She pulled one of the carrots from her bag and handed it over.

As fierce as he was, Brave was also quite a pampered, spoiled horse.

Julianna unlatched the stall door, wincing at the screeching of metal. The lads hadn't oiled up the hinges. Slacking on the job. She'd have a word with them about that when she returned.

"Back up, Brave," she cooed, until her horse moved enough for her to get into the stall.

Her bag of weapons and supplies were where she'd left them. Brave's saddle and bridle hung on the back wall. Another one of her requests from the stable hands. There were many times she had to hurry, and trying to locate her saddle and lug it down took too much time. Brave was her horse. Her responsibility and she didn't need anyone's help. She could saddle Brave as well as any man. No matter how much Robert argued with her about it.

Besides, if she were to ever get trapped somewhere, handling the weight of a saddle and knowing how to properly place it on a horse, was an important bit of knowledge she required.

Julianna ran her hand over Brave's mane, withers and back, loving how her palm glided over the softness of his fur. His muscles twitched, and Julianna smiled.

"Are ye ready for another adventure?" she asked.

Brave snorted and turned his head toward her, nipping gently at her shoulder.

"I'll take that as an aye."

Just as her hand touched the saddle, the doors to the stable opened and voices carried down the row to Brave's stall.

She gritted her teeth and ducked, backing into the front left corner where she knelt, hopefully to remain unseen. Above her head was a deep ledge attached to the plank boards beside the gate, mostly used for setting tools on when working with the horses. She hoped it would keep her hidden. Most of the stall was bathed in shadow. If they didn't look too closely, they'd miss her completely. Gratefully, Brave pretended as though she weren't there, went about munching on some hay, like it was completely usual for his lady to duck in his stall. Julianna pressed her back to the wood, wishing she could melt right into it, and tried to make out the voices. Sounded like one of the lads and…Ronan.

No, it couldn't be. What the hell was he doing in here?

Had he somehow figured out her plans?

Julianna shook her head, told herself to quit being such a ninny. There was no way he could have figured that out. No one could have. She didn't tell anyone, she'd simply disappeared. He probably had need of the lad for his own horse.

"This is Lady Julianna's horse, right here," the stable hand said, right above her head.

Julianna wanted to groan, her head hurt from the force it took to keep it in. She twisted her fingers in her skirts, closed her eyes like that might make her invisible. If Ronan spotted her it wouldn't be good. She'd have to knock him over the head with something so she could get away. Hurting him *again*, wasn't on her list of things to do. He just needed to leave on his own. She shouted at him in her mind to go away. Willed him to leave. It didn't work.

He stopped outside Brave's stall, and from the sounds of it, propped his elbows on the shelf above her head. She held her breath and leaned even closer to the wood. *Please dinna see me. Go away!*

"This is her horse, huh?" Ronan sounded just as shocked as every other man did when they found out what type of horse she rode.

"Indeed, sir."

"'Tis a bit big for a lass, isn't it?"

Oh, the brute! Thinking she couldn't handle a beast as magnificent as Brave.

"With all due respect, sir, Lady Julianna is one of the best riders I've ever seen. She has a way with horses, she does."

Julianna smiled, and caught herself from agreeing out loud.

"Is that right?"

There was no reply, 'haps the boy nodded.

"Well, I see the horse is still here."

"Did ye doubt it?"

"There's a bit of worry over where she is."

"Oh," the lad said, his voice filled with concern.

God's teeth! Why were they looking for her?

"I'll keep my eye out for her, sir," the lad said eagerly.

"My thanks. Let me know if ye see her, or if the horse disappears."

"I will for certes."

The voices receded, their booted feet making soft thudding noises on the dirt-packed, straw strewn lane.

Anger zinged through Julianna's veins. How dare Ronan come looking for her? As though she were his woman or something. One damn kiss, that's all it was, and she doubted he even remembered it. The man had been burning up with fever. Almost delirious. It had meant nothing. At least that's what she kept telling herself.

But, if she were honest, he'd laid a claim on her far before their kiss. They'd bantered back and forth, played this game of pull and push for weeks, maybe months. She couldn't recall. Didn't want to remember.

The man was not going to stand in her way.

No one was.

As soon as she heard the doors close and silence reigned for sixty seconds, she clambered to her feet, dusted off the straw and nearly stepped in a pile of horse manure. Wow. Close call, she could have sat right in it.

With eyes wide and a deep sigh of relief, she grabbed the horse's plaid blanket, saddle and reins and worked as quickly as she could to get them all into place properly. She covered most of Brave's body with the plaid, braided his hair and covered his face with a cloth meant to keep a horse's head warm. Every sound, creak, horse stomp and whine, she imagined Ronan coming through the doors and seeing what she was about.

He couldn't possibly know about her plans. So why was he concerned about her whereabouts? It was unnerving. He seemed to be more aware of her intentions than anyone else. If she believed in superstitions, she may have thought that kiss gave him that ability.

But that was not only unlikely, it was absurd.

And stupid.

She had to get that damned kiss out of her head. As if agreeing, Brave nodded his head.

"Oh, what do ye know?"

Julianna unlatched the gate and led Brave out of his stall. She guided him to the back door and opened it, peering out.

She'd come in when the sun was lowering in the sky, but it was now completely dark. Her luck was holding tight. Not a soul in sight. The biggest problem she faced was getting out the main gate and across the bridge. But if she'd timed it right, there would be an impressive amount of people leaving, and she could blend right in. Done with work for the day, they'd be heading out into the village to spend the evening with their families.

From within the satchel that she'd put her weapons, Julianna withdrew a plaid she'd acquired a few months ago, never knowing when she'd need to disappear. It was dulled in color, green and brown, ragged in places. She wrapped it around herself, forming a hood to cover her hair and most of her face. The excess in fabric hid her satchels and the sheathed sword she'd tucked within a fur lining between the saddle seat and strip of leather leading to the stirrup.

She braced her foot in the stirrup and mounted, then guided the horse slowly around the side of the stables that led to the gate, holding her breath with every step. It was paramount that she get out now.

People had already begun to stream from the castle and various work stations to go through the gate. Some on horseback, a few on donkeys, some riding in wagons pulled by either horses or donkeys, most on foot. They resided in Dornie, a short fifteen minute walk. Julianna nudged Brave into the pack of people leaving, with seeming ease.

No one bothered to look at her, save for a few uninterested glances. Even still, she continued to recite a prayer in her mind. She had to get across that bridge unnoticed. Ronan was obviously looking for her. Or was he just following Robert's orders?

The future king did request her presence often. She was his advisor, his protector. After having been gone for several days, he had most likely missed her counsel. And there was the tiny fact that she'd not been at the evening meal. Her maid was supposed to warn the Bruce she was not feeling well. Women's issues or some such. Something she'd never claimed before. In hindsight, that was probably a trigger for Robert the Bruce to seek her out.

She'd gone that morning and apologized, given him a recount of all that went on, and recounted to him the things she'd overheard, which weren't many. If anything, she'd only delayed them.

Which was why she had to fix the situation.

And why no one could stop her.

Julianna crossed under the gate. She didn't dare glance up at the guards. Anyone of them would have recognized her immediately. If anything, her abduction by the Ross clan proved to her that the guards were lax at checking who left and who entered. Even if she and Myra had been trussed up beneath a dozen bags of wool inside the back of a cart. Wouldn't they have noticed the moving wool? She supposed not.

Though she wanted them to be lax in their duties tonight, the future King of Scotland resided behind those walls, and their behavior was unacceptable. Security had to be tighter, there were lives at risk. When she returned, they would get a tongue lashing from her or Wallace. As much as she would like to let them have it, it would probably be best coming from Wallace.

Her horse's hooves clomped onto the bridge. She'd almost made it. Only a few hundred more feet to go, and then she'd cross beneath the second gate. After that, soft grass, and she'd be off.

"Halt! Ye there!"

She ignored the call. Her heart hammered in her chest. This wasn't the time to panic. They weren't halting her. It had to be someone else. No one, not even Ronan knew of her plans, even if he did have his suspicions. She had to stay calm. If she did she could ride right off the bridge and to freedom. It took all her willpower not to squeeze Brave's ribs so he broke out into a run. But with her breath held, she continued on.

"Stop!"

Saints! Not pushing her horse into a gallop seemed like the hardest thing she'd ever have to do. Only fifty more feet and she was in the clear. The voice sounded distant, not close enough to grab hold of her yet.

Then she heard the sound of running boots on the bridge. They'd seen her. *Dammit!* Beneath her thighs, Brave quivered. He sensed her need to run.

"Steady," she murmured.

An argument broke out behind her. She took a quick glance to see what was going on. A guard searched through the back of a wagon. She sighed with relief. Perhaps she wouldn't have to talk with them after all.

Moments later she was beneath the second gate. As soon as Brave's hooves touched the cold grass, she squeezed. He bolted forward, the wind knocking the plaid from her head. She didn't stop to fix it. Only leaned forward in the saddle.

Julianna had gotten away. She could complete her mission.

Ross would be a dead man.

Chapter Six

Where the hell was she?

Ronan had searched everywhere, and he was growing increasingly concerned. One lass could not simply disappear — and not just any lass, Lady Julianna.

The castle was vast, but he'd searched from the bowels to the very top. Every outbuilding had been thoroughly combed and he'd even had the well inspected.

Nowhere.

If the woman was half as talented as he suspected, it was entirely possible that she'd managed to sneak off the island. But he'd checked the stables. Her massive horse had still been there. Frowning, he realized he'd not asked if any of the other horses were missing.

Ronan sat down on a bench just outside the main doors of the castle. The wood seat was cold, but he ignored it. Leaned his head back on the castle's stone walls and stared up into the night sky. Thousands of golden stars dotted the inky black sky. Not a cloud in sight. The moon was full, lighting the courtyard.

He'd not told anyone of his suspicions and they'd probably all thought he'd gone mad trudging here and there. But Ronan didn't want to worry anyone. Especially if he was only worrying for naught. Could be she was holed up in a secret hiding place.

Why, though?

A dim glow from the stables seeped beneath the doorway, its shine beckoning him. His gut twisted and suddenly a sense of foreboding clouded over him. Pushing to his feet, Ronan all but ran to the stables, slamming open the doors. The groomsmen all stood in a circle, whispering frantically. *Mo creach!* He knew something was wrong.

When they saw him their eyes widened.

"The horse?" he growled.

"Gone," the head stable master croaked.

Ronan swung around and punched the nearest wall, his knuckles splitting under the pressure.

He stormed toward the empty stall to see if there were any clues. Nothing. Empty.

"When?" he asked.

The head stable master cleared his throat. "We noticed about half an hour ago."

"And no one thought to inform me?"

The man shook his head. "We looked about the courtyard, but she was already long gone. The gates closed. I suspect she left when the servants did."

Ballocks! Why didn't he put a special watch on the tower? His instincts never failed him and this time was no different. Why didn't he trust them? Why? Because he didn't want to be laughed at about his so called feelings for Julianna. Pride be damned. Now she was missing. Satan's Arse!

Pride be damned. Now she was missing.

"Keep your eyes peeled and let me know if ye see anything."

Ronan gritted his teeth and fisted his hands. Now he had the unpleasant task of telling Robert the Bruce that Julianna was missing. Not a chore he was looking forward to in the least.

The Bruce had already retired to his chamber for the evening to go over some maps with Wallace. Ronan would catch hell for interrupting them, but there was no other choice. Julianna's safety was important not only to him but to the Bruce.

Swallowing some of his anger, he lifted a fist and knocked.

"Enter." Wallace's growled.

Ronan opened the door and stepped through, bowing his head, hands behind his back.

"What is it?" Wallace asked.

Ronan glanced up to see the two men he admired glowering at him.

"Apologies for interrupting, but it is of the utmost importance." Ronan hesitated. He did not enjoy being the bearer of bad news.

"Well then," the Bruce said, putting a marker on the map, "what is it?"

"Julianna has gone missing."

The Bruce's eyes widened, and the muscles on the side of his jaw flexed. "Missing?"

"Aye, my lord."

"That lass will be the death of me," he muttered. "Are ye certain?"

"Her horse is gone. I checked everywhere. The stable lads as well."

"*Mo creach.*" Wallace grimaced.

"Ye have to go after her," Robert urged. He threw his map aside and fixed Ronan with a panicked stare. "Ye have to. Ross is still out there. Who knows how many more English are on their way. We've word there will be an imminent attack. We were planning to move camp. Ye must find her. "

"I will leave now."

"Bring her back to me."

"I will."

The stakes had been raised even more. They were planning to move camp. 'Twas the best choice given the fact that Ross knew where they were and would relay that information to Longshanks. None of them were safe anymore.

Ronan turned to leave.

"Wait," the Bruce said, stalling him. "Have ye any idea where she's gone?"

"Aye, I've an idea."

"Ross?"

"Aye."

"I thought as much. She apologized this morning for leaving a mess."

"'Twas not her fault."

"I know it. Ye know it. We all know it. But she doesna. Julianna is a stubborn woman. Born and bred to protect. She's a warrior, Ronan."

"That much I figured out."

"Ye know she is my protector."

"I gathered." Truth was, he'd not gathered that at all. He knew there was a special relationship, and with all the clues given him, Ronan had still been too mule-headed to think such. Now he knew, and it all made sense.

The Bruce nodded, glanced at Wallace. "I need her back. She is more than just my protector."

Did that mean she was his woman too? A searing pain clutched at Ronan's chest. He forced it to subside. If she was already claimed, there was nothing he could do about it, as much as the thought hurt.

"I will see to it she is returned to ye."

"To us. To Scotland. She belongs here."

Ronan nodded, watched Wallace give a subtle shake of his head. What did that mean?

He needed to find his cousin Daniel Murray. The man could help him in his search. That is, if his wife would allow him to leave her side. With Daniel and Graham, they could track her quickly, even if she had an hour or more gain on them.

"Ye must go alone." Wallace's voice stopped Ronan in his tracks.

Ronan frowned. "Why?"

"No one can know she's gone missing again. Tell the lads in the stable she was found in her rooms, ill." Wallace looked at him, his eyes crinkling at the corners with weariness.

"Ye've still not told me why." Ronan planted his feet, not willing to budge.

"I will explain when ye return. Julianna is too important. If news were to get out that she'd disappeared… Every enemy of the Bruce would meet ye along the road in a race to find her."

Ronan crossed his arms over his chest and stared at Wallace. They would have him go out alone to look for Julianna. When they knew the English and Ross men roamed close by. Slowly he shook his head. He had great confidence in his abilities to be sure, but to brave the wilderness on one's own during a time like this was nearly suicide.

Had not his own brothers and cousin run into many a skirmish only to barely come out alive—and they were damn good warriors.

"I know 'tis asking a lot. A great risk, indeed. Ye will be highly rewarded for her return. And ye can take my hound. Have her sniff the lady's things and she'll pick up her scent quick."

"All right."

Wallace stared at him a moment longer as if assessing he'd truly agreed. "All right, then. Come, I'll introduce ye to Lil Lass."

"Lil Lass?"

"Aye, my hound. Best nose in Scotland."

An hour later, Ronan was settled on his horse with Lil Lass by his side. The dog's name was a joke to be sure. She was one of the biggest wolfhounds he'd ever seen. A nightmare of a thing with feet as big as a man's and a snout as long as his forearm.

The dog lived up to Wallace's praise. She was silent as the grave, picking her way carefully through the darkened foliage. Nose to the ground, she led a path from the bridge straight into the woods. Every time her ears perked, Ronan grew still, listening. Sometimes there was nothing, others an animal crossed their path. Another time they hid from a man who walked drunkenly into a tree and fell backward.

Ronan didn't stick around to find out if he was friend or foe.

Admittedly, the dog was a better companion than any man. She would be an added guard, and her hearing and scenting skills were beyond the measure of any man. None could compare, and Ronan grew confident they would find Julianna before morning.

Lil Lass seemed to have picked up the infuriating woman's scent quite easily. Ronan wished he could smell as well as the dog. The brief moments he'd caught Julianna's scent were overpowering in sensuality. She smelled of leather and flowers. A unique combination that spoke of her individuality.

Once again he had the distinct sensation of her lips on his. A most vivid dream. Hot, plush lips.

"Och!" He yanked on the reins, halting Saint in his tracks.

Lil Lass stood stock still, her silver fur shining in the moonlight. One front paw was lifted slightly as though she'd literally paused in mid-step. Nose to the air she sniffed, then turned abruptly right. They'd traveled before on a well-worn path. The hound led them off into the less traveled woods. He had to slow his pace to keep the horse from tripping over any unseen vegetation. Thank the Lord it was winter and the normally lush trees were without leaves, and so the moon still lit their path quite well.

The dog's pace quickened, but Ronan wasn't willing to risk Saint's life or his own. Despite the bright moon, there was no telling what hidden roots or vines might trip up his steed. Lil Lass stopped every so often to let him catch up. A very well-trained dog, she was growing on Ronan with each passing minute.

Lil Lass stopped suddenly and sat down. She wagged her tail and looked up at Ronan expectantly. Ronan looked around. They were in the middle of the forest, surrounded by old firs, oaks and maples. Not a soul in sight.

He raised his brow at the dog and looked again. He still saw nothing.

What the bloody hell?

Deciding to take a closer look, Ronan dismounted from Saint, leaving the animal to munch on anything he found upon the ground. He inspected behind several trees. Not a soul. He peered through brambles. No one. Turning in a circle, Ronan was completely dumbfounded by the dog's seeming joy at having stopped here.

"What is it, Lil Lass?" he asked.

The hound cocked her head as if to ask him what he was talking about.

"Did ye find something?" After asking the question he felt like a complete imbecile. The dog was not likely to answer. "Come on, girl. Show me, Lil Lass."

Lil Lass stood and sniffed the spot in front of her, pawed at it and then sat back down, tongue out, tail wagging.

"Damn dog," he muttered. Ronan walked forward, scratched her behind her ears and then knelt to inspect the spot.

At first, in the light of the moon, he made out dead leaves, sticks and a few mushrooms, some grass. But on closer inspection, he noted that the poisoned mushrooms were all crumpled up. Like someone had squeezed the life out of them. The poison.

Julianna used poison on her weapons. Had she stopped her to rub more on them?

"Good girl," Ronan muttered with another pat to the dog's head, gave her strip of jerky for her efforts.

This was a good sign. They were on the right trail. However, they'd not yet spotted or heard Julianna.

Ronan was beginning to wonder if they would. The woman was a complete enigma. Vulnerable in one sense, but completely independent and dangerous even, in another.

When he found her, he would demand answers. Not only for why she ran off in secret, but also who she was. He'd let it go before. Just like everyone else, the mystery of her background had been what drew him to her, and was off limits. Understanding that, he'd not asked. Wasn't sure he wanted to know. Forced himself not to be interested, because showing interest meant he felt more than he should.

Now his life was on the line. Not that he minded. Ronan would have gone up against a hundred men to save Julianna. The thing was, he thought he deserved to know what her place was. Who she was.

And if she refused to tell him, he would get the answers from Wallace or Robert the Bruce. Ronan gritted his teeth. Wallace had promised him answers. But how could he be sure it wasn't simply a ploy to have him find Julianna? Ronan was one of the best at retrieving missing people, protecting people. His guess as to why they'd sent him out alone.

"Come now," he said to Lil Lass as he remounted his horse. They needed to keep on her trail.

Not knowing what exactly Julianna's stamina was, he didn't want to stop now. Most likely she'd run through the night. The woman had to know Robert would send someone out after her. Being aware of that, she would most likely go as far as she possibly could without collapsing.

Was it conceivable that she'd gained all her strength back so quickly? He'd only just retrieved her for the first time a week before.

Ronan growled as he urged Saint into motion and tossed Lil Lass another hunk of dried venison jerky. She swallowed it in one bite and then put her nose to the ground. Walking in a circle, the dog finally continued to the left. Off the path they'd been headed on before.

Had Julianna lost her way?

Ronan shook his head. She wasn't lost, because she couldn't have any idea where she was going in the end. He had a pretty good inclination she was going after Ross. That meant she had to find his old camp and track him from there. A spot she could easily find tonight.

Ronan would have bet a pouch full of silver that was where she was headed.

With renewed confidence, he urged Saint into a trot. They'd be there within an hour.

As predicted, they happened upon the spot where Ronan had first saved her. Half the tents were still standing. Others had come loose and hung from makeshift poles like dejected white flags, waving in the light winter breeze. The bodies had been removed by his men and buried. But the place was still scattered with remnants from camp. All the weapons were gone. Provisions taken. Tools, however, remained behind. A few blankets here and there, pots, a pair of boots, what looked like a whittled horse.

'Twas eerie and rather sad. Just looking at the abandoned camp one could assume those who'd occupied it left rather quickly.

Lil Lass sniffed around, stopping several times in certain spots, particularly outside of the tent Ronan had found Julianna in before.

He froze. Panic seized him. Was it possible that Lil Lass had taken up Julianna's scent from a couple weeks ago? No, no, no. God, let that not be the case.

Ronan dismounted, left Saint idle, and proceeded to whip back the fabric on the tents, allowing the moonlight to stream inside.

No Julianna. Lil Lass, sniffed around the edges of camp, again stopping and turning, appearing confused. Julianna's scent was everywhere. But she herself was not.

Ronan prayed she'd not met with foul play. That the scents were confusing because some were old and some were new. Had the lass gotten spooked and decided to take up the night somewhere else? That would be the smartest thing since the camp was exposed and she, only one person, could not take on a band of men. Or an army.

The other possibility was that she'd simply continued on. Caught the scent of Ross and moved forward.

"Ballocks," Ronan muttered under his breath. He stopped in the middle of the camp, hands on his hips and huffed a breath.

'Twould appear that tracking Lady Julianna would be a lot harder then he'd originally contemplated.

Lil Lass sat beside him, the heat of her body seeping onto his exposed flesh between his boots and the end of his plaid. He'd much rather have the heat of Julianna's body against his.

Patting the dog, he led her to the outskirts of the camp, hoping she'd pick up Julianna's scent going in another direction. But Lil Lass, continued to stop on the edge of the woods, then circled back into the camp.

The trail was dead.

Julianna was not here, and hadn't been. Somehow the hound had been misled.

Well, he wasn't going to get anywhere else tonight. He'd get a few hours of rest before day break, and then start anew.

A subtle shift in the wind had Lil Lass lifting her nose. And with it, Ronan too. He listened keenly. Could have sworn he'd heard something. Fabric scraping. Not the usual sounds he'd become accustomed to. Or the tents. This was different. He doubled back behind the tents and when he was well hidden, he looked up to the trees.

"Got ye," he whispered.

There perched high above camp, was the most beautiful, dangerous sight he'd ever seen. Julianna—a knife poised ready to strike in her hand.

Chapter Seven

What the devil was he doing here?

Julianna heard someone approaching. She'd not however in a million years believed it would be Ronan. She frowned down at him, contemplated throwing her knife. In the moonlight she was easily able to see her target and would not miss. Even if he did hide behind the tent. Was it possible he'd heard her when she shifted her position? The sound was slight, but to a trained warrior, it would have been noticeable. Moving couldn't be helped, her foot had started to fall asleep.

If the wind stopped, she could land a blow to his chest.

Then again, did she really want him dead? Her weapon was newly oiled in poisonous mushroom juices. With a deep, annoyed sigh, she sheathed the knife at her side and watched.

The fact of the matter was, seeing him made her heart race. Her fingers even shook a little. She hated admitting she was a little excited to see him.

Oddly enough, he was alone, save for the horse and the hound. Julianna had not seen Ronan with a dog before and guessed it must have been borrowed. Scenting her out. The dog had done a good job. Julianna headed this way for two reasons — one she hoped if they did send the dogs after her, they would give up when they reached here, guessing the dogs had come back to the place she'd been held captive. The second reason was it was easiest to track Ross from this point.

It'd been awhile since she'd tracked a man. A year or more. The past several months she'd been cooped up inside Eilean Donan. Even the name was starting to make her claustrophobic. Stuck on that island, nowhere to go. Bairn-sitting Robert.

Julianna wasn't going back now. Not with Ronan. She had a job to do. She'd see it done or else she'd be labeled a failure, and just might go insane in the process.

Ronan seemed to lose interest in the camp. He mounted his horse, whistled to the dog and took off in the opposite direction he'd come. Thank the Saints. He'd probably assumed she'd never been here, or at the very least that she was no longer.

Julianna counted to six hundred and then climbed down. With a solid ten minutes of Ronan being gone, she was confident he wouldn't come back looking for her. Although she wouldn't consider herself the best tree-climber, she was also not the worst.

It'd been a hobby of hers when she was a child. A way to hide from her instructors or from the other children who jeered at her. However unfortunate it was that she'd come by the skill, she was pleased to have maintained the talent.

To the right of the camp was a gully. Steep in parts, but not so much in others, she'd led her horse down into it to keep him safe. Knowing there were people looking for her — as far she knew Ronan could just be ahead of the party — it wasn't safe for her to stay here any longer.

Making haste, Julianna half slid, half ran down the hill, using all of her concentration on her steps not to trip or fall. A few well-placed roots and saplings helped her along the way. By the time she reached the bottom, she was no worse for wear. Brave munched peacefully on whatever it was he found beneath the pile of leaves. Grass perhaps.

She gripped his reins and glanced around. Getting down was easier with the horse. Climbing by herself had been difficult, it would be even harder leading a large animal.

"Come now, Brave," she said softly. "Time to fly again."

Her horse nodded his head and took steps to follow as she led him toward the incline. Glancing up, she wished she'd thought of a better place to hide the beast. Nevertheless, she wasn't one to give up.

With an encouraging word to the animal, she began to climb. Brave didn't appear to have any issues with the ascent. His hooves found sturdy placement at each move. They'd made it halfway when a sound from above made her stop dead still.

"Shh…boy," she whispered to the horse, rubbing his mane. Brave's flesh shuddered beneath her touch and he side-stepped to find better footing. He wasn't exactly in a good spot to stand still. They needed to keep moving.

Straining her ears, and peering up to the top of the rise, Julianna tried to decipher the noise. A shuffling. Like walking, but she couldn't figure out if it was one person, more than one, or just an animal. A sheer whistle had her shuddering. A call to someone.

Then voices.

And she didn't recognize them.

Not Ronan.

Saints!

Perhaps it would be better to go back down into the ravine and walk a ways until they found a better spot to climb.

She couldn't wait until those above decided to look over the hill. The moon shined too bright tonight to make them invisible and with the horse on shaky ground, she would easily be overcome.

Julianna listened a few moments longer. There was the sounds of metal clinking, shuffling, talking and a few more whistles. Enough to tell her that those above were settling in, not leaving. At least she was down here and not still stuck in the tree. That would put her in even more danger. She may have climbed a tree to hide earlier, but she'd no plans to stay up there the rest of the night. The discipline to remain unmoving would be draining enough, not to mention keeping herself perched precariously throughout the night without falling asleep. Already, exhaustion seeped in. She'd barely recovered from her last ordeal. Leaving when she did to go after Ross was not the best of her decisions, but one she'd made nevertheless. There was no other time that she could do it. No other way.

Thank goodness Ronan had already left. She'd never forgive herself for running off to capture Ross if Ronan was the cost.

Not that she cared for the man. Much.

She just didn't want him to be a casualty in her operation.

Brave appeared to sense her hesitation, probably felt the vibration of her worry through the reins. He nudged her with his nose, and Julianna gave him a gentle pet. Every moment that passed standing here put them further in danger. It was only a matter of time before Brave made a noise, or one of the camp settlers chose to peer over the ravine out of sheer curiosity.

The question was, how could she get out of here quietly? What was the safest path?

Obviously she needed more practice with stealth, and so did Brave. It'd been too long since they'd last traveled out to do so. A fact she would need to remedy when they returned. A long talk was overdue with Robert. Julianna understood her duty to him, to Scotland, but in turn, Robert needed to appreciate the need for her to keep up with her training.

The warrior inside her was close to being tamped down and Julianna could not let that happen. Another reason why marrying was out of the question.

Glancing up at the moon, she marveled at its brightness, its shape, wondered if there were any castles up there, someone staring down at her and speculating the same thing. A breeze tunneled through the gully and stirred the leaves around her feet. With the wind blowing, the noises of their moving would be harder to hear. She tugged on Brave's reins and pulled him carefully back down the hill, stopping and going with the blowing wind.

They made it down to the bottom without anyone sending up the alarm. For a moment, Julianna considered mounting the horse and riding him until she found a safer place to climb, but realized that it would most likely be safer for her to lead him a ways.

The wind picked up, rustling the trees and sending eerie whistles through the air. Every little noise had her jumping, an exercise in keeping her calm. Her nerves were frayed. She concentrated on keeping her breathing steady, slowing her heart. Remaining in control and not letting her imagination get the better of her. She truly was rusty when it came to sneaking about in the dark. A fact she detested admitting to herself.

Putting some distance between herself and the camp, Julianna began to feel more at ease. It would be best to get as far away as she could and then find a place for her and Brave to rest until morning. Her bones were starting to ache, her muscles to shake. If they didn't find a place soon, they would risk capture, for she'd surely collapse.

Julianna stole a moment to pull the wineskin of water from the saddle and took a long drink. The water helped a little, invigorating her to keep moving. The gully ended up being a lot longer than she'd estimated. And good thing too, it put her further away from the men who'd taken up residence in Ross' old camp.

Who could they have been?

Wouldn't it be just her luck they were actually Ross men? Julianna shook her head. Nay, they wouldn't come back. Not when they knew the Bruce's men would be after them. That would be the most idiotic thing they could do. Then again, perhaps knowing that, they decided the Bruce camp would not come looking for them there.

She debated leaving Brave here to graze and doubling back to check for sure. A bad idea, truly.

A shallow incline was on the right just a few yards ahead. Julianna increased her pace and began to climb. Brave had no problems gaining his footing. Moments later they reached the top. Staying still, Julianna took in her surroundings. They'd surfaced in the woods. Pine trees surrounded her, making it harder to see, their thick needles blocking the sky and the light of the moon. Closing her eyes, she listened carefully, zeroing in on each sound, becoming accustomed to it. A light breeze blew with a subtle whistle. Pine needles ruffled, pine cones knocked. A few small animals scurried. A larger one--'haps a deer, picked its way carefully through the woods. The crunch not big enough to be a human—at least she hoped. An owl or two hooted. In the distance, she heard the faint sound of a wolf howling.

The men at the camp were quiet, or least quiet enough that their sound didn't carry on the wind. They'd not lit a fire, for she didn't catch the scent of smoke in the breeze.

Brave pawed the ground, dipped his head to burrow within the leaves for a bite of sweet grass.

Julianna opened her eyes, adjusting to the darkness of the woods, letting the little light that seeped through highlight the tree trunks and branches, leaves on the ground. A swift breeze blew, broken up by the trees it felt like it was coming at her from all angles. She tugged her cloak tighter, made herself believe she was warmer than she was.

They were east of the camp, and the most likely direction that Ross had run. A village was a few miles through these woods. Kinterloch she believed it was called. A small holding previously ruled by Ross. A wooden keep was there, kept by his cousin. The soil was rich there. Crops aplenty in the spring. They even held a small market Julianna had been to a few times. As good a spot as any for Ross to seek shelter. No one would know of his treachery yet, and his cousin would most likely offer him shelter. Another reason why Julianna herself could not do the same. She could, however, find a place to hide near the village until morning and then sneak inside to see if Ross and his men were there. With the right fabrics—which she had—blending in was easy. If she made herself as unappealing as possible, men were not likely to pay attention.

'Twas an easy task. She often combed dirt through her hair to tame the red and gold. Smudged a bit on her cheeks to give the appearance of not having bathed in a while. Kept her nails nice and dirty. And the clothes. Her plaid was dull, worn. No one ever took interest.

In fact, even at Eilean Donan, when she'd given full care to her appearance and gown on a few occasions to look nice, only one man had taken notice.

Ronan.

Because he noticed her, she noticed him. Hmm…Not necessarily true. She'd noticed him the moment he crossed over the bridge. The way he sat his horse with superior strength and power. The way he could be serious with his men and then pass a look toward her that was both heated and mischievous at the same time. Every time he looked at her, a spark set off inside.

A spark that just now was making itself known. Why did he have to invade her thoughts? Take over as though he had a place there? Like she wanted him there.

Julianna gritted her teeth and took a tentative step forward. A branch cracked beneath her foot and she stilled, her entire body on alert for any sounds she'd not already become acquainted with.

There was nothing but the familiar, and so she took another step, tugging Brave along with her. They'd walked about five feet when the air changed. Became charged. Sensing her unease, Brave flicked his tail, perked his ears. He heard something as well.

Just a subtle difference, a whisper of someone passing through these parts just as stealthily as she attempted. Was it Ronan? Or a scout from those who'd made camp back at Ross' grounds. One outlaw would make it easier, but two or three would make it more entertaining. A challenge.

Julianna clenched her jaw and with her free hand slid her sword from within its scabbard beneath her saddle. She was prepared to protect herself and her animal. No one would get in her way.

Subtle crunching of leaves and sticks came from in front of her. If she had to guess, judging from the wind that carried the sounds, the person or persons were about thirty or forty feet away. She supposed she still possessed some skill after all.

Julianna went left. If whoever it was, was headed in her direction she was not going to continue in their path. Either they'd continue on, none the wiser to her presence, or they'd follow her. Once she determined their intent, she'd make her next move.

Urging Brave forward, she moved at a snail's pace to the left, easing between trees, over fallen logs and around thick brambles. She stopped every five feet or so to listen. At first the person continued on their path and Julianna had hope that she'd be rid of them. Three miles to Kinterloch would take her a couple of hours on foot, and she hoped to mount Brave at some point to quicken the pace.

But hope departed when the sounds of those who approached accelerated their pace, coming closer, echoing in the eerie forest air.

"Och," Julianna ground out under her breath. They *were* following her. While she'd enjoy the chance to practice her skills at weaponry, she *was* quite exhausted.

With furtive eyes, she looked around for a place to hide. Hiding was always harder with an animal as huge as Brave. His black coat was on his side as far as camouflage and while he was trained to maintain his silence at her command, she couldn't control everything. If he had to sneeze, the animal wouldn't have the forethought to keep it to himself. She glanced at Brave. Had he sneezed at all today? Not recalling an instance, she prayed it would remain that way.

Julianna sheathed her sword, mounted the horse and clicked her tongue. Whoever followed already knew where she was, she had to gain speed or else be a sitting duck.

From behind, the sounds of pounding hooves reached her. The one who followed had also mounted their horse.

"Damn! Faster, Brave," she urged.

Julianna used all of her concentration to avoid hitting low hanging branches and to keep Brave from tripping over fallen trees. Being followed was already a given, she need not listen continuously to their approach, it was inevitable.

Bursting from the trees she found herself crossing over a hilly glen, dotted with protruding stones that glimmered in the moonlight. The sky was vast and black, filled with diamond stars and a bright moon. The grounds grew rougher, and the approaching rider came closer. She didn't dare turn around for fear of slowing Brave's pace. Her mount breathed hard, his muscles rippled with excitement at being able to burn energy. His hooves dug deep in the ground, clumps of earth flying behind them.

With each stride, the glen grew into a maze of ever growing rocks, some as tall as a croft, until she felt like she could get lost among them. After one sharp turn, she yanked Brave's reins to the right, up and over the rocky hill and then down behind, where she abruptly stopped. Dismounting, she crawled up to the edge where she could look over and down onto the path she'd just tread on. The ground was cold and wet to her bare hands, and she could feel its chill seeping through her cloak and gown at the knees. The rider approached at a break-neck pace. His cloak was dark and flashes of his plaid were seen with every pound of his mount's front legs. He was adorned in weapons, and lucky for her—alone. He disappeared beyond the sharp turn. Good riddance.

"Pray dinna think to double back as I have done. God speed to ye, mutton-head," she mumbled, staring at the emptiness of the road below.

"And God-speed to ye too, lass."

Julianna froze upon the ground. Terror took over, seizing her breath and her heart. She was sure she'd been careful. Not careful enough apparently.

"Dinna get up on my account," the man said with a chuckle. His voice was deep, throaty and completely familiar.

"Ronan," Julianna said, pushing to her feet. She whirled around. Wiped her dirty hands on her cloak.

He stood on the ground, his horse ten feet away munching on grass. The hound sat beside the horse, tail thumping. Obviously pleased it had found its catch. Ronan tossed the dog a strip of something.

How had she not heard his approach? *This* mutton-head was deceptively better skilled at stalking then he'd let on.

Hands on her hips, she glowered at him, hoping the light of the moon showed her displeasure.

"What are ye doing here?" she asked.

"I could ask ye the same thing."

"Dinna bother. I willna answer ye." She crossed her arms over her chest, prepared to stare him down.

"All right, your choice then. Whether or not ye tell me makes no matter. I've come to collect ye, and I'll not leave without ye."

Julianna laughed then. Arrogant arse. Did he really think it would be that easy? "Ye'll have to catch me first."

Chapter Eight

Ronan widened his eyes, his gaze focused on the hellion before him.

"What?" he asked, a little dumfounded.

Even as the words left his lips, Julianna was flying. The woman leapt into the air, twisted and kicked him square in the chest.

Pain met with her impact. What in the hell? He grunted, stumbled backward but managed to keep his balance. Where she'd planted her feet ached something fierce. The woman had some power, he'd give her that. But he'd little time to reflect on it. As soon as she'd landed, Julianna was off. Gripping the saddle, she leapt onto her horse's back, not even using the stirrup.

The sight was both fascinating and flabbergasting. Had she that much muscle? Wallace mentioned she had training but... Ronan was stunned.

He could do it, most warriors could, certainly, but a woman? Again, it would appear, he'd underestimated her.

Ronan reached out, as though he'd be able to stop her with such a feeble move. She rounded her beast on him, the horse's huge head coming close, his teeth bared and chomping as though he would bite him square on the nose.

Having no other choice but to back up or be mauled, Ronan chose to live and took a few healthy steps backward.

"Wait, woman! For Christ's sake!" he shouted.

Julianna whirled her horse to the side, the mount's overlarge teeth no longer gnashing for Ronan's face. She was breathtaking in her anger and beauty. She glowered down at him, all fire, but then a subtle shift took place on the planes of her face. A smile formed and he felt almost like she'd kicked him in the chest once more.

He'd noticed before, oh how he'd noticed, but this was something different entirely. His every dream in a woman come true. How proudly she sat on that horse. Thighs clenched tight, hands fisted on the reins. The strength emanating from her was mesmerizing. What he wouldn't give to have all that power clenched and fisted around himself.

Och! Obviously other parts of him wished for the same thing. And quite fervently. Thank the Saints for his cloak, hiding the fact that his cock had grown hard and tented the front of his plaid. Ronan swallowed hard, willing his wayward member to dissipate. Julianna's sweet sheath would never be wrapped around his cock, his fingers or riding his tongue.

Oh, sweet goddess.

Ronan cleared his throat, hoping that would clear his mind.

"What the hell is wrong with ye?" Julianna asked, her furrowed brow deepening. "Ye look ill. Are ye all right?"

He cleared his throat again. "Aye. I'm all right. Now, get down off that horse."

She shook her head. "Nay going to happen, lad."

"Lad?"

A teasing chuckle issued from her most perfectly formed lips. "'Tis how ye're acting. What else would ye have me call ye?"

Lover? The most stimulating Highlander alive? How many things he would have her call him.

Ronan stopped himself from shaking his head. "I would have ye get off that horse."

"Well, now," she said, her small smile transforming into a challenging, triumphant one, "as I said, I willna be getting off this horse, and ye will have to catch me first."

The last word spoken, she kicked Brave and the horse lurched forward. Within seconds, she was gone, Ronan left staring at her back, her fiery blonde colored hair breaking free of her hood and catching the wind.

"Ballocks!" he hissed. Two fingers in his mouth, he whistled for his horse who quickly came to his side.

Ronan mounted and wasted no time in giving chase. Lil Lass loping behind. Julianna wouldn't get away that easily. He wasn't the type to give up a fight, a challenge and she'd issued one, no doubt about that.

Leaning over this horse's withers, Ronan gained speed. Where Julianna had once been a black speck ahead, she gained shape. He groaned at the sight of her bottom rising and falling from the horse, other more lascivious thoughts taking root within his imagination.

The woman was making him want to seek out confession, seek out a priest to rid him of the possession she'd done on him, and Ronan wasn't a religious man.

"Julianna!" he shouted to the wind, her name tossed back to hit him square in the jaw. The woman didn't even turn around to look at him.

Either she'd not heard him, or she was ignoring him. No matter, he'd not let her get away. He shouted to Saint, squeezed his thighs tighter around the horse's middle and held on as the beast surged forward. Julianna had an admirable mount to be sure, but not nearly as well-formed and trained as his own.

Saint was a horse in his own class. The highest class.

"That's right, now," he said, a laugh on the end. He was gaining on her, and thoroughly enjoying this game of cat and mouse.

Blood pumped through his veins, surging with a force that left him feeling almost like he was floating. Closer. Closer. He was almost on her.

Julianna did look back then, her plush lips forming an O of surprise. '

Ronan grinned at her. A smile that said it all—he was going to win and there was nothing she could do about it. "That's right, sweeting," he mumbled. "Ye'll be mine."

The words carried more weight than he'd intended. He'd only meant that he would win, that he'd gain control of her horse, of her. That she'd not be getting away from him. Had she heard? From her expression of bewilderment, horror, interest, it would appear she had. But the words hung heavy in the air around them, and the moment was quickly broken as she turned to face forward, leaning lower over her horse.

Her animal seemed to wrench energy from some invisible force and she pulled ahead. Ronan reached out, but too late she was no longer within his grasp.

He wouldn't lose her that easily. Not by mistakenly saying something that, unbidden, hit them both harder than he'd expected.

Saint, catching on that they were in a race, surged forward at a quicker pace, giving Ronan the upper hand once more. He plucked Julianna from her horse, settled her on his lap and slowed his horse to a stop. She smacked at him, jabbed him in the jaw and uttered words he'd never heard even some men say. For the first time, he was touching her. Her arse was taut, but supple as she bounced against his legs. Arms that were sculpted, firm, a back that had muscles he wasn't aware women could possess. Julianna was pure power in a woman's body. It was all he could do to not toss up her skirts and fully examine every inch. She continued to fight, ceaseless in her struggle to be free. But for all her bluster, she didn't actually hurt him. An act he knew to be purposeful since he was fully aware that if she wanted to, she could do some serious damage. Mayhap that meant she wanted to lose.

But Ronan couldn't think further on that. With two sisters of his own, four if you included his two sisters by marriage, he was not about to contemplate the female mind. He'd long ago determined they were a force to be reckoned with and a mystery no man would ever uncover.

Her own mount, which noticed the missing weight, slowed ahead and promptly went to munching on grass. Selfish animal. Ronan chuckled.

"I win." Unable to help himself, Ronan leaned forward to smell her hair. Horses, fresh air. Completely intoxicating.

Julianna slapped him hard on the face. A stinging slap that had him gripping her tight around the waist as he tried to recover from it, not wanting her to escape.

"That wasn't verra nice," he muttered.

"'Twasn't meant to be, ye boar!"

"What am I going to do with ye?" he asked, shaking his head slightly, and grinning. "Shall I bend ye over my knees? Give ye a spank?" He easily flipped her over, even while she kicked, and heaven help him, he slapped her firm little arse.

Glory be, it was the most erotic thing he'd done to date.

"Oh, ye fish-bellied, mottle head!"

"Mottle head?" he asked with a raised brow.

Julianna let out a frustrated groan. "Turn me over."

Ronan did so with pleasure. He wanted to see her angry face. Loved the way her eyes widened, mouth opened in shock. She didn't disappoint.

"What are ye doing? Do ye know what Robert will do when he learns of your treatment of me?"

Ronan shrugged and said, "Thank me?"

"Oh!" she shoved against him again, her long fingers pressing against his chest. Good lord, he liked that.

He liked everything she did, every little touch, even that slap.

Damn, he was getting too ahead of himself. But it was unstoppable. Ever since the day he'd first seen her storming across the bailey. She'd stopped to calmly speak to a few, then he'd seen her rail at another. A force to be reckoned with. 'Twas clear at that moment the woman held clout not only at Eilean Donan, but within the minds of every man and the few women there. One hell of a baker.

And she'd certainly captivated him.

"Dinna be angry with me," Ronan said softly. His words appeared to startle her.

She flinched and pulled back. "How can I not be? I left the castle for a reason. Did ye think I just went out for an evening jaunt?"

Ronan shook his head. "Nay, lass."

"I am no lass. Dinna call me that."

But she was a lass. And he wanted to scoop her up and hold her close. There he went again, unable to stop his thoughts from turning to touching her, holding her, protecting her. Somehow she'd wiggled her way inside him and he couldn't get her out. Wanted more.

"Lady Julianna, if ye would but tell me why ye've gone out into the wilds of Scotland unprotected, I may be able to help ye."

"I am protected."

"Before I came along."

She laughed then, a scathing laugh that made his belly twist. "Ye dolt, I can protect myself."

That stung a little. "But even more so with me here." He offered a smile, hoping to calm her. He liked when she was angry, but not when she was disparaging.

"I suppose ye're right. But if I were to tell ye why I've left, ye'd only take me back. That is why ye were sent after me, no?"

Ronan didn't want to lie. "Aye. The Bruce and Wallace both wanted me to come collect ye."

"And they sent ye alone?"

"Nay, I've got the hound as well." Lil Lass had followed well behind him as he chased Julianna and he admitted to being worried she wouldn't.

"A hound and a warrior to catch me. I can see they thought I'd get far," she said, the sarcasm in her voice overwhelming.

Ronan laughed. "Dinna think so, my lady. In fact, I'd planned on taking more, but Wallace made it clear to me why such would have only drawn attention."

"How so?"

"Ross wants ye, lass. If a search party had been sent out, every scout he's got within these trees would know it."

Julianna nodded. "Did ye happen to see who camped at his abandoned site?"

Nodding, he said, "A band of heathens."

She gave him a suspicious look. "Did ye know I'd gone down the ravine?"

Ronan's grin widened. "Aye. I hid in the forest and watched ye climb from the tree."

"Ye knew I was in the tree?"

"I confess, I did. Ye made a noise."

"A noise?"

"Aye. Mayhap your shoe scraped on the limb ye perched on."

Julianna scrunched up her nose and pursed her lips. "This little jaunt of mine has proven I need more practice."

"No way in hell," Ronan said before thinking.

Julianna's grunt of disgust was wholly expected. "Ye dinna own me, warrior. No man owns me and no man ever will."

Ronan didn't know if it was the vehement passion in her tone or the desire that kindled in her eyes. Whatever it was, it reached out and grabbed hold of him, propelling him forward. He slipped his hand behind her neck, threading his fingers into her soft hair, and tugged her forward as his face descended. When his lips touched hers, it felt like a fire ignited between them, consuming him. Julianna pulled back, mumbling against his lips but he wouldn't let her stop this kiss.

Not yet. He wanted a chance, wanted to see if this was everything it was built up to be in his mind, desired to see her response, to know once and for all if the passion growing between them, if the crackling air thick with need was real.

Ronan deepened the kiss, tasting her plump lips, teasing the crease of her mouth. He massaged her scalp with one hand and gripped tight to her waist with the other. He never wanted to let her go.

Damn…but he had to stop.

And then she responded.

A sweet, contagious mewl in the back of her throat. He answered with a growl of his own. Julianna opened her mouth, her tongue darting out to swipe at his before timidly retreating. He chased, stroking her tongue, teasing her, tracing every part of her mouth. She tasted sweet, succulent, a meal he could survive on for eternity.

The pressure of Julianna's hands on his chest lessoned from pushing to massaging as she felt the outline of his muscles. He tensed, never having reacted to a woman's touch the way he did with her. Desire curled deep inside him, ready to spring out with the slightest provocation.

"Julianna," he murmured against her lips, loving the feel and taste of her.

She whimpered, circling her tongue around his, her hands moving from his chest to his shoulders where she dug deep. He slipped his hand around her waist and pulled her flush against him. Her breasts crushed to his chest. So soft compared to the coiled tautness of her body. Softness mixed in with her muscle. Her nipples were hard, damned hard. Had to be or else he wouldn't have been able to feel those two taut points through the layers or their clothing.

He had his answer. She wanted him. More so, kissing her, feeling her breasts on him, he was once again struck with the sense of familiarity. As though this had happened before.

"Ronan," she whispered. "I swore this wouldn't happen again." Her fingers scraped lightly over his neck and into his hair.

What? He pulled back. "Again?"

In the moonlight he could see the dazed expression on her face, to which a part of him felt very satisfied for being the cause. The lucid part of him, however, was stuck on the word *again*.

Julianna nodded, looking a little confused. "Aye. When ye had a fever."

"Ah." That answered a lot of questions. "So ye took advantage of an invalid." He wiggled his brows. "What else did ye take advantage of?"

Gasping, she slapped playfully at his chest. "Ye are a brute. I didna take advantage of ye. 'Twas the other way around."

"How can a man in the throes of fever take advantage of a lass? Especially a lass as strong as ye?" He prodded the muscles of her upper arm. "I daresay ye had the advantage."

Julianna yanked from his grasp, a flash of insecurity coming over her. Was it possible she was ashamed her of physique?

That was an issue he would happily remedy. "Why did ye pull away? I like your strength." He stroked gently over her arms, wishing they were in a warm place and that it would have been all right to peel away the layers of her clothing and examine her further.

That, however, would be completely inappropriate. Kissing her was one thing, undressing her and plundering her tight little body was something wholly different. And likely to get him a knife in the throat by her and another from the Bruce.

With that sobering thought in mind he leaned back a little. Julianna's face turned placid.

"Ye're only saying that so as not to offend me."

Ronan grinned and winked. "I've nay problem offending anyone."

Julianna snorted. "That, I do believe."

However much he wanted to kiss her to make her realize how wrong she was in not believing him, Ronan had the gut feeling words would be best for her.

"My lady... I want ye to believe that if the Bruce did not stand between us, indeed if the whole of Scotland and England did not put a barrier between the two of us, I would strip ye of every inch of fabric and worship the length of ye."

Julianna's mouth fell open and she sucked in a quick breath. Speechless. He wasn't sure if he'd ever seen her that way. But her eyes were not void of reaction. Wide, they jerked to gaze from his lips and back to his eyes several times.

"I'm nay going back to the castle. Not until I'm done," she whispered, changing the subject away from making love.

A change he regretfully should thank her for. Else he turn her over once more and not only spank her, but lift her skirts.

"Tell me. Let me help ye."

She shook her head.

"I will make a deal with ye."

Again, she shook her head.

"Dinna be stubborn. I'm offering to help ye. If I brought ye back to the castle, ye'd only escape again to do whatever it is ye deem so important. I am offering to help ye, to provide escort."

Her mouth closed and she glanced away as if contemplating what he said. If she was actually going to give it some thought, he would let her. Ronan studied the landscape to make sure they were still alone. All was still. The sky was growing lighter, turning into a purplish grey instead of black. The sun would be fully risen within the next two hours.

Crossing her arms over her chest, she said, "Fine. Ye can come with me."

Victory. "Where are we going?"

"I am going to find Laird Ross. And I'm going to kill him."

Chapter Nine

Julianna tamped down the urge to clap her hand over her mouth, to pull back the words she'd just spoken. Ronan would force her to return to Eilean Donan now, an action which would in turn compel her to react.

A reaction she was sure to regret as would the steely warrior whose lap she perched on.

She could wallop him good in the temple, knock him out. Or mayhap less brutal, she could pull the dirk from her sleeve and make him put her down. But with the latter, he'd probably think he could overpower her, and Julianna did not want to inflict deadly force upon him.

Damn the man!

A wallop it would be. Just how should she go about it? She supposed she could play on his more desirous self and lean in for a kiss. He'd be none the wiser as she raised her hand to strike.

Julianna licked her lips, determined to be on her way within the next five minutes. Ronan's gaze followed the path her tongue took to wet her lips. Good. He was interested in kissing her some more. And, for heaven's sake, she was too. But no. She couldn't be caught up in the thrill of his mouth on hers, in the sensual, lightning-like exploration his tongue had taken.

Ronan lowered his face an inch, then stopped. Julianna stared at his chin, lightly touched his arm. She couldn't look him in the eye. Not when she knew this was all a ploy to get away. She almost felt sorry for him.

And herself.

"Julianna." His voice had taken on a husky tone. "We canna stay here. The sun is coming up."

She swallowed, trying to hold back the sudden sting of his rejection. 'Twas somewhat puzzling that he could want to kiss her, but sought to distract her away from the task. An act of self-preservation? Could be.

She wasn't going to give up though.

"I want…" How did one say they wished to kiss someone? She didn't want to appear too forward, even if it was only to make him let his guard down.

"Aye, my lady, I do too."

Oh dear, his voice was even lower, guttural. A sound that scraped tantalizingly along her nerves. Why did she have to want him so desperately?

She just had to remember what was more important—Ross and Scotland. Ridding the land of the treacherous bastard who'd threatened not only her life but that of everyone she didn't know.

"Then kiss me," she said, surprised at the sound of her own voice. This farce was affecting her far more than she wanted or appreciated.

Ronan wasted no time in answering her request. He growled, glanced away as though he hoped to change his mind, but not a second later he put his hands on either side of her face, guided her mouth to his and crushed their lips together. No gentle kiss was this. No exploration of each other. 'Twas pure, unadulterated passion.

And she nearly forgot to give him a thump on the head! Julianna tried to put her mind to rights as his tongue plundered her mouth. Tried to muster strength in her arms to lift one and put some power behind her swing. But her fingers trembled and every swipe of his tongue had her going mad with need, with thoughts of what this meant.

She was enjoying it too much.

Julianna fisted a hand, raised it, but then let it sink against his shoulder where she opened her hand and squeezed his muscle.

Shivers stole over her, racing up and down her spine and throughout her limbs. Her breasts grew heavy, aching with need and their peaks pebbled sending frissons of pleasure to pull at her core. Squirming against him, she worked to grow closer, to press herself to his chest, to feel the length of him, his warmth on her body.

A moan, a whimper. They were hers, coming from her own throat.

This was all his fault. Why did he have to be so charming? So good with his lips?

Her fingers trailed up his neck, around the back to tug at his soft hair. He did the same to her, and she felt herself melting another fraction.

No! She had to knock him out! Had to escape from his embrace, the hold he had on her mind.

The hound growled, an eerie warning that had them both scrambling apart. Julianna's breath came in rapid pants, her heart beat so hard she thought it might crack her ribs. She swiped trembling fingers over her kiss-swollen lips.

The dog had not ceased its growling and had jumped to its feet, hackles raised. Even their horses' ears pinned back.

"Someone comes," Ronan said so softly she barely heard him.

Julianna listened. Could hear the faint hoof beats in the distance. She nodded.

"We'll be faster if ye ride your own horse."

Again she nodded. And she could get away.

"Dinna try to escape me. I will only follow ye."

How had he guessed her plan?

Ronan nudged his horse over to hers and lifted her effortlessly, placing her on her own saddle. He gripped her chin, looked sternly into her eyes.

"Whatever the outcome is, know that I plan to help ye with Ross. I'll nay take ye back to the castle until ye've seen your mission completed."

Julianna's eyes widened. He truly would? She'd heard him say as much before, but had not believed him. The conviction, however, in his eyes was enough to change her mind. Ronan meant every word. That was a shocking revelation.

"Why?"

"We want the same thing. I'll explain more later. We must ride."

He was right, the longer they dallied, the less chance they had of staying out of sight of whoever approached.

"Follow me."

Ronan surged forward, his horse's legs loping in such an elegant way she froze for a moment to watch. Brave also had a beautiful gait. And while she was mesmerized by the animal's beauty, she was not frozen. Julianna realized with stunning clarity the reason why—it was Ronan on the horse. Tall, strong, powerful. He exuded raw power and sensuality. She shivered, shook her head and then urged her horse to move.

Ronan pointed toward another rise of rocks, and they wound their way up the hill, riding toward the rising sun. Julianna only took a moment to turn around, whoever approached was a tiny speck now and she hoped they didn't see her and Ronan and that if they did, they didn't care. With her luck, however, that would be too much to ask.

The wind whipped her hood and hair into her eyes and with it came a few stinging pelts of ice rain. Once again, her luck appeared to be the cause — for she had no luck.

Pulling her hood closer, she followed Ronan, keeping his horse's rear in her sights at all time. The ice rain found its way against her face, pinging against her forehead and cheeks, melting with the heat of her flesh and dripping into her eyes only to freeze upon her lashes. At least it was no longer completely dark. If she'd been blinded by icicles on her eyelashes and a nighttime sky, things would have been even worse.

"Come on!" Ronan called. His voice was urgent, made her nerves grate with fear.

Why was he acting as though their escape was crucial? She couldn't turn around to look, not with the way the ice and wind whipped. But she did listen. The wind whistled, the ice hit the ground, rocks and them with varying sounds. And beyond that the sound of approaching horses' hooves beat a rapid pace on the earth. They were being followed.

Julianna swallowed hard, growled under her breath. 'Twould appear that every man and his brother were out to keep her from her task. She'd not take it as a sign, but a challenge.

"We have to face them!" she shouted.

"Too many!"

Julianna took Ronan at his word. The hills grew steep, and soon their horses slowed with the exertion of climbing on slippery slopes.

"Almost there," Ronan called behind him.

Where was there? But she couldn't ask him, couldn't speak, was trying too hard to stay seated on Brave. Her saddle was wet and slippery and with each of her horse's jerky steps forward she slipped a little and had to tug herself back in place. Her arms and thighs burned from the exertion, and her hands stung from the cold. Her gloves were warm in winter, but in the rain...they could only take so much moisture and were beginning to freeze onto her flesh. Tears stung her eyes, threatening to spill.

Toughen up, she told herself. No time to worry over little things like sore muscles and frozen hands. She was a warrior. Warriors didn't cry over pitiful things like that.

Ronan certainly wasn't crying. He forged ahead. In the wilds of the Highlands, especially with enemies hiding within their own, to quit meant death. Julianna would beat death. Prove to Ronan that she was made of tougher stuff. That she was just as brave as he was. She didn't need him to provide protection, she could be *his* guard.

With renewed confidence she gripped the reins harder, tightened her legs and shouted for Brave to keep up his strength. Ronan called back his encouragement which made her smile, although it was a gritty determined grin. She kind of liked making him proud. Liked the way he called for her to keep up her courage.

The rise flattened out for a good twelve feet and curved around, a safer path given the weather, but Ronan surged ahead, continuing the climb. She understood why. Those who followed would see the easier path and think they took it. He was smart. A niggling fear that she would have taken the easier path droned inside her. But she couldn't be worrying about what she would and wouldn't do and what Ronan had chosen. Comparing the two of them was ridiculous.

And yet, it was hard not to. One of Julianna's weaknesses was her habit of comparing herself to others. To warriors, to other women. To the kitchen staff, to the ladies at court and even Robert. Examining each one and seeing their strengths and weaknesses was a practice she'd started back when her training first began. And if she was honest, it was really before then. She was a natural. Came out studying people. Hence the reason her parents insisted on this position for her.

For some time she'd considered herself lucky in that regard. The only bit of luck she had. And was a natural talent really a stroke of luck?

Julianna groaned inside. Why was she even bothering to have this conversation with herself? A weakness was not something to ponder and make excuses about. A weakness was something that needed to be conquered and since she was full aware of it, not in denial, she'd best start now.

Lifting her chin, she rode on. Ronan's horse slipped, his back hooves skidding a foot, give or take a few inches. Brave whinnied and she feared he'd rear up which would only force them both back down the hill.

"Steady!" she and Ronan both called to their animals.

Ronan's horse continued to slide backward, the rain having fallen hard enough to make the ground slick with mud. Julianna hauled Brave's reins to the side, going around Ronan in time before his horse caused her own to rear up. Ronan looked at her, and she found herself struck. His eyes were hard, indomitable and yet a flash of fear built inside them. His mouth was pressed thin, his lips white around the edges.

The man was determined to beat this slide. He would get to the top, that much was evident. What else was evident was that Julianna wanted to help him. She just wasn't sure how. Brave had steadier feet, and was able to dig his hooves deep into the mud, holding on for dear life.

"Come on!" she shouted to Ronan. "Grab hold!" She reached out her hand and he stared at it like she held out a rotten, maggot-infested limb. "Take my hand."

When his mount slid further, his skeptic gaze faded and he did grab her hand. She used all her strength in that arm and then some to hold on. The wetness of both their gloves molded into a tight seal, instead of simply sliding away. She was going to hurt tomorrow, but that mattered little. Letting Ronan and his horse fall behind was not an option.

Her legs gripped like an iron vice to her horse and with Ronan's impressive hold, she guided them both up the steep incline. There was no time to rest when they made it to the top, though her entire body shook from cold and fatigue. If they traveled much longer, she'd be in danger of needing saving. Julianna let Ronan have the lead once more since he seemed familiar with the land and because she didn't want to completely emasculate him. Having just saved his arse, she wasn't sure how he would react. Most men did not appreciate a woman's help. Especially hers. Julianna had learned to be more humble over the years instead of boasting of her victories.

Ronan appeared to have set his sights on heading west once more. Thank goodness. She didn't want to lose the ground she'd already made on Ross. Although they'd gone northward, at least they were still headed in the right direction. Having Ronan come along with her, although not her original intent, was starting to grow on her. He knew the area better. And, honestly, having him to assist should a fight break out wasn't a bad idea. He had, after all, come to her aid once before.

The man was probably also trying to impress Robert. Wanted to move up in the ranks. She could help him with that.

"We need to find shelter," she said, riding beside him.

Ronan nodded, but didn't look her way. "Aye. There is a place ahead."

"Ye're not thinking of that small village are ye?" Kinterloch was no place for them to hide.

Ronan did flash her a grin then, his gaze stroking her face for a split-second before turning back to the horizon with a frown. The man was so confusing.

"I'm nay an imbecile, my lady." His voice came out scathing.

Julianna's mouth fell open. "I never said such a thing."

"There are other ideas besides your own."

"I am well aware of that and perfectly willing to explore them, if I but knew what they were."

"Ye see? Ye canna allow me to lead the way after all."

Julianna huffed a breath. Mayhap the man was indeed an imbecile. Hadn't she let him do just that?

"I told ye, I have the same goal as ye. I want Ross dead. I want my revenge on him. And then I need to take ye back to the castle. Do ye think I'd sabotage that?"

Shaking her head, she held in an unladylike retort and instead said, "Apologies, Ronan. I did not mean to offend ye. I was merely hoping we were not going into the village because I believe Ross is seeking shelter there."

Ronan frowned at her then turned back to the road. "We are nay headed into the village. But there are a few abandoned crofts on the outskirts."

"All right."

He glanced at her a moment longer, but said nothing. They rode the rest of the way in silence. There was a cluster of three crofts closely built together, not a soul in sight. Even still, Ronan took his sword from its sheath and jumped from his horse.

"Will ye hold the reins while I check inside?"

Julianna nodded and withdrew her own sword, in case those who'd followed found them—or others lurked in the shadows. Within minutes of sitting still, the cold seeped deep within her bones and she shivered violently, teeth chattering. The sword grew heavy and hard to hold.

Ronan returned, eyeing her with concern. "Ye're freezing. Let us get inside and build a fire. They are still abandoned."

Julianna tried to climb down from Brave's back, but ended up falling instead. Her limbs just wouldn't work right. Ronan caught her in mid-air, his heat seeping both painfully and deliciously into her bones. "We need to get ye warm," he muttered and carried her the rest of the way inside, leading the horses behind him.

Julianna clutched to Ronan's cloak, willing herself to regain strength, but it appeared that even her stubborn will was failing in this respect.

Ronan yanked a dry plaid from his satchel and laid it on the ground. He set her on her feet, and her knees knocked together. She wrapped her arms around herself, rubbing furiously. Never had she been so cold. Had to be the ice rain. Normally, she sought shelter right away, she wasn't usually running away from fiends.

Ronan eyed her with a narrowed gaze. "Take off your clothes."

Julianna gasped, clutched her soaking wet cloak tighter to her chest. "Wh-what?"

"We need to get ye warm."

Very practical indeed, but completely out of the question. "Taking off my clothes willna do it."

"Aye, but getting ye out of the wet and into dry will. Do it now." His voice was stern. There would be no arguing with him.

"Turn your back at least," she sputtered.

Ronan rolled his eyes, crossed his arms, but did turn around. Julianna struggled with the heavy, wet fabric. It felt like an eternity went by and every few minutes she swore he would turn around to see if she was done, but he didn't. In fact, he was a perfect gentleman. With her clothes in a puddled heap at her feet, Julianna ripped the tossed plaid off the floor and wrapped it around herself.

She was still cold, although being dry eased her chill a little. Her icicle hair even started to melt a little.

"Ye can turn around," she said through chattering teeth.

Ronan did so, and had the decency not to look at her. His gaze was at the ceiling, then on the floor and then flicking around the room as he tried to gaze anywhere but at her. Julianna bit the inside of her cheek to keep from laughing.

"Can we build a fire?" Julianna prayed he'd say yes.

"Aye. I'll get the wood."

Ronan whirled around and sped from the croft as though a demon chased him.

Chapter Ten

God's teeth!

This was most assuredly a test. A test of his willpower, a test of his fortitude. Control. Ballocks, he needed to gain control!

Ronan raked his hands through his hair, flicking water this way and that. He was wet and should be cold, but instead his blood was hotter than a blaze. All because she'd undressed. Not even within his vision, but the idea of her taking her clothes off only feet away had nearly been the death of him.

Sweet Jesu, the woman was naked.

If he wanted to, he could sweet talk her out of his plaid, watch the fabric pool at her feet and then truly see, touch and taste her flesh. Oh, how he desired to do so. And it would be easy. She melted in his arms each time he'd kissed her. If he was good, and he knew he was, she'd be naked and beneath him in the next five minutes.

But he couldn't do that for many reasons. One, she'd most likely kill him afterward. Two, the Bruce would kill him if she didn't, and three… He just couldn't. Seducing her was wrong in so many ways, and the fact that he cared about the morality of the situation bespoke much. Was he growing soft? Ronan was a self-professed ladies' man. Charmed them into bed faster than a swarm of bees on a sweet smelling flower.

Ronan gritted his teeth. He couldn't be that way with Julianna. She wasn't a light skirt and she wasn't a woman willing to spread her legs for any man. The woman was most likely a virgin and should remain that way until the day she married.

And hell if he was going to be the man to marry her. Nay, that was certainly not going to happen. Ronan would never marry. Whatever lust he felt for Julianna had to end now. Leaning his head back, he closed his eyes and let the cold rain pelt on his face for a few moments, wishing it would clear his brain. Give him the miracle cure of no longer desiring Julianna and wishing to uncover her mysteries.

It didn't work.

"Och! Damn!" He stormed around the outside of the crofts, trying to find some wood he could use to build a fire. Most of the wood outside was wet, but he managed to find a few logs nestled beneath the pines that weren't completely soaked yet. He also found a few left inside the crofts no one had bothered to steal. With the prized wood huddled beneath his cloak he marched back to the croft he'd chosen for them to sleep in. The most kept together one. No leaky roof and a front door that hadn't been ripped off.

He'd kept the reason he knew of this place to himself. Julianna need not know that Ronan had come upon the place when he first traveled to Eilean Donan. She need not know that he'd witnessed the carnage that took place before his arrival. There were thirteen graves in a secluded spot behind these crofts. Men, women, children. He'd buried them all. Too late to save any of them.

Except one.

A wee lad. The poor boy was not more than six or seven, and without a family to look after him he would have died had Ronan left him behind. He took the boy with him to the Bruce's camp and put him in the kitchens to work. He didn't think anyone was aware what happened to little Tad, that Ronan had found him. He didn't want the boy to be pestered about it. Would make him sad or scared. Ronan had been that young when his own parents were murdered.

Everyone walked around giving him pity-filled faces like he was the saddest creature on earth. Ronan had hated it. Hated to see the pity in their eyes. Like he might perish because his parents had. If anything, their death made him stronger. Made him into the man he was today. A fighter. A warrior.

Ronan burst through the door of the cabin, frightening Julianna enough that she jumped and the plaid she'd wrapped herself in slipped a little off her shoulder.

He hissed in a breath at the sight of that tiny bit of flesh. Rounded with muscle, smooth and silky looking. She'd laid her clothes out flat to dry on the large square dining table. He tore his gaze away and turned toward the small hearth built in the far corner. A good eight feet away from her. 'Twas as far away as he was likely to get from her in such a small space.

Dumping the wood, he searched the room for a flint, but could find none. Luckily, he'd brought one. But it meant he had to step closer. The woman's toes peeped out beneath the plaid just a foot away from his satchel.

Long, slim toes, just as regal as the air she gave off but frighteningly white, reminding him of how cold she was.

"Toss me the satchel," he asked, finding that would be easier than having to step near her.

But, he hadn't exactly thought that through. As she dipped, now clutching the plaid with only one hand as a naked arm slipped out to grasp the leather strap of his bag, all sorts of lusty thoughts ran rampant in his mind. One false move and the plaid would be on the ground. Or slip and show more skin than just her arm.

His breaths quickened, heart beat erratically. He let out the breath he'd been holding when she tossed it at him. Barely enough time to react, he reached out before it hit him square in the face.

"Stop staring, ye brute." Julianna frowned, her brows furrowing together and daggers flying from her eyes. Her teeth chattering only served to lessen the rebuke. Showed that she was human rather than the goddess he believed her to be.

Her response was a good reminder to his libido that he needed to take a step back from her and this situation. They would never be together. That naked shoulder and those nude toes were as much of her flesh as he'd ever see.

Ronan nodded. "Apologies."

Julianna grunted. "None needed. I'd be offended if ye hadn't."

Ronan raised a brow. "Aye?"

"Aye."

He wanted to ask her why, but that conversation would only lead down a path he wasn't willing to take. Instead, he turned his back, carrying his satchel over to the hearth. Kneeling, he arranged the wood just so and then struck the flint. The wood smoked, too soggy to burn. Damn. But he wasn't going to give up.

Ronan stood and searched the croft once more, trying his best to ignore the minx dressed only in his plaid. Julianna did her best to stay out of his way too. She sat on the floor, her knees pulled up, the plaid covering every inch of her, save her head. Aye, he wasn't trying to look at her, but it was a little harder than simply pretending she wasn't there.

"While ye were out getting the wood I noticed some linens in that cupboard."

"Linens?" Did she wish him to bathe? That was absurd. He needed to get her warm.

"Aye. They will burn. Help catch the wood on fire."

"Ah," he sighed. "That may work." Ronan pulled open the cupboard and grabbed out the stack of old linens. He refused to think about the people that used it. Refused to imagine a time where little Tad's mother might have rubbed one on his head after washing his hair. He ripped the linens into strips and stuffed them in between and under the wood. After, he lit each linen with the flint, watching the fabric catch and burn, turning red then black. Flames erupted, and the wood smoked, but eventually dried out and started to smolder. It worked.

"Come closer to the fire," Ronan demanded. His voice came out harsher than he intended, but he needed it to. Needed to not sound like he cared, else she'd get the impression that he did.

A whisper of fabric was her answer. Moments later she was beside him, sinking to the ground. Her scent surrounded him. Subtly different with the rain, still wholly intoxicating.

Ronan glanced at her, unable to abide his own decision to ignore her. Her plush lips were blue around the edges and still her teeth chattered. Skin was deathly pale.

"This should help to warm ye."

She nodded, her gaze at the fire.

Ronan searched within his bag until he found a flask of Cook's spiced whisky.

"This should warm ye, too."

"Is that what I hope it is?" She gifted him with a charming smile.

A smile that made his breath catch. Ronan gritted his teeth.

"What are ye hoping for?"

"Cook's whisky," she answered.

Why did he wish she'd asked for something else? Perhaps maybe for him to hold her and rub some warmth into her flesh? Ballocks, he was at it again.

"Aye, that it is." He uncorked the flask and handed it to her.

Their fingers brushed sending a spark of lust to tingle through his veins. Ronan jerked back as though burned. But he couldn't take his eyes off her. She put her lips daintily to the flask, tilted her head back and swallowed. The way her throat worked as she drank had him imagining her throat doing other things. Wicked deeds. Acts that could *not* happen between them.

"Mmm," she moaned, handing him back the flask as she wiped the back of her hand over her lips. "That was lovely. I've been wanting some of her whisky since I was in Ross' camp."

"I'm happy to oblige. Let me know if ye want some more."

"'Haps in a few minutes."

"What happened there?"

Julianna pursed her lips. "Where?"

Ronan took a sip of the whisky, enjoying the burn in the back of his throat. "Ye know what I mean." They'd not discussed her imprisonment before, hadn't had the time, but now, here in the croft, all they had was time. And he meant to fill it up any other way than by kissing and touching.

"Aye. I knew what ye meant."

He was surprised she admitted it. Not surprised she didn't indulge him further.

"That lovely a time, lass?"

Julianna gave a short laugh. "Incredible."

"Ye jest, but I spoke in earnest."

"I know." She smiled and reached out a delicate hand — one that showed the length of her bare arm.

He stared at her limb, noting the elegant curve of muscles almost a contradiction to her delicate bone structure. The woman worked hard, that much was evident. More than just kneading dough. Ronan handed her the flask, avoiding her touch this time.

After taking a sip, Julianna flicked her gaze to the fire, her eyes clouding. "They were horrid. Barbaric." She huddled deeper into the plaid. "I was dying. They deprived me of food and drink. What they provided was not even good enough for a hound."

At that Lil Lass curled up beside Julianna. The massive dog was bigger than her, by a few stone or more. "Think she has fleas?" she asked with a little laugh, reaching out to stroke along the dog's back.

"Most likely."

"I dinna see anything jumping around. Nothing eager to nibble at my fingertips."

Not true. He was completely eager to nibble on her fingertips and any other part she wanted. "They lie in wait."

She smiled, her gaze meeting his for a moment, and he was struck with the power behind them. There was much more to Julianna than what met the eye. A thought he'd had more times than he could count.

"Dinna all beasts lie in wait until the moment ye turn your back on them?" Her words were deeper than what they meant on the surface.

"Indeed they do."

"Unless ye willingly allow them."

"Aye." What did she mean? Was she referring to fleas? To Ross? To himself?

"I'll not take advantage of ye, my lady."

Julianna's eyes widened in surprise before she shuttered them. "The thought never crossed my mind, Ronan."

He hoped that was because she would have willingly allowed him. With the heat of the fire and the whisky she'd consumed, Julianna's lips had turned back to a luscious shade of pink. He almost wished they were still blue, because now he could think of nothing more than kissing her again.

Food. They must eat. That would distract him—or at the very least keep his mouth busy. Ronan rummaged through his satchel and withdrew a few oatcakes, two legs of fowl he'd pilfered from Cook after the eve meal and an apple.

"I'm afraid we'll have to share the apple, but there is plenty of the rest." Ronan handed her an oatcake and the meat.

"I dinna like apples." Julianna took the offered fare and greedily bit into the meat. He watched, somewhat mesmerized, as she devoured the food.

"Hungry?" he asked with a chuckle.

Her face colored slightly and she smiled. "Starving, actually."

Ronan took a bite of meat, then asked, "Why dinna ye like apples?"

Julianna's lip curled and she gave him a look that said she'd been waiting for him to ask just that.

"Honestly, I dinna know. Haven't liked them since I was a child. 'Haps it was because we used them for target practice? Maybe I developed a fear that if I put an apple near my mouth I'd be a target?" She shrugged.

He raised a brow in question, then teased, "Ye're afraid of apples?"

"Och, I didna say that!"

"I think ye did. 'Haps ye're a distant relation to Eve?"

"Ye're a beast."

"And ye're afraid of a wee bit of fruit."

Julianna laughed. "Isn't there something silly ye're afraid of?"

"Warriors aren't afraid of anything," Ronan boasted.

That garnered him a fierce glare from Julianna. "Liar."

Ronan took a huge bite out of the apple, and wiggled the piece of fruit near her face. Julianna squealed and tried to lean back while holding her food and the plaid.

"Stop that!" Her laughter belied the grate in her tone.

"Come now, take a bite of my apple."

"Never." She shook her head and clamped her lips closed.

"Not even a teensy weensy bite?" He pulled his *sgian dubh* from his boot. "Even if I vow to annihilate the apple should it attack ye?"

"Not even then," she said with a laugh.

He slipped the weapon back in his boot and took another bite, a wide grin on his face. The woman was full of surprises. "Suit yourself, then."

"Ye've still not told me."

"Told ye what?"

"Now who is being elusive?"

"Not I," Ronan said with mock affront.

"Aye, 'tis ye."

"All right then, I shall tell ye something." Finishing off his meal, he leaned forward, rubbing his hands close to the fire. "I'm afraid of tomorrow."

"Tomorrow?"

He nodded. "No one knows what will happen."

"'Tis a fact."

"Aye. One that scares the hell out of me."

"Ye must be a verra controlling man." She raised a questioning, interested brow, picked at the remnants of meat on the bone of her dinner.

"Not entirely, but I dinna like surprises. I want to know what is going to happen and when. Unfortunately, we never know when tragedy will befall us. When someone close to us will die, or when we will be victorious."

Julianna was silent for a moment. Still. He glanced at her, saw that she looked poised to ask a question but then thought better of it. He could guess what she wanted to ask. That she'd want to know what tragedy had befallen him, but that was not something he wanted to discuss just yet. Maybe not ever.

"Do ye seek the aid of a wizard?" she asked.

Ronan could have fallen over laughing. Did she imagine him inside some hovel with a hundred year old man who stirred chipmunk eyes together with wildcat urine and told him what to expect when he woke?

"Nay, lass. Never have."

"Well, then ye canna be that afraid."

"I just dinna dwell on it."

"I suppose that is another answer to the problem. Dinna think of it. From this day forward, I willna think of apples." She handed Lil Lass the fowl leg and the dog jumped up and scurried to the opposite side of the room to devour it.

"A noble move, my lady."

"What? Not thinking of apples or giving the dog a bone?"

"Choosing to not let your fears rule ye."

"I hardly think I've let my fear of apples rule me."

"What does?"

"Rule me?"

"Aye."

The merriment left her eyes and she glanced toward the fire. He didn't think she would answer. Not when she'd shut down and looked so deep in thought. Ronan made sure the food was put away and brought out his wineskin. He took a sip of watered wine and passed it to Julianna. After a long draw she gave it back.

"Scotland rules me."

"Scotland? I suppose it rules us all."

She nodded. "Some more than others."

"Are ye the some?"

"Aye."

"Tell me."

Julianna shook her head. "I canna."

"I willna tell anyone."

Dipping her shoulder toward him, she gave him a coy look, a teasing smile curling her lips. "And, will ye offer me all your desserts for the next two years?"

Ronan winked. "I'll give ye whatever ye want."

Chapter Eleven

The man was tempting.

Too tempting. Julianna swallowed past the lump in her throat.

"All that whisky, I find myself growing tired," she said, annoyed with the way her voice came out sounding so breathy.

"We'd best get some rest. We can move out when dusk falls."

Julianna nodded. Traveling by night was for the best. They'd be less likely to be seen and most people would be sleeping — hopefully half or more of Ross' crew should they catch up to them.

The floor was hard, not nearly as comfortable as her bed at Eilean Donan, nor even the cot she'd slept on while prisoner.

But, she was exhausted, and the fire had finally warmed her toes and fingers enough she didn't think they would fall off.

Climbing to her feet, she reached for the satchel on her horse and pulled out the extra blanket she'd brought. Rolled up, it would make a nice pillow. Her gaze caught Ronan's form. He had no blanket.

"I thought to make this into a pillow, but now I realize, ye dinna have a blanket," she said.

"I dinna need one. The fire has me plenty warm."

Had she been completely selfish? "But your clothes are wet."

"Nearly dry now."

"Ye dinna need to make exceptions for me, Ronan, I can manage."

"I'm sure ye can, lass. Make yourself a pillow." He leaned his back against the wall, crossed his arms over his chest and closed his eyes.

Stubborn man. If he chose to freeze to death, she supposed it wouldn't be her fault, although she would miss his kisses. Julianna rolled her blanket before the fire and settled down. With the pillow, she was actually a lot more comfortable than she would have guessed. Exhaustion seeped well into her bones and though she blinked a few times, it didn't take her long to fall into a deep sleep.

She woke sometime later, surrounded on one side by the dog and Ronan on the other. But he was in the same spot. She however had somehow managed to scoot closer to him while sleeping. A play from her subconscious? Light streamed through the windows. Maybe mid-afternoon. The fire no longer blazed, but smoldered, its embers died down to red and black. The room was toasty warm. She no longer shivered, was indeed quite content. What had woken her? The dog let out a loud snore and Julianna suppressed a laugh. That must be what roused her. Feeling safe and warm, Julianna closed her eyes and fell back asleep.

The next time she woke, light no longer filtered in from the windows and the fire was completely out. The room was still warm, although she sensed the temperature had lowered judging from the cold on the tip of her nose. She however, was warm, hot even.

Mortification filled her and with it a sense of arousal. Her leg was tossed over Ronan's thigh. Her arm wrapped around his waist, her naked breasts pushed up against his side and her head on his chest.

God's teeth! She was nude and plastered to the man. Julianna's breath hitched. Ronan shifted, murmured something, but he didn't appear to be awake yet. As quick as she could, she rolled over, only be stopped by his fingers curling around her arm and hauling her back.

She gritted her teeth, glanced up at him. His eyes were closed, breaths steady. If he was awake she would have given him a new scar to rival any others he might have. Bastard. Apparently, fever was not the only thing needed to provoke him. Even in his sleep he was a lusty fool. Under different circumstances—as in an entirely different life—she would have snuggled closer. Perhaps explored his body, begged for a kiss.

But this was reality, and she wasn't about to lose herself in his embrace yet again—especially with no clothes on. As if his subconscious sensed her thoughts, he draped an arm around back, caging her to his side. His warmth surrounded her, drugged her, stomach jolted and God save her, her nipples hardened.

Reaching to the hand resting on her hip, she lifted it with two fingers in an effort to disengage herself from his hold, but the man actually pulled his hand from her grasp, grunted and tugged her closer.

A soft chuckle from his lips had her shoving him hard and then jumping to her feet, scrambling for the plaid to cover herself, but somehow the fabric had gotten caught beneath his large frame, and so only a few feet of it came up. She used the barely there scrap to cover her breasts and between her thighs, but the rest of her was completely exposed. In fact, the air was quite chilly against her bare bottom.

"Get off the plaid, ye bastard!" she screamed, yanking on it with vigor.

That only made Ronan laugh more. While he did roll away so she could yank the rest of it around herself, he did not stop laughing.

"Och, lass, what a lovely sight in the morning."

The nerve! She only growled back at him. Turning her back she stomped to the table to see if her clothes were dry. Mostly. Damp in a few spots, she could deal with that. At least they weren't soaked and once she was dressed, she'd no longer be on display for Ronan the Brute.

"Come now, my lady, dinna be sore with me."

"How could I not be? Ye stole my covering and touched me inappropriately."

"Hardly. Ye were the one who curled yourself around me. Not my problem ye were nay wearing anything when ye did it."

"Ugh… Turn your back," she ordered. Hearing his boots scrape, she dropped the plaid and yanked the chemise from the table.

A low whistle came from behind.

Staring at the ceiling and willing this moment to be forever erased from either of their memories, she fisted her hands. "Ye didna turn around, did ye?" Her voice was void of emotion, thank the saints.

"Nay. I meant to, but ye did not give me time."

"Do it now."

"Aye, my lady."

Oh, saints preserve her. The man had just gotten a full view of her bare arse. Heat seared a path from her belly, up over her chest and neck and landed full force into her cheeks. Fingers trembling, she wrenched on her chemise, hearing the fabric tear a little. She wanted to scream. To stomp her feet. To run from the croft. To hurl a knife at Ronan — but not have it actually hit him, just scare him. A lot.

"Lass, if ye like, I can strip down and let ye see me? Then we'd be even."

She didn't know whether to be offended or to laugh. The man certainly had a way to take her from rage to something less. Calm wasn't quite where she was at yet.

"That will not be necessary."

Ronan chuckled. "Are ye decent yet?"

"Nay!" She grappled with the plain gown she wore, and then her *arisaid*. At least her soft wool hose were dry. They were one thing she indulged in. The finest wool in Scotland — actually produced by Ronan's family. The fabric was silky soft and graced her skin in a melodious whisper of indulgence. One glance at her plain gown and even her dull chemise, nobody would guess she wore the best of hose. This particular pair, she'd embroidered thistles on. They made her feel special, reminded her that some small part of herself was still a woman.

"Dinna fash, I was only jesting."

Julianna let out a sigh and turned around. "I know it. I'm sorry I didna wait to make sure your back was fully turned."

"No need to apologize, lass. I assure ye, offended was the last thing I was feeling."

Julianna bit the inside of her cheek to keep from smiling. She shouldn't like what he was saying. Should be scandalized, but if she were to be honest with herself, she liked how he flirted, showed obvious interest in her. But she couldn't encourage him. That would only lead down a road she wasn't prepared to travel—no matter how much he made her heart flutter.

"Have ye anymore oatcakes?"

Ronan smiled—a smile that said he knew what she was doing. Julianna resisted the urge to roll her eyes at him and instead folded up the plaid she'd borrowed. He rummaged through his satchel.

"I've got plenty."

"Just one is fine," she said.

She handed him the plaid in exchange for the oatcake, glad to have one less stale than the ones she had packed.

"Thank ye for letting me use the plaid."

"Ye're welcome. As much fun as it would have been to see ye traipsing around the croft without it, I dinna think I would have survived."

"How so?"

He shrugged. "Probably would have done something that had ye throwing one of your poisoned daggers at me."

Julianna smiled as she bit into the oatcake. Not as stale as she thought it might be. "That's a fact and my aim is true. Ye might have come out of it missing one or more of your prized parts."

"I've only one prized part," he drawled with a wicked wink.

"For shame!"

"What? Is a man not allowed to prize his fighting arm?"

Heat infused Julianna's face. She couldn't believe she'd been referring to the man's shaft when he'd been talking about his arm. As if waking up pressed against him this morning wasn't enough mortification for one day. Julianna seemed bent on embarrassing herself further. She clenched her hands, resisting the urge to press them to her face to quell the heat.

"Nay. I prize my own as well." Her voice came out sounding strangled.

"Of course, there are other parts of me I prize."

"Oh. I suppose everyone likes more than one thing about themselves," she mumbled. There was no way she was going to have this conversation with him. Could see where it was leading.

"Aye. I also like my other arm, for I can use it with almost the same skill."

Julianna smiled tightly, and then went to gather up her own blanket from the floor. Lil Lass had managed to curl her large body into a tight ball upon it. After a battle of wills, Julianna was finally able to get the fabric from beneath the hound who glared at her as though she'd threatened her well-being.

"Will ye nay play along?"

Julianna shook her head as she rolled the blanket and shoved it into her satchel.

"And why not? 'Tis fun. Dinna ye like to have a bit of fun?"

Julianna whirled around to face Ronan head on. She put her fisted hands on her hips and frowned at him. "I like to have fun just as much as the next person. But do ye nay recall why we are here? I have a goal in mind, not just the desire to spend the day here with ye."

Ronan's joyful smile fell. He raked a hand through his hair and looked at her like she'd grown two heads. "I know why we're here, Julianna."

She opened her mouth to berate him for calling her by her given name. Not once had she given him permission to do so.

But Ronan spoke first. "The fact is we almost died yesterday. We almost died a couple weeks ago. We could die later today or tomorrow. I but sought a few moments of laughter with a woman I highly respect."

Well if he didn't know how to make her feel guilty and like a sour old crone. And she felt like she'd tossed his fear right into his face.

"But if ye prefer that I dinna jest with ye, that we remain focused and plotting at all times, so be it. I'll not have ye railing at me. A shrewish woman is not attractive."

Julianna's breath escaped her in a rush of anger. Did he just call her a shrew? And unattractive?

She was speechless. The man had managed to make her feel guilty and horrid all in the matter of a minute. Seemed hardly fair.

"I do prefer it." Her voice was clipped and she turned from him, intent on giving Brave a carrot and slipping his saddle back on. The sooner they were on their way the better.

Ronan ignored her, going about the same chores. When they'd both readied their mounts, he led the way outside, checking first to make sure they were alone. Though it was dark and the moon not as bright, the area appeared clear. They mounted their horses and headed west. As they were only a couple of miles or so outside Kinterloch village, they kept to the trees in case any stragglers caught them on the road.

Julianna cleared her throat, the silence becoming unbearable. Ronan looked over at her and raised a brow.

"We'll be at the village in a few minutes. How do ye propose we go about finding out if Ross has been there or still is?"

Ronan looked her over. "His men will recognize ye. Even with your plain gown."

Julianna frowned. "Aye. And ye broke into their camp. Will they not recognize ye, too?"

"The men I came across all died. But even still, if Ross and his men have been staying in Kinterloch, they've most likely made friends. His cousin holds the town. Either of us asking questions will get back to them."

"What do ye suggest? We wait for a drunkard to stumble across our path and ply him with questions?" Julianna peered through the forest. They'd been lucky not to come across anyone. Almost too lucky.

Without making it look too obvious, she started to study the trees. She wasn't the only one that could hide up a tree.

"The idea has merit."

Julianna laughed softly. "Aye, but who's to say he tells us the truth?"

"'Haps he's only looking for a few extra coins for his next flagon of whisky," Ronan added.

"Exactly." However sarcastic their conversation, it was amazing how much they fed off each other.

"Here's what I think," Ronan started. "I say we smudge our faces with a bit of dirt, head into town looking for a meal or a place to bed down. We'll not ask any direct questions, simply see how it plays out. Listen in on a few conversations."

A glint of silver in one of the trees caught her attention. Just as she'd suspected.

"I dinna think that will be necessary," she said in a whisper.

Ronan jerked his gaze her way. "What?"

"Remember where ye found me yesterday?"

"Aye," he said slowly, his gaze leaving her to look subtly into the trees.

"I think we'll find our answer there." Julianna kept her voice low.

"Agreed," Ronan murmured, and then a little louder said, "I have to take a piss."

"All right. Let us stop a moment." Julianna kept her voice raised as well.

The flash of silver she'd spied earlier moved, and with it she saw at least four others.

Five against two. Numbers she could handle. A challenge to be sure, and she'd probably mess her hose, but she'd been itching for a good fight.

They stilled their horses and dismounted. Julianna held up one hand, showing that she'd seen five in the trees, and Ronan nodded his agreement.

"Well, get on with your piss, then," she said, trying to keep the laughter from her voice. At the same time, she felt her wrists to make sure both her daggers were in place. Two long needles held her hair in place. Her sword was easily within reach on the horse and she was determined to stay where she was so she could grab it. Ronan's sword was strapped to his back and she suspected he was equally outfitted in weapons on his body.

"Och, still your mouth, wench," he said.

Julianna's lips itched to smile, but she kept them in a frown and answered him with, "Better hurry else your goose's neck gets chewed up by a wildcat."

Ronan raised a dubious brow and Julianna had to look away for fear of laughing. He made a big, loud, clumsy show of walking toward the nearest tree, whipping up his plaid, and lord help her, he actually started to relieve himself. She turned away, not wanting to witness such an act, and was glad she did. The men who'd been hiding were all coming down the trees, their backs to her.

Pulling a needle from her hair she took aim and whipped it through the air toward the closest fiend. There was no sound, other than his shriek and the heavy thud as his body hit the ground.

"What in blazes was that?" she called out, pretending to jump in a circle, frightened.

Ronan whirled around, claymore in hand, the rage on his face no longer a joke. He was furious in truth and looked just as deadly. Glad she was to have him on her side. The four other men jumped the remainder of the way from their respective trees and swaggered toward them, swords drawn.

The clear leader stepped forward. "Evening."

The Highlander's Warrior Bride

Ronan did not respond and neither did Julianna. Lil Lass growled, her ears perked up and hair on end. Ronan waved his hand using the signal Wallace had shown him, meaning stand down. The dog obediently sat on her haunches, but did not take her eyes off the men.

"What are ye folks doing in the woods when 'tis dark?"

Again Ronan did not answer and Julianna followed his lead. She didn't want to show the men she knew anything about fighting. The longer they thought her to be a weak link the better chances she and Ronan had of taking them all out. She studied each one of them, observing the state of their dress, physical forms, weapons. They all looked healthy enough, clean enough to show they took care of themselves, had a camp at least if they didn't live in the village. Their clothes too looked halfway decent. Each held a sword and she was sure they had as many concealed weapons as she and Ronan.

"Are ye mute?" the leader asked.

Ronan only sneered.

"I'll take that as a no."

"Take it for whatever ye want. We want no trouble," Ronan said evenly. He stabbed the tip of his sword into the ground and held both his hands out to the side. "Let us be on our way."

"What way is that?"

Ronan nodded his head toward the village, whose lights could be seen just beyond the trees.

"Kinterloch? There's nothing for ye there." The leader did not surrender his weapon, but continued to hold it out, as if warding off Ronan's approach.

"Why's that?" Ronan asked. "We only seek food and shelter. We'll move on in the morning."

"Is that your wife?"

Ronan nodded.

Julianna bristled. The man was changing the subject and she didn't like the path he was taking. Imagining herself as Ronan's wife was a fantasy she could not indulge in.

"Why dinna ye go ahead to the village then and find some food and shelter, we'll keep your wife here until ye get back."

Her stomach flipped and she crossed her arms over her chest, putting each hand inside her sleeves to feel her daggers.

"Not going to happen." Ronan gripped the handle of his claymore and pulled it from the ground.

Chapter Twelve

If these whoresons wanted a fight, then by God, Ronan would give them one. He'd say the four of them had heavy ballocks to try and pick a fight, but unfortunately for the idiots, they had no idea who Ronan or Julianna were.

Poor bastards.

"Well, if ye willna leave her here, then I'm afraid we're at an impasse." The leader twirled his sword in his hand, obviously confident in his skills.

Ronan stole a glance at Julianna. A mask of indifference covered her face. Her hair had fallen on one side, giving her normally tightly wound knot a lopsided look. He had an idea if he looked at the man lying prone on the ground that there would be sharp object protruding from his body.

"I suppose we are," Ronan said, keeping his voice even and not edged with the anger he felt.

"Do ye know what I like to do when I come to a stalemate with another?" The leader turned his head and smiled at first one of his men and then the other two who stood on the opposite side.

Ronan did not give the man a response. He took the time the man used to stroke his own ego as an opportunity to assess their weapons and their weak points. Each had a sword and knife, and from several bulges in their sleeves, hidden weapons as well.

"I like to take down the man." He walked forward a step, trying for menacing, but it wouldn't work. "Then I like to take his woman down—have the man watch me work my sword on her." With the word *sword*, he grabbed his crotch and jiggled it.

Ronan raised a brow, expecting Julianna to put the fool out of his misery, but she seemed just as equally preoccupied with assessing the situation.

Enough was enough, however, Ronan was growing bored. "Get on with it then. My belly growls and I'm in need of a pint or two of ale."

The leader stopped his speech and gave Ronan an odd look. Obviously he was surprised by Ronan's lack of concern, but it was too late to back out now. The man had stated his threats in plain view of his men. If he were to back down they'd think him a weakling.

"Jonas, get the lass. Mattie and Birch, ye're with me."

Ronan did grin then. Only one man for Julianna to put out of his misery. Perfect. He raised his claymore and steadied his feet. These bastards wouldn't live long. His only regret was that he'd be concentrating on his own battle and would miss seeing Julianna skewer Jonas.

"Aye, boss," Jonas said, taking his sweet time to saunter toward her.

Ronan wanted to encourage him to speed up, or at least to wait until he was done taking care of Boss, Mattie and Birch. Och, well…

Boss held back while Mattie and Birch lunged at him. Ronan easily side-stepped, turned halfway and sliced through the back of Birch's thigh. The man went down with a howl and clutched at his bleeding leg. Instead of running at him full force again, Mattie turned in a circle. Boss continued to hang back, watching. Would probably run as soon as Mattie was done for, or maybe enlist the help of Jonas.

Nope. The sound of the other man grunting behind him, and Boss' shout of dismay gave Ronan the added push to lunge toward Mattie. The man froze, and Ronan didn't have the heart to kill him, so instead he knocked him hard on the head and the man fell beside a still screaming Birch. With the hilt of his claymore he put Birch into a deep sleep.

"Who are ye?" Boss said, backing away.

"Just a couple of travelers in need of food and shelter," Ronan said with a sneer on his face.

Boss shook his head. "Nay."

"Aye."

"I dinna believe ye. Dinna come any closer." He held his sword out, waved it, slicing it through the air. Ronan continued forward.

"I thought ye wanted to play?" Ronan said with a mock pout.

"Now, if ye just let me go… I… I can take ye to a powerful man. He'll give ye coin. Food. Whatever ye want."

"Who is this powerful man?"

"He's a laird. A powerful one."

"Ye mentioned that already. But how do I know ye're telling the truth. We heard tell that the village was held by a vassal. That wouldna be the laird ye speak of."

Boss shook his head. "Ye're right, but he is housing my laird."

"Housing?" Poor maggot had no idea the information he was spewing out.

"Aye. Laird Ross."

As soon as the words were out of his mouth, a whistling sound sliced past Ronan's ear. A knife sunk into the man's chest and he fell to the ground his eyes wide, face going pale. Within seconds, foam pooled on his lips and he fell flat.

"What did ye go and do that for?" Ronan asked. Frowning, he turned toward Julianna with his hands on his hips.

She shrugged. "He gave us the information we wanted. Canna have him going back to the village and telling Ross of our approach."

"Did ye not realize I left those two alive?"

"Really?" she said, annoyed. "Couldna handle it?"

"Didna see the point," he answered.

"Fine. Have it your way. I was taught to leave no witnesses. We'll hide the dead and tie these two to a tree. They willna be able to escape and tell Ross about us and it will give us time to get into the village to find him."

Ronan nodded, liking how she took the lead. A strong woman was hard to come by, especially one who could fight like she did. His cock tightened in response. Damn if she didn't have a way of making him want her, even in the midst of the carnage they'd created.

He snorted with disgust for himself, wiped off his claymore and sheathed it. Julianna had ripped a strip of fabric off of Birch's linen shirt and wrapped it tight around his wound.

"If ye can get the three dead ones hidden, I can tie these two to a tree."

"Think ye can haul them? They are nay slight men."

Julianna only smiled at him as though indulging a small child. "Ye have no need to worry about me, Ronan."

"All right." If she wanted to play that she could maneuver those two men, he would humor her. He'd hide the dead and then come back to help her. The lady sure was confident. Cocky even.

When Ronan returned, she'd sheathed her weapons, fixed her hair and…tied the two men to the same tree. Both were still knocked out and she didn't look any worse for wear.

"Are ye ready?" she asked, mounting her horse. Julianna glanced back at him, worry crinkling her eyes. "Ye look like ye've seen a ghost. Are ye all right?"

"I should give ye more credit, my lady. I didna think ye could do it."

She smiled and clucked her tongue. "I know. Most men dinna think a woman can do the same things. I try not to tread on boots too often, but there are times when even your manly ego must get over it."

Ronan laughed. "Your tongue is ever sharp." And he wanted nothing more than to grab her off that horse and kiss her fiercely. How could he arrange that?

"Get on your horse. We've made it past Ross' scouts, but there is still a village to be breached."

"Spoken like a true commander."

She batted her lashes and held her hand to her chest. "Would ye like it better if I said it like a lady? Oh, kind warrior, would ye please oblige me and mount that well-built, noble stead, so we might —"

"That'll do," Ronan said with a roar of laughter. "I dare say, ye are lucky to be traveling with me, else ye might have been among the dead."

"For more reasons than one," she said softly.

Without thinking Ronan reached out and touched her leg, giving her a gentle squeeze. His eyes widened at the same time hers did, and he moved quickly to pull away, but Julianna stilled his hand, gripped it tight, holding it place upon her muscled thigh.

"Thank ye, Ronan," she said.

"For what?" Damn if his voice didn't croak like a lad of fourteen.

"For coming with me."

"I'd never have let ye go alone."

She reached out and stroked his cheek, her thumb brushing tenderly back and forth.

"Julianna," he managed to say, but his words were cut off when she leaned down and swept her lips over his.

"Dinna say anything," she murmured against his mouth. "Just kiss me back."

No sweeter words had ever been uttered from a female's lips. Ronan wasted no time in taking possession of her mouth. He licked greedily at her lips until she opened for his entry. They both let out sighs of satisfaction as their tongues touched. An urgency took hold of Ronan. He slid his hand up her thigh, gripped her hip, grabbed the other one and lifted her from the horse. He held her in the air, pulled tight to him so he could feel every lush curve and supple muscle against him. Julianna was a goddess to be sure.

She wrapped her arms around his neck and went a step forward by wrapping one leg around his hip. *Saints!* He was going to come undone. He slid his hands beneath her bottom, pulled the other leg around his hip and held her like that. The heat of her sex seeped through both their clothes making his already fiery blood burn hotter. Just this one kiss, this one indulgence. They both needed it. Needed this sense of being desired by another. A sense of intimacy. Battle-rush coursed through their veins and it was obligatory for them to find a way to let it out. After one faced death, one wanted to feel alive.

Her breasts were crushed to his chest, nipples hard. He grunted at the impact of her body, a sudden aching pang whizzing through his shoulder. Gripping her weight in one hand, he slid his other up her ribs to cup a plush swell. They were soft, round, warm. God what he wouldn't do to feel their silky weight, naked in his palm. Ronan thumbed over her nipple, reveled in her indrawn breath.

Julianna scraped her nails along his scalp and the back of his neck, massaged deep into his uninjured shoulders. Her thighs were clenched tight around him, making him shake with need. Cock hard, his turgid flesh pulsed, begged, to sink within the heated channel she teased him with.

He had to stop now if he was going to. While he still had a thread of control left. He was very close to coming unraveled completely, thrusting her against a tree while he took what she offered. Ronan tried to pull away, to take his lips from Julianna's but she only leaned in closer.

"Not yet," she said, her breathy tones stroking so enticingly along his nerves.

How could he say no? How could he deny her what she wanted? What he'd craved for months. Ronan didn't want to answer that question, because at some point in the next three minutes he would have to do just that, or end up with Julianna pinned to an aged oak, her skirts yanked up and himself buried deep inside her.

Just the image he'd embedded in his mind was too much to bear. He yanked on her skirts, planted his hand firmly beneath a smooth thigh. And groaned. It was perfection. Hell, he'd known that when she'd dropped her plaid in the croft. Her backside and legs were firmly formed, but with a feminine curve that made his mouth water. Touching them only made what he'd seen come alive more vividly in his mind.

Her skin was warm, silky and trembling. Was it fear or desire that made her quiver? Unsure of which and not willing to risk it being fear, once again he pulled away. Their eyes locked in the dark. The moon shone, making the whites of her eyes glow, the centers dark.

"Ronan," she whispered, her teeth also gleaming in the moonlight.

Their hot breath puffed between them.

"We have to stop," he said, his voice gruff.

"I know we should." She kissed the corner of his mouth lightly.

"Aye." Ronan couldn't help himself, he slid his lips along her chin to her ear, tugged gently at her earlobe. "We must."

Julianna tilted her head to the side and moaned. "Must we?"

That got his attention. "My lady, dinna ye know what happens between a man and a woman?"

Julianna let out a throaty laugh. "Why, Ronan, ye are trying to be a gentleman."

"Now is not the time for laughter."

"But 'twas funny." Her fingers curled through his hair and tugged.

"Ye make my blood fill with fire," he growled, nibbling on her lower lip.

"Ye do the same to me." She flicked her tongue out to tease his.

"Dinna ye understand? If we dinna stop, I will take ye."

"Please," she murmured.

"But that is only the right of your husband."

Julianna leaned back and locked eyes with him once more. "First of all, warrior, I am not married and I dinna plan to be. Second, ye willna be the first man I've made love to."

Shock ricocheted through Ronan's body. "What?"

"Which part?"

"Well, both."

Her teeth shone in the moonlight when she grinned. "Ah. I seem to have shocked your senses. A first for ye? I feel a sense of accomplishment."

"You're a wench."

Julianna laughed again, toyed with his hair. "My duty is to Scotland. My brother willna allow me to marry and I've no interest."

"Your brother? Who is he?"

She rubbed her nose against his. "No one ye need concern yourself with right now."

"But I may have need to concern myself with him later."

"Then I will gladly bring ye to him."

Ronan frowned. "And the other? Who dared to claim what wasn't theirs?"

Julianna snuck in a kiss, her tongue toying with his and he nearly forgot they were talking as stimulating sensation filled him once more.

"Tell me," he said against her mouth.

"'Twas not more than a squire a couple years ago."

"Lucky bastard," Ronan said with a chuckle. "Even still, I canna."

He respected her, wanted more for her than a heady coupling in the woods.

"Then we'd best be on our way to the village." Julianna's voice was filled with disappointment, even a little rejection. She slipped from his arms, and smoothed her skirts.

He didn't want her to feel that way. If the circumstances were different, he'd have taken her already. Nearly had. But Ronan refused to be another notch in her bedpost—one that didn't offer her what she deserved, which was commitment. Hell, if he'd gone through with the deed just now he would have demanded a meeting with her brother, and then begged for her hand. Would have been the right thing to do, even if neither of them wanted to marry.

True, they were suited for one another. He could count on her to have his back and vice versa. They made a good team. He didn't need to convince himself of that. And he was damned attracted to her. More so than he should have been.

"My lady, I—"

She held up her hand, stopping him. "Dinna say a word, Ronan. I was caught up in the moment as were ye." She spread her arms out. "Look what just happened? We were caught between five men. 'Tis easy to see that the both of us were overcome with emotion."

Was she so easily able to brush off their encounter? 'Twas almost offensive, save for the way her eyes darted about. The way she refused to lock onto his gaze. She was avoiding him. The first sign of someone lying. Well good. He didn't want to be only one so affected by their kiss, by everything.

"Aye," he agreed. "Let us ride then."

"Might I have a nip of that whisky first?"

A damned fine idea. Ronan pulled the flask from his satchel and handed it to her. Still, she avoided his gaze, went out of her way not to touch him by tossing the corked flask back. Ronan took a long draw, realizing the flask was nearly empty. They'd better find Ross and make him suffer before the night was through, else he'd need to stop for a refill of whisky, and no one made better whisky than Cook.

Chapter Thirteen

Julianna watched Ronan guzzle the last of the whisky. While she wanted to begrudge him the luxury, it was *his* flask and she'd no claim to it. Besides, the last time she'd taken more than one sip from his flask she'd ended up naked and plastered to him. Not that she was faring much better sober.

Her thigh still burned where he'd grasped her. Nipples were still hard and the one he'd touched tingled. Lips were another story all together. Her body was a traitor.

They mounted up and continued on as though nothing untoward had happened—neither the skirmish nor the kiss.

Julianna preferred it that way. Talking wasn't something she could readily do. Just wasn't any good at it. And it made her uncomfortable to share her feelings. So why did she keep stealing glances at Ronan? Watching the way he gripped the reins, the way his thighs flexed against his horse's body? Why did she wish they traveled during the day so she could study him in more detail?

Because she was a fool.

Only fools wished for things they couldn't have. But what was it, exactly, that she wanted?

Julianna couldn't quite put her finger on it. Wasn't ready to accept that the moment she'd first seen Ronan, the second he'd kissed her, she was forever changed. If she gave that notion another thought then she'd be worrying over whether Ronan felt the same thing, and if a future together was even a remote possibility.

Oh, who was she kidding? Those very thoughts were already circulating in her mind.

Stealing another glance his way, she chewed on her lip. A few more minutes and they'd be in the village.

"What is amiss?" Ronan asked, giving her a sideways glance. "I can see ye looking at me."

"I'm nay looking at ye."

"Then why do your eyes keep turning this way?"

Julianna suppressed a smile by biting her cheek. "Ye're mistaken. The darkness is playing tricks on ye."

"I'm accustomed to seeing in the dark."

"Then ye might want to re-accustom yourself."

Ronan chuckled. "Ye've a mouth on ye, I'll give ye that."

"I willna take anything ye've got to give."

"Come now, I meant no offense."

"I'm nay offended." She shrugged, playing nonchalant.

Ronan stopped his horse, took hold of her reins forcing her to stop as well. He waited to speak until she looked at him, and when she did she almost sighed. The man was too handsome for her own good.

"Look, 'tis obvious ye've something on your mind. Why not share it now so that we go into the village with clear heads."

Julianna clamped her lips closed and stared at him. If he wanted this to be a battle of wills, so be it. She'd never share the things she'd been thinking. Especially not with him. Fanciful notions. That's all they were.

Ronan let go of her reins and ran his hand through his hair, scrubbed it over his face. The move was something she'd come to see him do when he was thinking hard about something he wanted to say. She chose to wait patiently for him to speak. Silence spanned between them for several heartbeats.

"I've not been handling—" He stopped and took a deep breath. "Ye are a lady. I think."

Julianna rolled her eyes. "Aye."

"Though ye are a kitchen servant."

"Aye."

"'Tis a front."

"Aye." She'd never told anyone this much before. 'Twas not as terrifying as she thought it would be.

"Well, then. Ye are a lady, and a man should not take such liberties with a lady, unless he is—"

Julianna waved her hand, dismissing his words. "We've already established I have no husband and most likely willna."

His eyes remained fixed on hers and he didn't speak for a few moments. Drawing his brow together, he asked, "Why?"

"I already explained that," she said, slightly exasperated.

Ronan shrugged. "I know. But, 'tis just, ye are a verra passionate woman. A strong, intelligent woman. A prize for any man."

His words brought unwanted tears to prick the backs of her eyes. "But ye forget something, Ronan. I'm a warrior. No Highlander wants a warrior bride."

A flash of something crossed his face, but in the darkness, she could not quite make out what it was before his face was once more clear.

"I think ye're wrong," he said softly.

Julianna laughed, trying to cover her emotions with mirth. "Then ye've been removed from reality for far too long."

Ronan frowned in earnest. "And ye do not give yourself enough credit."

Julianna straightened her spine, feeling his disapproval keenly. "I give myself credit where 'tis due. I'm not one to linger in fancyland."

"Lass, ye dinna understand." His voice was gravelly, like his words were getting caught in his throat. "I said ye were a prize."

There was no use in arguing with him, he didn't understand what she was saying, and she didn't want to read into the words he was saying. Julianna bowed her head and graciously said, "Thank ye."

Though most of her training had been as a warrior, Julianna was still taught how to behave like a lady and when given a compliment a lady always gave her thanks.

"Ye're welcome."

Hoping that he was finished, she nudged Brave forward.

"Wait, ye have not told me what was bothering ye."

If he was willing to tell her he thought she was a prize — however harebrained an idea it was — she could certainly give him an answer.

Stilling her horse, she turned back to him and lied, straight-faced. "I was wondering how many men we'd encounter in the village. We easily took down five this eve, but we will no doubt come across more than that."

Ronan's face fell, his lips curling down slightly. No doubt he'd hoped for something more from her, since he'd been willing to put his mind out there, but Julianna was not ready to open up. Already he knew too much. Any more and she'd be putting him in danger, not to mention her own heart.

There was a subtle shift in the way Ronan sat his horse. He stiffened, seemed taller. Julianna could tell he was putting a protective wall around himself. Just as she'd done. There were so many things they had in common it was almost tragic they couldn't pursue their obvious desires. Well, actually he wouldn't pursue them. As wanton as it was, Julianna had been completely ready to lift her skirts. To her, making love with Ronan was not only something she wanted to do to quell the physical burn that ignited whenever he was near, but also to quell the emotions racing rampant in her mind. She hoped to put herself at ease by giving in to at least one thing, if she couldn't have the whole of him.

The squire hadn't been a lie. She had given him her virginity. But she'd been in love. Even thought she was pregnant for a few scary weeks. Turned out to be a false alarm. Her woman's cycle had never been regular. The incident had been enough to scare her away from Ben forever. He'd been heart broken, and so had she. The lad had probably gotten into his head there could be something between them. That they'd been in love. That said love would conquer all.

Foolish notions of two young, naïve people.

Julianna knew better now.

Ronan was the first man she'd offered herself to after Ben. When he rejected her, she felt the pain of it acutely. Hadn't expected it. Didn't all men dream of a lass lifting their skirts willingly? Ronan was known to be quite a rogue, at least that was what she'd heard whispered amongst the staff. She was fairly confident there was not another warrior named Ronan within Robert's camp.

Either he spoke the truth and was far more admirable than she'd given him credit for, or it was her. She repulsed him somehow. He'd seen her naked behind. Perhaps he preferred a softer woman. Her physique was not exactly what could be called womanly. Boyish, mannish even.

"We'll assess the village afore we make any moves," Ronan said, his voice taking on a practical tone. "If Ross is not there, no need for us to alert the overlord, his cousin, or scare any of the villagers."

"A sound plan." Julianna cleared her throat. "And if he is there?"

"We take him out."

"And fight off those who surround us?"

"Nay. We'll inform his cousin of Ross' treachery, remind him of his duty to Scotland and ask for his assistance. Pray that his cousin respects his own hide more than his blood. Ye are right, we canna take them out by ourselves."

Julianna nodded. However much she'd borne Ronan's rejection, why was she now getting the feeling that he was the one feeling spurned?

She had to get it together. Her mind was so clouded with Ronan she wasn't thinking straight. An easy target was what she would become if she didn't settle her mind. Ronan out. Duty in. She repeated the notion in her mind over and over as they continued on the path, exiting the woods and leading their horses onto the dirt-packed road. The wind blew gentler than it had the night before, almost a soft, cool caress against her burning skin. Stars filled the skies, and the moon was not nearly as full as the previous night. Not a cloud in sight, as though the storm from yesterday never happened. The weather was so unpredictable. Much like a man.

Julianna grinned at the thought as she gazed toward the village. The buildings dotted the land like black blobs, each with its own shining golden light seeping through windows. Swirls of silver smoke caught the moonlight and curled from their rooftops as everyone had a fire in their hearths.

The manor house was substantially larger, yet not as impressive as one of the many castles she'd seen. Was Ross ensconced inside? His feet curled up before a fire, wine in one hand and a wench in the other. The image made her snarl. The devil-man was probably making that poor wench's life hell.

No matter, Julianna would put him out of his misery soon enough. Glancing at Ronan he gave her a nod and they urged their horses into faster gaits. Though dusk fell early, most people would soon be climbing into their beds if they weren't there already. If they showed up too late they would only be turned away.

They reached the wooden gates of the village easily enough. One guard stood atop, and gazed down at them with leery eyes.

"We are hoping for shelter," Ronan called up.

"And who might ye be?"

"Just two travelers looking for a warm bed. We'll cause ye no trouble. We'd be glad even for a straw bed in the stable, if there is nothing else."

The guard grunted. "Ye look a little too well to be just a traveler."

Ronan laughed. "I am well. We travel to see my brother."

"Who is your brother?"

"No one ye'd know. He lives in the Lowlands."

"Far away from home?"

"Aye. Married a wealthy farmer's daughter, but had to promise him labor in return."

How easily he made up a story. Not even a single tell-tale hint that he was lying.

The guard laughed at Ronan's story. "Poor bastard. Are ye going to offer up your labor there as well?"

"That and my wife's," he said, hooking his thumb in Julianna's direction.

Once again she was made to be his wife. She had to lower her head so the guard didn't notice the flash of anger in her eyes.

"Well, then I suppose we could offer ye shelter for the night seeing as how ye'll be worked to the bone for the remainder of your sorry life."

"Our thanks."

Did the guard realize how much his words sunk into Julianna's mind? Well, obviously no. The man didn't know them from Adam. Not until she met Ronan did she dream of a different life. Not until she'd met Ronan had she thought that she was not happy. That there was more to life than protecting the future king, more to life than taking her brother's orders.

The thoughts were disturbing and she hated the reminder.

Thankfully, the gate was wrenched open, wobbly and rickety. The townsfolk were lucky that not too many were interested in attacking their little hole in nature, because Julianna was fairly certain she could have taken down that door with one kick.

Ross must have realized that when he came here. What made him stay? Unless he thought that no one would look for him here. Or perhaps he'd been able to turn his cousin's mind against the Bruce. Worse still, he paid the man to protect him. Even crueler, perhaps Ross had taken hostages to ensure that the town protected him.

With a sinking feeling in the pit of her stomach, Julianna had a strong intuition that the latter was exactly what was happening here. She flicked a nervous gaze at Ronan, trying to catch his attention, but he didn't take notice, or else he ignored her.

"Ronan," she whispered harshly.

He did glance at her then. "What is it?" he asked in a similar tone.

"I need to speak with ye forthwith." Julianna tried not to make her wondering eyes too obvious, but she had the sudden feeling they were being watched closely. Almost as though people peered from the cracks in their shuddered windows and doors. Faithfully taking in every feature of Ronan and Julianna to report back to Ross.

She imagined them brandishing pitchforks, knives, wooden cooking spoons, chairs and whatever else they could get their hands on. The hair on the back of her neck rose.

"We need to leave," she whispered without looking at him. Her eyes locked on the guard from the top gate. She'd turned around to look up at him and the eerie smile upon his face was enough to make her blood run cold. "We're about to be served up on a platter, I can feel it."

From the corner of her eye, she watched Ronan stiffen. His fingers flexed on the reins and he stopped, leaned down the side of his horse, closest to her, as though studying his leg.

"I feel it too. But I dinna know how we can leave."

Julianna made the pretense of studying his horse too. "They have yet to close the gate. We could make haste and charge through it."

Ronan nodded. "I fear that may be our only option."

A door creaked open and a man with a hideous face stepped out, his body silhouetted by the light within his small croft. In his hand was a small axe.

"We'd best do so now," Julianna said. She smiled at the armed man to throw him off balance. It worked. He stumbled in his path and gave her a look, as though second guessing himself. Good, while his guard was down it was time to act.

Julianna swung Brave around, pulled her sword from beneath her saddle and charged the main gate. The guard on top's evil smile fell and he worked without success to notch an arrow, the shaft slipping from his fumbling fingers. She smiled up at him as she passed under. From behind her, she heard the sounds of an angry mob, and a thunderous roar from Ronan.

"God, please, let us get clear of this mass of followers!" she cried up to the heavens.

Hoof beats pounded behind her, and she chanced a glance to see that Ronan came up quickly toward her. A horde of weapon brandishing men ran after them, shouting obscenities and shaking their sticks in the air. But they were only on foot, they wouldn't be able to catch up to Ronan and Julianna.

An arrow whizzed by her cheek landing in the ground a few feet in front. Brave ran it over. Seemed the guard had finally gotten his arrow notched. Leaning low over her horse, she urged him to run faster. The man may have missed the first time, but there was no telling if his mark would be true the second time around.

Pain seared her thigh.

She'd been hit! Julianna didn't stop. Didn't look to see what the damage was. They had to get into the trees. They had to get to a point where they were safe. After seeing the town, she wasn't sure where that would be. Robert the Bruce was up against a lot more than just a few wayward earls. Those even in his backyard appeared to have changed sides — or at the very least were willing to do so for a price, possibly their lives.

They broke through the trees and Julianna used her sword to block the branches that swung dangerously toward her face. Her thigh throbbed something fierce, making her hands shake. Still, she didn't let go of the reins. Neither did she stop.

"Whoa!" Ronan called. "Ye can slow down. They'll nay come in here after us."

Julianna slowed her horse, and when she'd come to a stop with Ronan beside her, she glanced down to her thigh. No arrow. Must have grazed her. Tentatively, she touched the spot. A tear in her skirts, clean through her chemise. Warm, stickiness met her fingertips. Another fraction of an inch and the arrow would have been fully embedded.

"Ye've been hit?" Ronan lifted her hand, his eyes widening as blood glinted from her fingers in the moonlight.

"Nay, just a flesh wound."

"Still an injury. Let us wrap it up."

Julianna nodded, lifted her skirt slightly and ripped a strip from the bottom of her chemise.

"Let me," Ronan said.

"I can manage," Julianna said sharply.

Ronan tilted her chin up with the tip of his finger. His gaze softened. "I know ye can manage, but every now and then we have to accept help from others. Trust others to have our best interests at heart. Even warriors. Ye can trust me, lass."

Julianna swallowed. Why did he have to be so damn smart?

"All right." She handed him the strip of linen and when he took it, their fingertips brushed, sending a spark of the earlier sensations she'd had. Sensations that contradicted themselves in mind, being both wanted and unwanted.

Slowly, she lifted her skirts, until her thigh was exposed. A gash about three inches long marred her flesh.

"'Tis a shame the fool marred your skin."

Julianna shook her head, and smiled full of pride. "A warrior is never ashamed of her battle scars."

Chapter Fourteen

Viewing the blood on Julianna's thigh had made Ronan see red — fury so potent he'd literally gone blind with it. The sheer urge to whirl around and run through the bastard who'd drawn her life's essence was overwhelming. Miraculously, it was the lady herself who calmed him. She didn't seem fazed by the wound. Instead, she was proud of it.

A warrior is never ashamed of her battle scars.

How right she was. Plenty of times, Ronan had admired the knotted, white lines on his body. Recalled each wound, who had put it there and with what weapon. He too recalled how he'd retaliated. Julianna didn't have time to retaliate, but he had a feeling she would soon. One way or another. Something he'd learned about her, besides her passionate nature, a calculating force to be reckoned with lay beneath the surface.

Damn, if she didn't arouse his ardor. Never in his wildest dreams did he think he'd meet a woman like her. Even when his eyes had first cast upon her, he'd only been mystified. Wished to pursue her because of all the intrigue that surrounded her. But now... Now he wanted to peel away her layers — clothing and mind.

"What are ye smiling about?" she asked, scowling at him in that way he so adored.

"Nothing," he said with a shrug of his shoulders.

She tilted her head and studied him. "I think we'd best get back to that croft. And at first light, we need to make haste for Eilean Donan."

"What is your plan?"

"I think we need to discuss with the Bruce and Wallace. We need reinforcements." Disappointment filled her voice and a slight crease marred her brow.

"I know ye wanted to do this on your own."

Her lips pressed together and she shrugged. "I did. But I'm nay such a fool as to admit that I can."

"I would never call ye a fool." He knotted the strip of linen onto her wound.

"Thank ye."

"No need to give thanks, my lady."

"I know it, but 'tis due all the same. Ye've put your faith in me. Trusted me. That is important to me, and so I give ye my thanks."

He inclined his head to her, and pushed her skirts back in place.

"When we reach the croft, I can take a better look at the wound. Dress it more properly."

Julianna nodded. "I'm afraid I may need ye to burn it."

Ronan bit the tip of his tongue. The last thing he wanted to do was burn her flesh, but he wasn't going to argue with her, that wouldn't get him anywhere.

"Let us hurry, afore they rouse their horsemen to come after us."

"Aye. There's no telling if they had more scouts in these woods."

They clucked to their horses and hurried back the way they'd come. Just under an hour later, and nary an incident more, they made it back to the small cluster of crofts that housed them the night before. Ronan dismounted and checked each one to be sure there were no squatters. When all was safe, he led his horse into the larger croft with Julianna following. Ronan used his flint to light a candle.

"I'll wipe down the horses and get them settled if ye want to fetch some wood for the fire."

Ronan nodded. "Bar the door."

"I dinna think that's necessary."

"All the same, 'twill make me more comfortable."

Thankfully, she didn't argue with him. It appeared they were leveling out their ground together, each knowing when the other was right and no longer arguing for the sake of it. Ronan resisted the urge to grip her hand, pull her into his embrace before he left in case they never saw each other again. There could be no embracing. Having made that clear earlier, he was certain she'd be sure to keep her distance. And it would be safer for them both that way. He didn't know who her brother was, and didn't want to start a feud with the man. 'Twas also obvious they both had their objectives in life and a relationship wasn't a part of it.

With a last longing look, one in which she returned, dammit, he lurched out the door. He would just have to make sure he made it back. The sound of wood scraping against the door eased his mind. She'd done as he asked.

Ronan set about getting the wood and searching for any other useful items. He didn't tarry long, worried about her wound. It most likely pained her something fierce. And then he remembered with stinging clarity — they'd run out of whisky.

Ballocks!

He knocked on the door, and it was quickly opened by Julianna. She peered out, eyes wide, her sword drawn. No prettier sight had he ever seen.

"Ye're back." She stated the obvious with a sigh of relief in her voice.

When he entered, Ronan noticed pain etched around her eyes.

"Lass… I dinna have any more whisky."

"Then 'tis a good thing I took some off a couple of those rogues." She rummaged through her pack and held up two flasks, a smile curling her lips like she'd found a great prize.

"A good thing, aye. I'll light the fire, then we'd best address your wound."

Her smile faded and she nodded. "Aye."

"Does it pain ye?" he asked, setting the wood upon their older ashes. They wouldn't need the fabric to help light the fire this time.

"A little."

Ronan smiled. She most likely understated her pain. "Come sit."

He spread out a plaid on the floor, and she settled upon it, her legs stretched out before her.

"This feels different in the candlelight than the shine of the moon," she said, suddenly appearing shy.

"Och, lass, ye're a warrior. Show me your wound." His gruffness seemed to calm her, and she smiled, pulling her skirt up just enough to show the bloodied strip of linen tied to her thigh, and healthy helping of her curvy leg and fancy hose. He'd not expected to see such finery on a woman who cherished her weapons over her gowns.

But he didn't have time to admire her; the linen was soaked with blood. Damn. If the wound was still bleeding, then he would have to cauterize it. Bleeding still after so long meant it was deep, and her body was having a hard time staunching the flow. In a perfect world, they'd have a healer sew it up with nice poultice of healing herbs to ease the pain and hinder infection. But alas, it was the two of them inside a dead family's croft with naught but the supplies in both their packs.

"I'll need some more of your linens," he mused.

Julianna nodded and ripped off several more strips. "This chemise has gone to waste anyhow, might as well use as much of it as we need."

Ronan took the strips from her, wishing he could at least boil a pot of water... Though he had a pan, he didn't have as much water. Just the little bit left in his waterskin and he'd not had time to refill. The well between the crofts had been blocked by a bolder—probably by the same men who'd destroyed those who lived here. Normally, he was so much better prepared, but having to run for their lives for at least three occasions in the last twenty-four hours, he'd had more on his mind than refilling water.

Lucky for them both, she'd had the presence of mind to take the whisky.

"Hold still, lass." Gingerly, he used his dirk to cut off the bloodied linen.

Julianna hissed, her muscles tensing, but she remained still. He tossed the linen into the fire and gazed at the wound. It gaped open, an ugly gash, but did not appear to be bleeding much.

"Looks like ye may not have to burn it," he said, relief in his voice. He'd not wanted to do it. Didn't want to cause her the pain, and couldn't bear to be the one who hurt her further — even if it might save her life.

"I was afraid with our riding I'd torn it open more, but ye did a good job tying it in the woods." Her voice was soft, breathy and he wondered if she was feeling faint.

"Here, take a sip." He held one of the flasks to her lips and watched as she took a healthy gulp. "Now, I need to pour it on your leg. Want something to bite on?"

"Are ye offering yourself?" Julianna's lips quirked in a tease.

Ronan laughed. "Nay, not with the wound ye're likely to leave."

"Aw, I willna bite hard."

Ronan grunted his disbelief. "I've seen a man bite a leather strap clear in two."

"A belt, good idea." Julianna hastily untied the belt at her waist and put the end of it in her mouth. "Do it," she said around the leather.

Ronan gazed into her eyes, hating what he was about to do, but knowing it was necessary. He poured.

Julianna's eyes widened, jaw clenched and her lips turned white. She spit out the belt and screamed at the top of her lungs. He ducked to the left when her hand flailed out, fisted and aimed toward him. Ronan jumped to his feet and backed away, trying not to laugh.

"Hell of a reaction, lass."

"Arsehole!"

He did laugh then. "I told ye 'twould not feel good. What of your other wounds, have they nay been cleaned with whisky?"

Julianna clenched her teeth and took some long jagged breaths. "I was passed out. I'm sure they were, but I dinna remember."

"Well, now ye've another tale to tell." He chuckled some more and handed her the flask to sip on. "Although, would have been a more entertaining story if ye could say ye clobbered me. I supposed if ye want to add that, I could rub my chin during the telling."

Julianna smiled, raising the flask to her lips. Before she sipped, she said, "I think I will."

After she'd had a moment to breathe, and take quite a few sips of heady liquor, Ronan knelt beside her once more. He studied the wound. Although a few droplets of blood beaded to the surface, it appeared to have otherwise finished its flow for now. All the soaking of the linen must have happened quite soon after he wrapped it. But he'd made sure to tie it tight, and that had most likely aided in stopping the flow.

"I dinna think I need to burn ye. I'd like to wrap it up again and as soon as we reach the castle have the healer take a look, make ye a paste."

Julianna nodded. "Agreed."

Ronan tied the linen strips to her wound, taking care with her leg, but knotting it securely. "Ye were brave today, my lady."

"As were ye."

Ronan stoked the fire and then settled down beside her.

"We make a good team."

"Perhaps I'll allow ye to be my second." Her voice held a teasing edge.

"I might take ye up on it. I'd let ye have my back. The way your gut told ye we were going to be attacked was plenty enough evidence for me." He took a pull of the whisky, feeling it warm his belly. "Well, and the way ye fought in the woods. Your aim is true, and your intuition stellar."

Ronan grabbed his satchel and pulled out some oatcakes.

"Hungry?"

She shook her head. "Not truly."

"Will ye eat just one at least? Ye lost a bit of blood and your body could use the sustenance to regain its strength."

Julianna nodded and took the offered oatcake, munching on it like a child who abhorred their supper. Ronan clenched his jaw to keep from laughing. She looked every bit like Tad did when he was fed oatcakes.

"I can feel your laughter," she muttered.

"How so?"

"Ye tremble a little, and ye keep clenching your jaw, but aside from that, I can see it in your eyes." She flicked her gaze toward his, locking her sights on him. "Ye have a good game face, Ronan, but I've gotten to know ye over the last few months. My training is in studying people. I can read ye, even if ye dinna want me too."

Why did her words make his blood surge with desire? Was it the fact that she'd been studying him, watching him, that she was actually interested enough to do such? Or was it that she'd understood him. Connected with him on a different level.

Only his brothers, Magnus and Blane had ever meshed with him, been able to read his mind. Even his sisters Lorna and Heather weren't able to read past his placidity when he wanted to hide. His cousins Daniel and Brandon came close. Friends since they were bairns, the men had grown up together, seeing each other often enough to have lived in the same castle.

But even his brothers, sisters, cousins—they were blood. On some level, he expected them to understand him. They'd spent intimate years together. He and Julianna on the other hand... Though there hadn't been years, there did seem to be this potent connection—a bond between the two of them that went deeper than a few heated kisses. It scared the hell out of him.

And captivated him.

"What if I said, I wanted ye to read me?" Ronan inched a little closer, not daring to touch, but enough that they shared heat.

Julianna shuttered her ash-colored eyes for a minute, her long lashes sweeping over her cheeks. When she lifted them, her eyes brimmed with tears, glittery in the fire-light.

"It may be the whisky, or maybe the pain, I dinna know which, but I would say I want to. I..." She licked her lips, blinked rapidly. Her hands fiddled with her skirts. "I like ye, Ronan. Ye make me feel things I've longed to. But at the same time, ye make me suffer, for I know they are far from within my grasp." Her last words were said in a whisper, and she swiped at the tears that escaped to land in glistening streaks on her soft flesh.

Ronan didn't know what pushed the words past his lips, but the moment he opened his mouth, they spilled out like the confession of a man long lost. "They dinna have to be. I am here. Take hold."

She shook her head, looked away. "Ye dinna understand. I canna. The whisky's gone to both our heads."

He felt her dissent like a physical blow. How could she deny them both when it was so obvious they could make each other happy? He wasn't sure if it was love, was almost certain it couldn't be. But that didn't mean someday they wouldn't have it. What he was convinced of, was that they should be together. He gripped her by the shoulders, forcing her to face him. Her body moved easily in his hands, no struggle. She wanted him to touch her, to show her how it could be different, didn't she?

"We can make this work," he said.

"What? What will we make work?"

Her question was pointed, and he didn't know if he had the right answers, only that he wanted to try.

"Us, this." Those two words uttered, he claimed her mouth with his, taking in her earthy scent and the taste of whisky on her lips.

Julianna struggled at first, but then she sagged against him. Wrapped her arms around his neck, tilted her head to deepen the kiss. Rushing sensations like those after a battle surged in his veins. Victory was within his grasp. But he wasn't sure what the victory was. That she'd kissed him surely. But was he truly ready to accept what he offered? Hell, yes. And ballocks, no!

Truth was, Ronan was a confused mess. Whenever Julianna was around, his mind went in a thousand different directions. To ensure the realm was defended, loyalty to the Bruce and to Wallace, duty to family. All of those things he was capable of doing with his eyes closed and his sword arm tied behind his back. After all, he could fight just as well with his opposite hand. And now there was Julianna. A protective impulse coursed through him where she was concerned. He would battle to the death. He would go up against anyone who dared to harm her. No one was safe should they mistreat her. Ronan's affections were, or at the very least his obsession with her, was that intense.

Her tongue stroked over his, filling him with a deep urgency. His cock grew hard, pulsed with the need to bury deep inside her. He groaned when her breasts brushed his chest.

"Oh, Ronan…"

He had to put aside all the notions running rampant in his mind. Now was not the time to assess his mind, his feelings. Now he had a beautiful woman in his arms. A woman who wanted his attention, and who he craved in return. They could talk on their future in the morning on the ride back to Eilean Donan. For now, they would just languish in each other's embrace. But kissing was as far as he would let it go.

Perhaps even a few touches. She'd been injured. Needed her rest. If they were to take things any further it would seal both their fates, and with the amount of whisky they'd drunk and the life threatening battles of the last twenty-four hours, neither of them was in any kind of position to be making life changing decisions.

Julianna's fingers kneaded his back, trailed a path up his spine to his shoulders. "Make love to me," she murmured.

Chapter Fifteen

Julianna hadn't meant for the words to escape her lips. For indeed, she *wanted* Ronan to make love to her, dreamed about it, thought about it constantly, but in reality? Make it real.

The heart wants what it cannot have, she reminded herself bitterly. But being in his arms—it took her to another place, made her feel whole inside.

And now that the words were uttered, she didn't want to pull them back. With stunning clarity, she realized that her heart had taken the lead and asked for what she would never have had the ballocks to request.

She pulled back from his kiss, her hand on his chest where she could feel his heart racing as fast as her own. Gazing into his eyes, she saw mirrored in them all the desire, need and fear that she felt. "Make love to me," she said with conviction. "Here. Tonight."

"But…"

Julianna shook her head, pressed her finger to his lips. "Dinna make excuses. I let ye do that before. We're both adults, and while there are others that rule us day in and day out, here we are alone."

"But my conscience is still here," Ronan said, though his voice did not hold the same persuasion it had in the forest.

"As is mine. And 'tis clear."

Ronan narrowed his eyes. "How?"

Julianna smiled, scrunched her hand a little on his chest, feeling his muscle flex beneath her fingers. "I am nay like other women, Ronan." She realized with those words he might think she was labeling herself a wanton. That was not the case. She bit her lip realizing her mistake. How did one go about explaining? "Ye see, I may never marry. I canna. 'Tis the reason I am what I am. The reason I took a lover some years ago. But that doesna mean I dinna want to feel…something. To be close to someone."

Ronan placed his hand over hers, squeezed. "I know how ye feel."

"Ye do?"

"Aye. I know naught of your circumstances, and I canna compare myself to ye. I can marry. Indeed, my family wishes it, but, I canna allow any woman into my life. She would only get hurt."

Julianna glanced down at their hands. Studied the veins lining the back of his overlarge one. He completely engulfed her. Even with that simple touch she felt closer to him.

"Ye said before, that ye thought I was a prize," Julianna said, taking a chance and glancing back up. Ronan's gaze bored into hers.

"Aye. I still believe it."

"Well, I believe ye're a prize as well. A prize any woman would be glad to have. Dinna hide behind your sword and the fear that ye may hurt someone should ye be called back to the earth. Anyone who's had the pleasure of knowing ye is better for it."

Ronan's eyes darkened with some emotion she couldn't decipher.

"Then we are a pair, the two of us. Ye believing ye can never marry and me refusing to." He grinned, a little lopsided, and she felt a tug on her heart.

"Precisely the reason I wish to make love. There is no one I'd rather share such intimacy with." And no one who promised to be so delightful at it. Just his touch, the press of his lips on hers had her quivering. What would it be like if he were to take it a step further?

"Julianna, I confess to the same desire… And believe me when I say I've had to restrain myself. Ye are exquisite, everything I've ever dreamed of."

"And yet…" she urged, wanting to hear the whole of it.

"I have too much respect for ye to take ye like a common woman upon the floor."

"Let there be no doubt—I'd not let ye take me like a common woman."

Ronan raised a brow in question.

"I would let ye take me like the woman I am—a noble warrior."

She watched with fascination as he swallowed—her words having affected him greatly.

"Will your brother kill me?" he whispered, pulling her hand to his lips.

"Likely, if he were to find out."

"Who is your brother?"

Julianna averted her gaze. If she were to tell him, Ronan would toss her on her horse and demand they return to Eilean

Donan at once. "Not someone I want to be thinking of right now."

Ronan frowned at that, lightly bit her pointer knuckle. "Why will ye not tell me?"

Sooner or later, Ronan would figure it out, but she didn't want to talk about it right now. "I will tell ye when we return on the morrow."

"As he runs me through for taking what isn't mine?"

Hearing him say the word *taking* brought to mind all the things she'd fantasized about doing with him...

"Ye canna take what has already been freely given, Ronan. But I assure ye, I willna be running to tell him. And I'll not be begging for your hand."

"I'm not certain if I should be offended or not."

"Why would ye be offended?"

Ronan winked. "Most lasses beg for more after having me in their beds."

A teasing glint entered his eyes and Julianna loved seeing his lighter side. He was such a strong and powerful man. Serious, deadly. Gentle when caring for her wound, passionate when kissing and touching her. To see him tease was just another side of him that plucked at her heart.

"That confident?" she teased back.

"Oh, aye." He leaned forward, just a breath away and whispered, "I can make ye beg too."

A heated flush swept from the top of her head down to her toes. Her thigh pained her no more. She was sure he could make her plead. Hadn't she already begged him to make love to her a few times now? The man had every right to be confident.

"Prove it," she countered.

Ronan grinned wickedly. "I love a challenge."

Before she could respond, he licked her lower lip, tugged it with his teeth. Frissons of hot desire fired, pooling at her center. Dear Lord, she refused to supplicate.

Maybe she should make him be the one who pleaded for more. Aye, that sounded like an excellent choice. Julianna captured Ronan's tongue between her teeth, sucked it into her mouth. He growled, a deep vibrating noise that caused her sex to clench. Stroking up her arms, he gently massaged her shoulders, her back, the sides of her ribs — and then the undersides of her breasts.

Her nipples were hard, taut, aching for his touch, but he didn't go near them. Instead drove her crazy by stroking everywhere else. He was good...very good. They'd barely gotten anywhere and already she was melting. Now she knew why those few women at the castle ran after him panting.

Who knew what the future held? She dared not think on it another moment. Tonight he was all hers.

Julianna gently broke their kiss, pushed him back and sat up on her knees, winced slightly at the sting in her thigh. Without taking her eyes from his, she unhooked the belt at her waist, took her time to undress. Peeling away every inch of fabric slowly, seductively. Watched his eyes widen, then grow heavy. His chest rose and fell at a faster pace. As much as he wanted to remain in control, his desire grew with each peel of her clothing. Julianna tossed her gown aside, knelt in just her chemise, realized how threadbare it was, that her hardened nipples jutted against the fabric, that each dusky circle was clearly visible. Ronan's eyes were riveted to the spot, and she wasted no time in taking advantage of that. She arched her back slightly, and then took hold of the ribbons at the center of her chest.

"Wait," Ronan said, his voice gruff. "Let me."

Julianna stilled her fingers and waited. He took hold of the ribbons between his thumb and forefinger. Tugging slowly, the sound of the ties swishing as they loosened seemed to echo in the room. He rose to his knees, so they faced each other, both kneeling.

Heart pounding in her ears, Julianna found it hard to breathe. She was nearly naked. But felt completely exposed. Her chemise untied, the sides fell apart nearly to her navel, exposing the expanse of her cleavage. Ronan ran a finger from the dip in her throat, down through the valley of her breasts to her belly. Julianna drank in a breath, sucked in her belly. Her skin pebbled and she shivered.

"Ye're softer than I imagined," Ronan whispered. He leaned forward and kissed her collarbone. Trailed his lips, nuzzling her as he went, down between her breasts. His fingers gently traced the lines of a scar above her breast, once again taking away her breath. A knife wound three years prior. "I had thought ye'd be taut, rough, but ye're not." He sounded amazed. "When ye dropped the plaid this morn, I was amazed to see such femininity." He touched another one on her shoulder, a mace, its jagged points had dug deep and hurt like hell.

"Did ye think me masculine?" she asked, starting to feel a little self-conscious. Her fingers rested on his shoulders and she leaned more of her weight onto her uninjured thigh.

"Nay, never. But ye're so strong. I just didna think a woman could be strong and…sensual. But ye've proven me wrong. About so many things. Even your scars. They tell a story of a woman full of strength and bravery. I admire ye."

Heat flushed her cheeks and she looked away, not sure how she was supposed to take his words. Ronan lifted her chin with a finger, forcing her to look at him.

"My words still hold true. Ye're a prize. A treasure that walks amongst us. A goddess, Julianna. None of us have realized what an honor it's been to be in your presence. And not just because of this gift ye're giving me. I'm—" He shook his head. "I'm no good with words, my lady."

Her heart skipped a beat. "But ye are."

Julianna pressed her palms to his face, feeling the stubble on his cheeks tickle her skin.

"I've never talked so much to another woman. I feel a fool."

Julianna laughed softly. "Again, ye're in good company. Enough talking. Now kiss me."

Ronan pulled her taut against him, hands wrapped around her waist, and brushed his lips over hers. He was gentle at first, as if testing the waters. It was sensual, slow, their tongues melded and stroked as though they had all the time in the world to taste one another.

Julianna gripped the back of his *leine* shirt and tugged it free from his plaid, splayed her hands on the bare muscles surrounding his spine. Knotted scars laced his back and met her fingertips. Battle wounds. The sign of a true warrior. He was warm, sinew, pure strength. It was as though her touch ignited something inside him. He took her mouth with thrilling vigor. Oh, this was the Ronan she knew, the power and passion behind his kiss that made her weak and strong at the same time.

While she ran her hands up along his spine, dug into his shoulders, Ronan too continued his exploration. He hooked his thumbs into her chemise and tugged it over her shoulders and down her arms, trapping her. Excitement filled her, consumed her. He was no squire. Ronan knew just how to touch her to make her sigh and they'd barely done more than kiss. Or maybe it was the way he breathed. Every caress, his scent, his very being.

Julianna tugged his shirt the rest of the way from his plaid, so she could feel his abdomen—another rippling expanse of tight, masculine muscle. When she splayed her hands over his bare chest, Ronan hissed a breath against her lips.

"Och, lass..." he murmured, trailing his lips from hers to form a provocative path along her chin and neck.

Where his lips touched, she burned. She wanted him to feel the same way. Julianna pressed her temple to his shoulder and her lips to his corded neck. Another hiss of breath came from Ronan. He licked at her flesh, and she mimicked the moves, the tip of her tongue darting against his salty flesh, before she pressed her lips there for a gentle suck. His scent invaded her nostrils and did something odd to her insides. 'Twas as if, just the scent of him could leave her undone.

Before she could ponder more on how much he fascinated her—more so than anyone she'd ever met—Ronan cupped her breasts and brushed his thumbs over her taut nipples.

Julianna gasped, thrust her chest forward, filling his hands more fully with her breasts. He was warm, and yet she was covered with puckered flesh and chills swept through her at an alarming rate. Coupling with the squire had been fun, exciting, but never had he elicited this sort of response from her. Making love to Ronan was an entirely different experience, one she could see why women begged for more. If it weren't for the fact that she'd sworn not to do it, she might be indeed begging already.

Ronan slid his mouth from her neck and kissed between her breasts, nuzzling the fleshy mounds. His hot breath caressed over her flesh and she whimpered. Wanted him to taste her nipples. They ached for that very thing and she couldn't understand why. The squire had never kissed her breasts. He'd touched them, played with her nipples but never—

Searing hot velvet touched the peak of one breast. Julianna cried out. Eyes she hadn't known were closed flew open and her gaze settled on Ronan's red tongue flicking over her nipple. She watched, mesmerized as he circled around the peak, flicked over it, then sucked it into his mouth. *Holy...* All thought left her, and she was nothing but a mass of hot, wicked sensation.

She gripped the back of his head, threaded her fingers into his hair and held him in place. "Dinna stop," she moaned.

Ronan chuckled, rolling his tongue in decadent swiftness over her flesh. Telling him not to stop wasn't considered begging was it?

She didn't know. She didn't care. If she lost the challenge that didn't matter, as long as he kept doing what he was doing.

With trembling fingers Julianna let go of Ronan's head and explored his chest, finding his tiny nipples. They were hard, and when she gently pinched them, he groaned. What would he do if she put her mouth there?

They still knelt before each other, and so Julianna gently pushed him. "Take off your clothes and lay down," she whispered against his neck.

Ronan looked up at her, surprise in his eyes. Her courage was coming in spurts and when she looked at him it dissipated. But only because she was worried she'd say or do the wrong thing. Ronan was the expert at lovemaking, not her.

"As ye say, my lady." Ronan scooted back a few inches, took the pin from his plaid, tossed the long piece of fabric behind him, and then pulled off his shirt.

Julianna sat back on her heels and watched as his golden skin, with a sprinkling of light hair was revealed to her again. Her breath caught and she felt light-headed. Ronan was beautiful. Could have been sculpted from stone, except she knew when she touched him, though he was thick with muscle, he was also warm and pliable. She traced the pink scar near his shoulder—from her thrown dagger. It'd healed well, but she still wished she'd thought before throwing.

"Dinna worry over it, lass. I would have done the same." He smiled and stroked her cheek. His touch was comforting, and she was glad he didn't hold any hard feelings at her having injured him. "Besides, I've never been scarred by a woman. 'Tis my most treasured scar."

Julianna laughed, bit her lip. "I'm still sorry, all the same."

Keeping his plaid in place, he lay down on his back, the fire light casting dancing shadows on his form.

Did he think she would change her mind? Was that the reason for keeping his plaid on? Perhaps. But she also found she liked the element of mystery. She could explore parts of him at a time. Hide the element she wanted more than anything inside her.

Every few minutes she did get a little scared, but deep down, she wanted this. Wanted to feel him inside her. Wanted to be loved, if only for tonight. She'd led a life of loneliness, and judging from the way it was unfolding, she would continue to live that way. Except, for right now. Tonight she would pretend that life was different.

Julianna took her time walking on her knees, taking in every inch that he'd revealed and recalling the moments she'd studied him before while he'd been full of fever. She stopped when she was beside him, and sat back on her heels. Staring at his chest was too much temptation. She skimmed her hand over him, feeling the now familiar expanse, but seeing it too.

"Do ye remember kissing me when ye had the fever?" she asked.

Ronan slid his hand over her arm and tugged her closer. She braced her hand on his other side, leaning against him rib to rib.

"I remember dreaming of it."

"'Twas real." Julianna was surprised at how soft her voice had become.

"And 'twas verra good," he said.

Her lip curled in a smile. "Aye."

"Come here."

She didn't hesitate in leaning down to kiss him, liked that he was allowing her to be on top, giving her more control.

While he kissed her, he slid his hand beneath her chemise, stroking a burning path from her calf to her thigh. Julianna shivered, kissed him harder. When he reached her buttock, he squeezed. She sighed. He caressed her hip, her bare ribs, belly, the undersides of her breasts, and each touch was soft, but so potent in its power and pull. Her sex was damp, and clenched, waiting for him to fill her.

Ronan slipped his hand between her thighs, gently spread his fingers forcing her to open her legs for him. She did so without hesitation, moaned when he slid a finger through her wet folds, and stroked over the hardened nub of her pleasure. The man was even good in this way. Her sex clenched and her insides trembled. She swished her hips forward, wanting more of the wonderful sensations he stroked from her. Needing it. Refusing to beg for it other than with her body.

But then he pushed a finger inside her.

And she cried out—gasped and bit her tongue to keep from telling him not to stop that as well.

"Ye're so wet. Even if ye dinna want to beg, your body weeps for more." Ronan's voice was deep, evocative and slid over her body with the same pleasure as his hands.

"And what of your body?" she asked, her voice equally husky.

"Give me your hand," he said.

Julianna held out her hand and Ronan guided her over his plaid to grasp his erection.

"Oh!" She recoiled at once in fear, but made herself grip him tight. Another thing she'd not done with the squire. Theirs had been hurried couplings.

A warrior did not retreat in battle. With a little smile of triumph she squeezed his shaft, thick as a spear and long. Dear God, he was impressive. Growing bolder, she stroked up and down, the fabric of his plaid bunching in the most irritating way.

"Will ye take off your plaid?" she asked.

"Aye, gladly." He smiled and winked, taking her breath away.

Ronan gripped his belt, a move she found wholly enticing, and unhooked it. With swift movements, and a lift of his hips, he whipped his plaid from around his body leaving him nude and completely exposed.

Julianna's eyes widened as her gaze narrowed in on his glorious…body.

"I'm nay entirely sure I can handle that," she said, bemused.

Chapter Sixteen

Ronan pressed his lips in a smile, trying not to laugh at the serious, worried look that had come over Julianna's face.

"I assure ye, 'twill be all right," he said, trying to soothe her.

The moment she'd gotten a look at his cock, the woman had lost all sense of pluck that she'd been radiating in waves. Ronan was proud of his cock. Bigger than most, but he knew how to work it, which was what really kept the ladies pleased.

"I dinna know," she mused. "The squire wasn't…"

Ronan chuckled. He took her hand and placed it on his shaft, gritting his teeth at the warmth of her lithe fingers encircling him.

"Ye handle it perfectly, lass."

She smiled at him, stroked her thumb over the tip. Dear God, he was going to lose it. Just from her touch. There was something about having *her* be the one to touch him. Meant more than just the corporeality of it. Went deeper inside him. Something he wasn't willing to explore just now.

"Your skin is soft, I'd thought it would be rough," she said with wonderment.

"What exactly did ye do with the squire?" Ronan raised a brow, starting to become skeptical of not only the squire's skills, but whether or not he existed.

Her reaction to him was so raw, so new, almost as though she'd never been with a man afore now. Even in the firelight he could see her face color slightly.

"Dinna be shy, lass." He stroked her arm, feeling her flesh prickle with each glide of his hand.

"'Twas quick."

"He didna touch ye the way I do?"

Julianna shook her head.

"Did ye find your pleasure?"

Her brow furrowed. "I think so."

That meant most likely not. "An explosion here?" he asked, slipping his hand back between her thighs and stroking her nub.

Julianna's head fell forward slightly and she gasped. "Nay."

"But ye liked...being with him?" Ronan was trying for delicate. Julianna was such a strong woman in so many ways, but when it came to lovemaking, she appeared fragile and innocent. He didn't want to scare her or scar her for that matter.

She nodded. "Aye."

He smiled, caressed her pleasure nub in circles, all the while her eyes rolled, lips parted. She didn't stop stroking him either, a problem he'd need to correct. If she kept at it, he wouldn't last long enough to make her experience any better than what the squire had shown her.

That wasn't his style. When Ronan brought a woman to bed, she was left wanting nothing.

Swiftly he disengaged them, flipped her onto her back—careful of her thigh—and loomed above her.

"What are ye doing?" she asked.

"Making love to ye," he answered, nuzzling her neck and then biting her earlobe. "If I were to let ye continue your play, it'd be finished before we started."

"Ye...liked that?"

"Oh, aye, lass. I liked it verra much."

Julianna sighed, and though he didn't look at her face, he could hear her smile. He liked the sounds of her sighs, craved to hear more of them. Nuzzling a path between her breasts, he kissed her belly, hiked her chemise up over her hips, and then pulled her to sitting to take it the rest of the way off.

Ballocks... She was naked, glorious. Beautiful. Golden in the firelight. The front of her was just as well formed as the back. A tight, flat belly, lined with slight muscle—he'd never seen such on a woman before. Julianna worked hard at her trade, and when they left here, he would demand to know exactly where she got her training—the whole story this time.

Her breasts were round, full, perky. Just as soft as they looked. Her hips were trim, thighs long and sculpted, and a triangle of reddish hair graced her mound. Ronan stroked over her thighs, running his hands from her knees to her hips.

"Julianna, ye're exquisite," he whispered.

She lay back, opening her thighs and revealing the pink petals of her sex. Ronan's breath caught. He glanced up at her face. Her eyes were heavily lidded, cloudy with desire, and she watched him, studied him. There was trust in every angle. Trust. This woman was placing her most valued possession in his hands. For her body was truly a treasure. The offer, her response, 'twas so overwhelming. His chest grew tight, and every muscle coiled, ready to spring. He made a vow to himself, he would make her cry out with pleasure again and again.

Her features relaxed and she smiled. "Ye look worried, Ronan."

"Never," he answered, winking. "Just canna stop looking. I suppose I'm making a muddle of our first time." He slid his hands up and down her warm thighs. Realized too late he'd said first time as though he expected subsequent occasions.

Julianna sucked her lower lip into her mouth, and gripped his arms at the elbows. She tugged. As much as he'd teased her before, Ronan wasn't going to make her beg, if anything, he was the one desperately in need of her touch.

"Ye still have time to make up for it," she said with a teasing lilt. "I'm nay going anywhere."

And dammit if he wasn't going to make up for it tenfold. Ronan knelt between her thighs, feeling the warm length of her strong legs on his hips. His cock pulsed, and he swore it was harder than it had ever been before. Julianna's eyes riveted to the spot where the tip of his erection dropped lazily onto her mound. Where there had been fear earlier, hunger filled her gaze.

He leaned his weight on an elbow. Her hot, wet cleft cradled his shaft and he winced the pleasure was so excruciatingly potent. Closing his eyes, he laid claim to her mouth, trying to distract himself from what he really wanted, which was to bury himself in her hot center.

Tremors passed through him as she massaged his back, arms, hips. The women he bedded were eager lovers, but it'd always been quick—however satisfactory for both ends. He'd never taken so much time with a woman, never had a woman take so much pleasure in simply touching and kissing him. Making love to Julianna was a whole new experience, one he felt almost virginal at. They touched, kissed… And talking. When had talking become part of bedding? Certainly he could whisper naughty phrases and demand equally naughty actions, but to simply talk, to get to know one another, to actually care. Lord, she was taking over his mind.

And frighteningly, he enjoyed it.

Ronan was falling for Julianna. Had been since the moment he'd fastened eyes on her. Pulling away from her mouth he kissed his way back toward her lush breasts, and then lower. He was going to pleasure her with his mouth. Her feminine scent teased his senses, made his mouth water.

When he kissed the very top of her mound where her soft curls began, Julianna gasped and clenched her thighs tight on his head.

"Nay, Ronan."

"Aye, Julianna."

He pried her thighs open and breathed hotly over her folds, listening to her try and stifle a whimper. "If ye dinna like it, I will stop."

He glanced up at her, saw that she bit her fist and nodded.

"I think ye'll like it," he said, teasing her folds with the tip of his tongue. One glance showed him she again nodded, still biting her hand. Ronan chuckled, then dove in for another taste. He teased, probed, licked. Julianna's muffled whimpers grew to full out cries of pleasure. With his thumbs he pealed her folds open giving him full access to her nub of pleasure. God, she tasted like Heaven. Slick heat, and feminine sensuality. He suckled her nub, flicked his tongue over it, nuzzled her folds, made love to her with his mouth.

Julianna's thighs shook and she clenched tight. The fist that had been in her mouth lay buried in his hair, holding his mouth tight to her center. Her hips bucked beneath him, and when he slipped a finger inside her hot velvet, her muscles squeezed him tight. She was close…

Ronan didn't let up. Continued his push and pull, until Julianna broke apart beneath his ministrations.

"Ronan!" she cried out as her body shook violently. She sat up with the strength of her climax, eyes wide, mouth opened in surprise, cheeks flushed pink.

He smiled, a curve of pure male satisfaction. "I told ye, ye'd like it."

She nodded slowly. "Aye... 'Twas...magic." She licked her lips. "Can I...do the same to ye?"

Ronan's cock surged, and the thought of her luscious lips wrapped around his length nearly had him undone right then and there. "Next time," he croaked out.

She nodded, readily accepting there would be a next time. Hell, they were both living in another world right now. Reality would set in soon enough, and Ronan wasn't about to ruin the moment with thoughts of tomorrow. He slid up her body until they were nose to nose.

"I want ye so verra much," he whispered.

Julianna responded by lifting her hips, and nibbling his lower lip. "Take me."

Ronan tilted his hips, his cock pressing against her slick heat. He surged forward, burying himself in one full thrust. She was exquisitely tight, surrounding him at once in a cocoon of pleasure. His forehead fell against hers and he couldn't move, just breathed, trying to focus, to push away the release that hovered on the brink.

"That feels so good," she murmured, moving to kiss at his neck.

If she kept doing that... Ronan gripped her chin, moving to claim her mouth, if only to stop the heated torture of her mouth on his flesh. She flexed the muscles of her sex and tilted her hips, nearly upending him. He groaned.

Ronan gradually withdrew, then plunged back inside. He wanted to go slow. Wanted to drag out their pleasure, but she felt so damn good... And she was moaning, her fingers clasping his back, hips rising and falling to meet his. Julianna was a natural at lovemaking. The very best he'd ever had.

He kept his pace and thrusts measured, calculated to draw out her pleasure, but Julianna was a wildcat, writhing and demanding. As soon as he felt her sex clench tight and begin fluttering, Ronan knew his intent to make love to her all night was lost, she'd had him undone. He gritted his teeth and plunged ahead, riding out her climax. One more. He could give her one more.

"Oh, Ronan," she gasped. "So good…"

Tremors shook her body, and his own shivers took hold, pleasure radiating from the base of his spine and surging forward. Nay. He wouldn't finish yet…

Ronan squeezed his eyes shut against the pleasure that took hold of his body and possessed him. He pressed his lips to the crook of her shoulder, licked and nipped her skin, sucking on her earlobe. Swirling his hips, he arched up inside her, hitting that spot he knew would bring her to fruition once more. Julianna gasped, cried out. Their bodies were slick, sliding against one another in heated passion.

"Oh!" she cried, then clamped her teeth on his shoulder, biting not so gently. Once more her body surrounded him in a heated climax.

Ronan did not hold back this time. He quickened his pace, thrusting deep and hard. His release hit him like gale force, slamming into him with a power he'd never before known. A heady, low moan escaped his throat, and his entire body vibrated into hers.

"Julianna!" he roared, before collapsing on top of her.

Conscious not to crush her, he held himself on his elbows, but left his forehead against her shoulder as he waited for his breaths to steady. Their lovemaking had been earth-shattering. Life changing. Euphoric. Shocking. Damned good.

"Julianna," he murmured again, then kissed her lightly on the lips, stroked the strands of hair that stuck to the sides of her face back. "That was…"

"Stunning."

He nodded, kissed her again. Felt his heart clench.

She was his Julianna. *His*. Never would he let another touch her. Brother be damned; he'd claimed her and under no circumstances would he let anyone take her from him.

Chapter Seventeen

Julianna blinked open her eyes, stretched her arms wide, and then realized with alarm that she was completely nude and her covers had disappeared.

A quick glance around the croft showed that Ronan had left, and moment of panic seized her. Had he left her there? Her fears quickly subsided when he came through the door seconds later—replaced by mortification as she rolled onto her belly in an attempt to hide her bosom from him. Followed by a wince as she rolled onto her injured thigh. She scrambled to gather the billowing length of wool fabric covering the floor. His plaid.

Where were her clothes?

"A lovely sight in the morning," Ronan said cheerfully.

Before she could fully cover herself, he playfully swatted at her bare bottom.

"Why did ye let me sleep in so late?"

The sun was shining through the various cracks in the croft and at some point, Ronan must have opened the single window to let in some fresh, although frightfully cold, air. They were supposed to leave at first light, not the nooning.

"I couldna bear to wake ye. Especially when I knew how much ye could use the sleep." His devilish grin and wink were a pointed reminder of just *why* she would have been tired.

A flush covered her skin, and instantly her nipples and between her thighs tingled. Just looking at him reminded her of their night together. The exploration, the effect he'd had on both her mind and her body.

How could she let him go now?

She'd have to have that talk with her brother. Assure him that she wouldn't leave her duties behind, but that she wanted more. Thought she'd found what that more was, in Ronan.

She frowned as she stood, the plaid gathered about her shoulders. But going to her brother was impossible if Ronan didn't feel the same way. Julianna would never force a man's hand, and Ronan had not mentioned wanting to be tied to her for life. In fact, hadn't they made it clear to each other that they were both indulging themselves? Disappointment sliced through her anew. They had done that very thing and she'd not go back on her word. Not in a million years. Not even if a knife were held to her throat. She had too much respect for Ronan. A bond she didn't want to break.

Though, he had mentioned something about *again*, which implied this was not a one-time deal. Julianna wanted to groan but kept it locked up inside. No need to trouble him with her fickle female mind—one that seemed to have sprung upon her when he walked into her life. Before now, everything had been cut and dry. Black and white. Now there appeared to be shades of grey that were so varied on the spectrum she felt like she was living inside a storm cloud.

Spotting her clothes neatly laid out on the table, she teased, "Did a bit of maid's work, did ye?" The question helped to lighten not only her mood, but appeared to amuse Ronan as well.

He laughed. "There ye have it wrong. I merely moved them out of your reach so I might admire your form for a wee bit longer."

Julianna tossed him a mock cantankerous expression over her shoulder, making sure the plaid dipped a little to show her flesh.

"Then ye succeeded."

His face turned serious. "I never fail to get what I desire."

"And neither do I." There he had it. She wanted him. For more than one night. He'd made the comment, and she'd interpreted it for herself. Ronan was her mission.

But as she slipped into her clothes, Julianna couldn't help but wonder at his choice of words. Was she merely a conquest?

Ballocks and bloody hell!

What the hell was he thinking saying something that ridiculous? Ronan wanted to turn back the hands of time and crush those words before they came out of his mouth. Had he really just made her sound like an easy bedding?

He'd have to watch his back extra carefully because she was sure to run him through with one of her poisoned weapons. Ronan eyed her warily. Waited for the explosion.

But when she turned around, her face was serene, expressionless. And that scared him more than when he'd seen the bloodied bodies of his parents in the wagon the Sutherland clan had brought their retrieved remains home in.

Her expression meant so many things—she did not care about him at all, that *he'd* been the one easily seduced. Hell she was a warrior. It wasn't entirely unbelievable that she would have picked up a few bad warrior habits, like bedding anything willing.

Ronan looked down at the ground as he contemplated that. He didn't believe it. Didn't want to believe that. Her passion had been real. Tangible. The pain of her having used him cut deeper than he ever wanted to admit.

Worse than being rejected was that maybe she believe he had in fact been the one thinking such. Nay, he couldn't have her believing she was merely a conquest.

"Julianna," he started, stepping toward her. He'd taken the horses outside to graze, had planned on coming in and waking her, serving her breakfast. "I hope we might break our fast together before we leave. I've not much in the way of fare, but—"

She held up her hand cutting him off. "There's no need. We can eat on the road. We are well behind schedule."

Ronan tried to keep his face from falling, but her clipped tone, and obvious dismissal, wounded his pride. He supposed he should have known that last night was the one and only time they'd share intimacy. One he'd never forget and would haunt his dreams for the rest of his years, however long they might be.

The way she studied his face told him she'd seen his reaction. Damn. He'd always been good at hiding his emotions. Except around her. Ronan swiped all emotion from his face with a run of his hand from his forehead to his chin. Julianna gazed at her toes, then back up at him, her features softening somewhat.

"I'm sorry, Ronan," she said. She crossed her arms over her chest, and he got the distinctive impression she was trying to protect herself as much as she was trying to distance herself from him. "I didna mean to be...rude. 'Tis simply that...last night..." She heaved a breath and he wasn't sure he wanted to hear what else she had to say. She gave him a forced smile.

"'Twas a wonderful night. But the truth is, that our being together didna erase the fact that Ross is a few miles down the road and that he's built up a whole new army with or without his cousin's aid. Mayhap even brought more earls to his side. We must return to Eilean Donan."

He nodded. How could he have forgotten the danger posed to the nation? This was why he shouldn't get involved with a woman other than the lasses willing to give him a few moments of pleasure. Being with Julianna had nearly made him forget the state of their nation.

The Bruce, Wallace, Scotland, his entire family, they all depended on him. And in a way, so did Julianna. He'd let them down. His gut twisted, and his hunger for the morning meal suddenly dissipated.

"Then, let us ride."

The morning sun on her face wasn't as much of a welcome as it normally was. Julianna left the croft with a heavy heart. Her feet felt dense as she trudged toward Brave. Ronan had already saddled her horse. The man was…nothing short of amazing.

And she felt like a total wench. The look on his face when she declined breakfast had wrenched her soul. Almost as though he really did wish more. Had the same feelings. She'd thought it impossible, but it appeared that he might actually feel the same. Then he'd shuttered his face. Hidden his feelings from her. Felt like the first time he'd tried to hide from her. And that hurt.

She'd give anything to change what had to be done. Would even give up her position within Robert's camp. That thought made her realize something wholly abhorrent. Her stomach actually clenched. She was… She was…

Nay. Julianna shook her head, grabbed the reins, and threw herself on top of the horse. She gazed over at Ronan, who seemed just as disturbed as her when he mounted. His face was a storm cloud.

She was in love with him.

Would wait until the end of time for him.

Would give up her life for him.

When this was over. When Ross was in his grave, Julianna would beg for Ronan. Would fight to have him by her side. Make him see that they were perfect for each other.

She stared up at the clouds. *God, if ye're up there, hear me. Keep Ronan safe. He's mine.*

Julianna wasn't much of a praying woman. There'd been too much she'd seen. Too many times she'd questioned God's existence. But if he was up there, looking down on her, she hoped he heard her prayer.

With a glance at Ronan who appeared to be waiting for her to move, Julianna squeezed Braves sides and urged him in the direction of Ross' old camp.

They took the way they'd come, and hid on the outskirts of Ross' old camp, waiting for a sign from within. Those who'd camped there before did not appear to still be there, but that didn't mean they weren't coming back. Julianna and Ronan rode silently, their horses trained to step lightly, through the camp and continued on their way.

By later afternoon, when the sky had just started to turn grey with the coming dusk, Eilean Donan loomed before them, ever mysterious in the way she emerged from the mist and surrounding water.

Instead of being thrilled to be back with those she'd grown close to, Julianna felt a sense of doom. The way the crenellations jutted into the clouds didn't make her feel secure; she felt closed in. Suffocated.

Her entire life had been devoted to Scotland, to Robert. Before now she'd lived, breathed, eaten duty, honor, commitment. Never questioned it, save a few times she could count on one hand and always for selfish reasons that she'd soon pushed aside as childish desires.

But wanting Ronan… That was different. Didn't feel childish. It was something she'd tried to deny herself. Truly.

Well, actually not very hard. He was the one thing she wanted to allow herself to have. The man. The hope he brought with him. The way he made her feel. Special, cherished, desired. Even thinking about it, her heart soared, feeling constricted within her ribcage.

And why couldn't she have both? Aye, he was a distraction, but if she knew he would be waiting for her at the end of the day, wasn't that something she could overcome? There were so many challenges she'd dealt with. Her upbringing, training, having never met her mother and not seeing her ill father in over five years, depending on Robert and he, in turn, depending on her.

This was her life. She was Julianna, warrior, guard to the future King of Scotland.

But she wanted to be Julianna, wife of Ronan Sutherland.

She stole a glance at Ronan, shocked to see that he too was looking at her. He opened his mouth as if to speak and she tried not to lean forward in her eagerness to hear his voice. They'd not spoken since leaving the croft.

"What is it?" she asked, her patience losing out.

"Last night…" He trailed off and she worried the words she'd spoken earlier still stung him.

"Aye?" Julianna tried to make her voice soft, encouraging.

"I discovered something."

That was an odd thing to say. She raised a brow in question, but her reaction didn't seem to sit well with Ronan. He shifted in his seat, shook his head.

"'Tis not important. Ye promised ye'd tell me who your brother is when we returned to the castle. I'll have his name now. Who are ye?"

Julianna gazed back over the horizon, watched the mist as it curled up and out of the water like greedy mystical fingers. She breathed in the scents, cold, wintry, but soothing all the same. A promise was a promise. But she wasn't sure that Ronan was truly ready to hear what she had to say.

"Julianna?"

She gazed back at him. Took in the determined set of his jaw.

"Dinna make me wait longer, lass."

Julianna sighed deeply, gripped the reins of her horse tight. Brave's skin trembled beneath her and he flicked his mane. She loosened her hold, and bit her lip, finding she needed something to clench, be it her hands or her teeth.

Julianna had never told a soul what she was about to tell Ronan. Robert knew obviously, and her father. Her tutors as well, but they were long dead. On this earth she and two others were the only ones who truly knew who she was. Who her mother and father were, her siblings. The rest were kept in the dark. For Robert's sake. For her own.

Ronan let out a huff, and flicked his horse's reins, Saint taking four steps before Julianna had the nerve to open her mouth.

"Wait, dinna leave. I mean to tell ye."

Ronan stopped his horse but didn't turn around. "Lass, ye were the one who pointed out that we'd urgent news to relay, that we have a battle to prepare for." His voice was filled with exasperation. "Now ye stall on a simple question. How hard can it be to simply say —"

"I am Julianna de Brus." *The Bruce's own sister.*

There, she'd done it. Julianna heaved a deep sigh, feeling lighter. But what weightlessness she felt soon dispelled. Ronan said nothing. His shoulders appeared stiffer, and he sat unmoving.

"Did ye hear me? I'm Jul—"

"I heard ye, my lady." His voice was strained, like he had to force out each syllable.

Julianna felt like he'd punched her in the heart. Her chest hurt, and her eyes stung. He was angry. Why?

"Ye lied."

Julianna blanched. "I dinna lie."

Ronan whirled around atop his horse, his face contorted in anger. "I put my trust in ye. Laid ye on your back and had my way with ye."

"'Twas not like that."

"And ye think, Robert the Bruce is going to see it any other way? I slept with the king's sister."

"Half sister."

Ronan's hands flew up to the heavens. "Does it matter?"

She shook her head. It didn't. To her and Robert it had never mattered. She was older by four years, and he'd always been her little brother, even if her mother was his father's lover.

"Dammit, Julianna! Ye could have told me."

"And what?" she asked, her lips curling into something very close to a sneer. "Ye wouldn't have wanted me? Is my name so repulsive?"

Ronan shook his head, raked his hands through his hair.

"'Tis not that, my lady."

"Stop calling me, *my lady*."

"Ye once made sure I only called ye that."

"We're well past formalities, Ronan Sutherland."

He nodded. "If I'd known ye were his flesh and blood, I'd not have made love to ye. Ye're right. But 'tis not for lack of wanting. Nor desire. I *want* ye, Julianna. I crave ye. Feel lost when I dinna know where ye are. But he is the future king. He will want more for his sister than what I am."

"Ye're a fool. And ye dinna listen. Robert doesna want me to marry. I'm too important to him."

Confusion and pain roared inside her head. She couldn't face Ronan anymore. Found it easier to turn away. Suddenly, she was desperate for her bedchamber, for the solitude it would provide.

"Let us away. 'Tis nearly dark." She didn't look to see Ronan's reaction. Didn't wait for his answer. With a kick of her heels, Brave was heading fast down the road toward her brother, Robert the Bruce.

Chapter Eighteen

The lump sitting large in Ronan's gut was painful. He couldn't believe what Julianna had just told him. All these months he'd lived at Eilean Donan. Been the right-hand man to Wallace and the damned Bruce! No one bothered to tell him that Julianna was Robert's sister, even if she was only his half-sister. Flesh and blood all the same!

Fury lit a torch inside his veins. He felt duped, used. But most of all, he felt stupid. He should have seen it, shouldn't he? Noticed their similarities. Were there any? He guessed they did have the same stubborn streak. Maybe the same color eyes? He couldn't quite bring to mind the color of Robert's eyes. Though he knew her eyes were a dark grey like storm clouds. Probably why his moods were so turbulent when he was around her.

Julianna rode ahead, her back stiff. She sat her horse regally. And she should, being the sister of the future king. Damn, what a fool he'd been! He'd spread her thighs wide, tasted the fruit that graced between. And all the while she knew who she was. If her brother found out... There'd be no fight, no forced marriage, Ronan would be hung from the nearest rafter—after being drawn and quartered in full consciousness.

Taking a ragged breath, he pushed Saint into a gallop in order to catch up with Julianna. He might be angry at her, might feel that she betrayed him, but he was still responsible for her safety. Robert and Wallace both charged him with bringing her back. Less than forty-eight hours later he was indeed returning with her. Albeit, there were a few more secrets revealed and wagon-full of hypothetical baggage they were bringing back with them.

He had to believe that Julianna wouldn't be telling Robert anything, and so, for today, he would give his report, meet with the men and prepare them for taking siege of Kinterloch. Then he'd eat his evening meal and retire to bed early. After they'd cleaned up the mess with Ross and the village, he would approach the Bruce and do the right thing. He would offer for Julianna's hand. No matter what she said, or his own feelings— he'd made a vow that she was his. And, betrayal or not, *he* was not going to go back on his word. Even if she didn't know about it.

Oddly for the time of day, there was no one on the road. The hair on the back of Ronan's neck prickled. Something wasn't right. Julianna, for once, seemed to be acting more on emotion than instinct.

He leaned low over Saint and whispered in his ear as he nudged him with his heels. The horse lowered his head and increased his speed. Ronan pulled his claymore from his back as he charged.

Julianna, probably hearing his increased paced, whirled in her saddle, eyes widening, mouth falling open. But Ronan's instincts were not wrong. As soon as she'd taken her eyes off the road, a huge tree trunk was launched into her path.

"Julianna!" Ronan called.

She pulled her sword, whirled her horse around but not in time. Brave had begun to leap over the tree, and Julianna was tossed roughly to the ground. Brave made his jump, continued to run a few feet, but then dutifully stopped and waited for his mistress.

The tree hadn't fallen by an act of nature. A group of about half a dozen vagabonds jumped into the road. An ambush.

Ronan only took a second to make sure they were not men of the Bruce's camp before he took action.

"Go!" he shouted to Julianna. Thank God, for once she didn't argue but scrambled out of the way.

Ronan was on the men half a second later. On foot, they were no match for him. One tried to spear his horse in the chest, but Saint always rode with a plate of armor in the sensitive spot that felled many horses. The man's spear split in half, and Saint trampled over him. One down, five to go. Ronan arched his sword, sliced through one on his right side, wielded the reins to the left and felled another. From his peripheral, he saw one had notched a bow, but a whizzing through the air caught the man in the throat — Julianna's pin. Lil Lass leapt onto another man, knocking him to the ground where he remained unconscious.

The final maggot, snarled, a dagger in one hand and a sword in the other.

"Why dinna ye get off that horse and fight me like a man?"

Ronan sneered and prepared to jump off the horse, when a knife hit the man in the chest. His eyes rolled back into his head and he dropped to his knees.

Well, that was no fun. He kind of wanted to fight the man.

Ronan glanced at Julianna and nodded his appreciation. Her lips were thin, brows furrowed. She nodded back. He jumped from his horse, checked the woods on the side of the road to make sure all was clear, then reached a hand down.

Julianna shook her head and attempted to stand, falling once, but shoving his help aside once more. "I can do it," she said through gritted teeth.

"I know it, lass. I just wanted to help."

"I dinna need ye."

Her words stung. Ronan knew she didn't need him. Hell, she didn't need anyone, but it didn't mean that it didn't hurt any less.

She finally stood, rubbed her rear which probably hurt like the devil from her fall, then limped over to the fallen tree limb, which had to be a foot and a half thick. Lifting a leg over it, Julianna sank, straddling the trunk.

"What are ye doing, lass?" Concerned, Ronan hurried toward her.

"Leave me be. I hurt my arse is all."

He tried not to laugh. "I'll make sure ye get a warm bath when we arrive."

"I can manage on my own." She glared up at him. Looked away. Bit her lip. "I'm sorry," she grumbled toward the ground. "I should have known something was wrong, but I was too tossed up in my mind. Your fault, by the way."

Ronan reached out and touched her shoulder. He gave her a gentle squeeze, then gripped her chin, urging her to look at him. "Julianna, we are not each other's enemy."

"From the way ye looked at me when I told ye of Robert, ye sure showed the opposite."

"I was surprised. Hurt."

"It doesna matter. Let us be on our way."

He nodded. Cook's spiced whisky was calling his name. Julianna may be tough as steel, but she was still a woman. And if he learned anything from his sisters and his sisters-in-law, it was that women were likely to change moods quite often and there didn't appear to be much he could do to change it, save accept it, and offer his support.

That didn't appear to be at all what Julianna wanted from him. As he watched her limp toward her horse, he realized with a start, that while he thought he knew her, felt a deep connection with her, what she'd revealed and what she still kept hidden made her appear to be much a stranger.

Though she limped, Julianna hooked her foot into the stirrup and swung up on the saddle with ease. She glanced back at him, studied him a moment longer than he would have suspected based on her dismissal.

"Are ye coming or not?" she asked haughtily.

Ronan nodded. "Aye, my lady."

He leapt onto Saint's back and hurried toward her, his mount taking the jump over the log with ease. They'd have to send men out to clear the road, else someone with a wagon would be blocked. The ride to the bridge was silent, but thick with tension. Ronan wanted to ask her so many questions, to pry her back open like he'd done at the croft. To return *that* Julianna to him. The one that was carefree, happy. This Julianna was serious, mysterious and a ripple of anger lay just beneath the surface of her steady façade. 'Twas in fact that ripple that kept his mouth shut.

"Ronan," she said, breaking the silence, when the first clop of hooves sounded on the bridge.

He glanced up at the castle. Men stood upon the battlements, arrows notched and aimed, but when he waved, they retracted their weapons, called for the gate to be opened. Lil Lass ran ahead and through the gate, disappearing.

"Aye?"

"Not a word to Robert. We've enough to deal with."

Since she'd brought it up, Ronan felt speaking on it was fair game. He glanced at her, gave her a serious expression and said, "Aye, lass, ye've got my word. But I will speak with ye on all matters when we've taken Ross down."

She nodded, glanced away. He hated that she couldn't look at him. Had he made such a bad impression on her? Ronan frowned. They drew closer to the gate, which was slowly being opened.

"I want ye to accept my apology," she mumbled.

"For what?"

She sighed, like he was hauling unwanted words from her. "For keeping it from ye. I hope ye can understand that I did it for Robert's safety. 'Tis my duty."

Ronan nodded. He didn't want to understand. But he could. There were secrets that families kept for their protection. Several his own family kept. He couldn't begrudge her that. "I dinna blame ye, lass. 'Tis only…" He didn't want to travel down the road that had gotten her riled up in the first place. She didn't seem to understand his own feelings of betrayal, and maybe they were selfish because she'd only done what she thought was in the best interest of her brother and herself. "Never mind, 'tis not important."

Julianna didn't question him, though her astute eyes studied him shrewdly.

"I will report to the Bruce," she said, her voice firm, shoulders squared.

"I have my own report."

"Ye can report to Wallace."

"All right." He was in no mood to argue with her. In fact, his mood was going rather south.

They crossed under the gate, which was quickly closed behind them. As soon as they were through, stable hands came out to attend the horses, and servants took their satchels and weapons from the mounts, bringing them into the castle.

Graham nodded to Ronan from a group he must have been training in the courtyard.

Wallace and Bruce approached with quick steps, the latter's expression one of fury. Ronan could see now, looking at the set of Robert's eyes and the glower he gave Julianna, that they were indeed related.

"To my study," he ground out.

Julianna didn't say a word, but lifted her chin, and swept passed all who'd come to greet them as she made her way into the keep.

"My lord," Ronan called.

The Bruce stayed his steps and turned toward Ronan, Julianna did as well, an imperceptible shake of her head. Ronan jogged forward and whispered into his future king's ear.

"The lass is well. Only meant to clean up the mess that is Ross. We've bigger problems. I will discuss them with Wallace, and I believe Julianna wishes to relay them to ye."

Robert nodded, his face placid, then turned and followed Julianna inside.

Wallace came up beside him. "What was that about?"

"I fear he is verra angry at her."

"Aye, and well he should be."

Ronan nodded. "For certes, save she only thought to do her duty."

Wallace glanced at him, a mirthful curve to his lips. "Ye like her."

Ronan glared. "Mind your own business."

"She is partly my business."

"I'll not discuss my personal feelings with ye, unless ye've decided to become a housekeeper and not the general."

Wallace laughed. "Ye've a way with words. Come inside and give me your report. Ye've a visitor too."

"Magnus?" Ronan's older brother was laird of their clan, and he missed him fiercely. It was hard to be away from his older brother for so many months, having previously seen him nearly every day of his life. Away from their home, but Ronan had to forge his own path, and when Wallace had invited him to help train the men, he'd seen a bright future ahead of himself.

"Nay. Your cousin Brandon Sinclair."

Ronan smiled. He'd not seen his cousin in a while. "Has he come to join us?"

"Aye. Brought nigh on two dozen warriors."

Ronan nodded. Brandon was also a laird, known in the north for their stealth. Ronan wouldn't have to train Brandon's men, they were elite.

"Go clean yourself up, ye smell like shite, and when ye're through, come to my chamber to give me your report. I'll have Sinclair and Murray join us as well."

Ronan nodded. The bedchamber that had been given to him when he was injured was still made up and a fresh basin of water placed on the table. He made quick work of washing up, didn't bother to shave as he wanted to get the report out of the way, the plans laid and a whisky in his hands. He donned a clean *leine* shirt and plaid, laced up his boots, put on his weapons and then went in search of Wallace's chamber. The man's room had to be the second largest in the castle as the Bruce's was the biggest.

Ronan was admitted upon knocking. Wallace's chamber not only housed his bed, but a large trestle table, currently covered in maps, scrolls, parchment, quills and ink wells.

Daniel, Brandon and Wallace glanced up from the map they poured over and nodded toward him.

"Glad to have ye back," Daniel said.

"Aye, I was wondering what was taking ye so long," Brandon teased. "Even had Wallace here wondering if ye'd run off into the sunset with the lass."

Dead God if his cousin only knew how close to the truth he was. Ronan laughed him off, stepped forward and gave his cousin an arm shake and heavy pounding on the back. After their masculine show of affection, Ronan got serious.

"Ross has taken up several miles away within Kinterloch. He's turned them against the Bruce. 'Tis only a matter of time before they attempt an attack."

"'Twould appear, I arrived right on time," Brandon said with a rub of his hands.

"Aye, and glad am I for ye to have our backs." Ronan glanced from his cousin to Wallace. "What would ye have us do?"

Chapter Nineteen

"Ye dinna understand!" Julianna paced the length of her brother's chamber, her face hot with fury.

"I understand perfectly," Robert shouted back, slamming his hands down on the table. "Ye left your station. I needed ye here, not traipsing about the countryside."

Oh, he didn't just say that... Julianna whirled on him, and hissed, "I never traipse."

"Gallivanting, playing the hero, committing suicide, what would ye call it?"

She marched over to his table, slammed her own hands down and said with deadly calm, "Saving your arse."

Robert straightened, scrutinizing her in a way she'd never seen him do before. "And what if while ye were gone, Ross had backtracked to Eilean Donan? Ye would not have been here to do your duty and ye'd have taken one of my best men with ye."

Julianna scoffed. "I didna take Ronan with me."

Robert raised a brow, folded his arms over his chest. "Aye, but ye did. The moment ye left with no one to guard your back."

Julianna sliced her hands through the air, in an attempt to end the topic. "'Tis of no matter, we've returned and there are more things to discuss than me setting out to finish what I started. Ross is a menace and needs to be sent to his maker."

Robert shook his head. "I see ye will not understand that ye are at fault. 'Haps it would be best for ye to spend some time in your chamber. I'll have Wallace give me another guard."

Julianna's mouth fell open. He couldn't seriously be considering locking her up, relieving her of her duties. A crushing blow. Her stomach knotted and she had to use all of her power to stay upright rather than doubling over.

"Ye canna mean it," she said, her voice lowered.

Bruce glowered at her. "Aye, I do. Ye may be my guard, but who do ye think looks after ye?"

Julianna shook her head.

"Me, lass, me." The tone of his voice, quiet and exasperated, shocked her.

Robert had always been her brother. A fact she'd never forgotten, even if she wanted to; it was impressed upon her. He was her charge, though they were not far apart in years. In all this time, she'd never once thought he was looking out for her. At best, she'd thought, when it came to her, he did things for his own good.

"When I left Eilean Donan, I did so with ye in mind, Robert. I wanted to take Ross out of the equation. In retrospect, I suppose 'twas foolhardy to have done so without telling ye."

Robert squinted his eyes. "Are ye just saying this because I've threatened to lock ye in your chamber?"

Julianna shook her head, a small smile curving her lips. "One thing the two of us have in common is our stubborn streak, brother. If ye would make good to your threat, there is nothing I could do, save figure out a way to escape. My words would be meaningless right now."

"Aye, that they would."

She hoped he was confessing he'd not truly meant them. Julianna hastened to continue. "I was furious with Ross, for his treachery, his treatment of Myra, of myself. I knew he planned to come after ye again. I could think of nothing but putting an end to it, and so I left. But I was not gone long when Ronan came upon me. It wasn't until we reached Kinterloch that I comprehended the depth of Ross's machinations."

Robert uncrossed his arms and came around the table to stand beside Julianna, his countenance had turned from irritation at her to the flat expression he used when discussing Ross and any of the other men who went against him.

"Tell me."

"I fear he's turned his cousin, the overlord of Kinterloch, against ye. At the very least, his cousin is doing Ross' bidding whether he sides with him or not. Ronan and I were attacked upon entry. I believe either we were recognized or they somehow knew we'd taken out their scouts."

"Ye and Ronan work well together," Robert said with a frown.

"Aye, 'tis a good thing." She straightened her shoulders and hoped he didn't notice a change in her temperature. The mention of Ronan always made her body heat, and talk of them working well together went way beyond a simple skirmish in her mind.

If Robert took any more meaning to her words, or saw more in her than she hoped to reveal, he didn't let on. He turned from her and paced, checking his map once or twice. Julianna knew not to speak when he started his walking. He was most likely devising some sort of plan that he would ask for her advice on momentarily.

While she waited, she glanced toward the shuttered window. Wished she could open it up and breathe in the fresh wintry air. She hated to be cooped up in the castle. Hated the drafts and the stifling air of being inside.

Robert finally turned to her, fisted his hands on his hips and declared, "Ronan and Wallace will lead the men to the village."

She opened her mouth to protest, but Robert stayed her with his hand. "Lass, if ye go with him, then everyone will know of your role here."

Rolling her eyes, she folded her hands before her, trying to look demure. "Do ye not think they already do? When I left, ye sent one of your best men after me. Let me go with Ronan. I know the way well. I was there. I can help to lead the men. And should Ronan…fall, I can be there to continue on." The man had better not fall! She'd bring him back to life just to kill him herself if he were to succumb to some battle wound.

Robert pursed his lips in thought. "I suppose ye are right, but—"

"'Tis better they know my true role and grow to respect that than to believe what they already do."

"And what is that?" Robert asked with a raised brow.

"Half the castle thinks I am your mistress."

"Absurd!"

"But true."

"I supposed I can see where they'd get the idea. All right, ye will travel with Ronan."

Julianna nodded. "And what of protecting Eilean Donan?"

"Daniel and Brandon can see to it."

"I will speak with Ronan. We will leave on the morrow."

"Nay, lass. Let me speak with Ronan. When I've had a chance, ye can meet the men to discuss your strategies."

Julianna nodded, not wanting to argue. She hastened from Robert's chambers before he could change his mind. When she arrived at her own bedchamber, a hot bath waited for her. A relieved sigh escaped her, and she tore off her clothes, anxious to sink within the steamy depths. Ronan had made good on his promise.

She stepped to the wooden tub, lined with a thin linen, and climbed inside. Gingerly, she sat down, waiting for the sting of water to hit her covered wound, but thankfully, it had begun to heal itself and the pain was only a dull ache.

The water was warm. Heaven. Sinking beneath the surface, she wet her hair and lathered it lazily with the lemon-scented soap left for her. It'd been so long since her last bath. Mostly she'd had to scrub using water from the cold basin. Not that baths were not available, she could have probably had one every Sunday if she wished, but working the kitchens and guarding Robert took a lot of time, and in order to keep a low profile, she'd never ask for such an indulgence. As it was, those at the keep already looked upon her oddly for the counsel she kept with their leader and the chamber he afforded her.

Now they would all know the truth. Some would accept it as news they'd already suspected. Others would be angry that she'd lied, and resent her. Some may even be downright resistant. But she hoped, prayed, that whatever reaction they had, they had it quickly and all went back to normal. She didn't want to be known as the Bruce's sister, she wanted to be recognized for who she was. Family or not, she was a person.

With the revelation of her identity, questions would lurk, scorn would be slung her way. After all, Julianna was a bastard. Her mother had been her father's lover. Apparently, he'd met her mother in the Holy Land while fighting the crusades. She was a servant to one of the lords. They'd fallen in love, and her mother had brought her into the word before taking her leave of it. Her father brought her home with him, when he had to take the news of his comrade's death to the man's widow. Her mother and father fell in love, and married within the year. But Julianna was not forgotten. Instead, her father took her under his wing and trained her to be his little warrior.

A tear slipped from Julianna's eye as she remembered her father fondly. For all his brutishness, and his insistence on her being a hardened warrior from a young age, he truly was a great man. Until Robert chose for Scotland to be a separate entity from the English. Their father, for reasons Julianna could only decipher as greed, sided with the English.

But at least he'd given Robert one thing before betraying him—Julianna. She'd forever cleave to her brother's side and that of Scotland. Her father's treachery was truly heartbreaking, and not something she chose to think on often. In essence, she'd been orphaned by both her parents. And now the tears would begin. Ducking her head under the water she held her breath until she was sure she'd no longer cry. When she surfaced and incessant knocking pounded at her door.

"What the devil?" she muttered, grabbing for the linen towel beside the tub. She'd not even had a chance to full enjoy her bath, and already someone was seeking her out.

She supposed she should be grateful they were, as Robert very well could have decided to pull her from the ranks completely.

"Who is it?" she called.

"'Tis Ronan."

"Oh," she gasped, standing up and clutching the linen to herself. "What do ye want?"

There was silence on the other side of the door for a few moments and she feared he'd left.

"Will ye nay open the door?"

"Nay."

"Nay?" he sounded confused, and Julianna suppressed her laughter.

"I am not…decent."

Again a long pause. "I dinna mind."

She did laugh then, albeit quietly. Again she wished she had a robe. Julianna wrapped the towel tightly around herself, her wet hair dripping onto her shoulders. 'Twas not decent at all for her to answer this way. The linen was damp and see-through.

Her plaid. She pulled a clean one from her wardrobe and wrapped herself in that, making sure she was covered from head to toe, then opened the door.

Ronan stood just outside the door, his shoulders nearly as wide as the doorframe, and a teasing smile on his face.

"I see ye took precaution to bundle up. May I come in?"

She shook her head. "What do ye need, Ronan?"

"I wanted to see how ye fared? And I brought ye this." He held up a small linen sachet with a medicinal herbal scent coming from it. "For your wound."

She winged a brow. "I am fine. But thank ye." She took the sachet and sat it on a side table, eager to put it on her wound. And eager to get warm.

"All went well with…the Bruce?"

"Aye. Have ye not spoken with him? He seeks ye."

"Not yet. I was speaking with Wallace and my cousins."

Julianna nodded.

"Will ye not tell me what he wants?"

She shook her head, droplets of water sprinkling onto her cheeks. "Nay. He wished to speak with ye first."

Panic flashed on Ronan's face and Julianna rolled her eyes. "Dinna fear for your freedom. He only wants to talk with ye regarding Ross."

To her surprise a slight blush colored Ronan's cheeks. "All right. Is there anything ye need?"

"A robe," she said a little sarcastically.

Ronan chuckled, reached out and stroked the plaid where the fabric met her neck. The tip of his finger brushed her skin. A shiver spiraled up her spine and she bit her lip.

"I think this suits ye more than a robe," he said with a wicked grin.

"All the easier to get me out of?" she teased right back.

Ronan's eyes widened marginally, lighting with desire. "Aye. There is that."

He stepped toward her and she took a step back. "What are ye doing?" she asked, her voice uncharacteristically small.

"I want to kiss ye, Julianna. And I dinna want the world to see." He closed the door to her chamber with his foot.

She'd not even noticed how far he'd backed her into the room until that door closed. Leaving them utterly alone.

"Does anyone know that ye came to my chamber?" she asked.

Ronan shook his head leaning nearer; his hand snaked around her waist and tugged her close.

The last time they'd seen each other, she'd been cross with him. Tried to push him away, but it didn't appear that her viperish attitude worked on him. Only seemed to pull him closer. Literally.

He'd had a bath too. His scent was intoxicating and she closed her eyes, breathing in his fresh, clean aroma, underplayed with masculine tones. Ronan's scent. She licked her lips, tilted up her face. He pulled her flush against him so their pelvises touched. A shudder passed through her, and her legs became a little unsteady. She wanted to reach out and hold onto him to secure herself, but if she did, she'd drop her plaid.

Why hadn't she at least put on a chemise? Had the more wanton side of her hoped for this very occurrence?

Probably. Because she tingled everywhere—from the tips of her toes to the hair on her head. She parted her lips, about to ask if he would kiss her when Ronan descended the rest of the way, claiming her mouth in a soft, yet fully sensual kiss. His warm lips pressed to hers, her lower lip between both of his. Ronan stroked his tongue into her mouth at the same time she flicked hers out to meet his. He tasted good too. Like sugar and spice.

Julianna recalled he liked sweets. Had probably indulged in some confection before coming to find her. But thoughts of anything sweeter than being in his arms were soon gone when he fully pulled her into his embrace. She could feel his hard length jutting through his plaid, and pressing hotly against her quickly dampening center.

How easy it would be to simply let go of the plaid, let it drop on the floor and lead him to her bed where they'd make love for…hours.

In another world. In this one, Robert would send someone to find Ronan if he didn't show up at his chambers soon. Not that he'd look here, but it was too risky.

Keeping hold of her plaid, she managed to push against his chest. "We must stop," she said breathlessly.

Ronan's eyes were heavily lidded, his lips full and wet from their kiss. She wanted nothing more than to lick them, nibble them, and feel them on every forbidden part of her body. But they couldn't. Not now.

"Aye, I know." He took a step back, raked his hand through his hair. He turned a mischievous grin on her. "I simply canna help myself when I'm around ye. Especially when ye keep presenting me with your near nakedness."

Her cheeks burned and she clutched the plaid to her tighter. "Ye make it seem like I keep seeking ye out, but ye are here in my chamber, and when we were at the croft…well…" They'd both wanted it.

Ronan's grin was lopsided and he nodded. "Well, indeed."

Julianna turned her back on him and walked across the room toward her hearth. Her toes had started to turn numb against the cold plank floor, no matter that the rest of her was a flaming mass of desire. She held up each foot individually until her toes were warmed. Ronan didn't leave, but he didn't say anything either. He simply came to stand beside her, warmed his hands. Theirs was a comfortable silence, the kind borne to those who were naturally at ease with one another. The thought both annoyed her and startled her. She didn't want to be comfortable with him—it lent too much to the thoughts she tried to avoid of the possibility of a future together.

After her chat with Robert this afternoon, she was even more determined to prove herself as his guard and Ronan was only going to get in the way of that.

But still, she was stunned to feel so contented around him. Julianna never felt so relaxed and on edge at the same time with anyone. The man had to have bewitched her. He was, after all, a Sutherland. Rogues at heart, handsome to a fault, charming the skirts up on every woman who walked their way. Though she'd not met his brothers, their reputations preceded them.

Julianna was aware that it wasn't entirely fair to judge Ronan and his brothers on courtly conjecture. But to be fair, rumors did abound. Ronan's eldest brother, Magnus, had stolen his bride from a battlefield—and out of the arms of her betrothed. Although, Julianna had heard the bastard was English so Magnus was doing the lass a favor. But his other older brother, Blane, had stolen his bride from the church. What kind of man corrupted a nun? What would Ronan do? Steal the king's sister for his wife? She gasped, it would be perfectly within the pattern.

"What are ye thinking about?" Ronan asked suddenly.

"Nothing," Julianna said a little too quickly. She cast a glance at him to see that he looked skeptical, but didn't mouth it. "I was…merely wondering what ye were still doing here?"

She tried for haughty, but in all actuality, she was curious.

"I was hoping ye'd admit to me—" Ronan broke off when Julianna whirled to face him.

"What?" she asked, eyes widening.

"I was hoping ye'd tell me what the Bruce wants." The way he flicked his gaze toward the fire and then back to her made Julianna question his true motive.

What did he really wish for her to reveal? Her feelings? Her desire for another kiss?

"I canna. Now ye must go. If someone were to find ye here...even just a servant, rumors will quickly escalate and Robert will have us both whipped or worse."

"Worse? Do ye truly think he'd be so cruel?"

Julianna laughed with a bit of bitterness laced in. "I never presume to guess what Robert will do. But I know he's a stubborn arse, and vicious when crossed."

"I'll keep that in mind." Ronan grabbed her by the elbows and pulled her close. "But if I'm going to be punished, I think it should be for more than a mere kiss."

And he claimed Julianna's mouth with a carnal ferocity that made her knees buckle.

Chapter Twenty

Ronan kissed Julianna with a passion he'd not known he possessed, and she kissed him back just as fervently. Almost like they both worried this might be their last kiss. But it couldn't be. He wouldn't let it.

Her mouth was too sweet. Too perfectly fit his own.

This was his woman. Damn, he couldn't be thinking like that unless…

"Tell me to stop," he said, his voice gruff.

"Stop," she said breathlessly, but pressed her mouth harder against his.

Mixed signals. How, he wanted to continue kissing her. To toss her onto the bed and ravish her, but that wasn't the right thing to do, and though he was normally a rogue with the ladies, for Julianna he wanted to be different. Already, he'd taken what she offered.

"Tell me ye dinna want me," he said, sliding his lips to her chin and then her earlobe. "Tell me this is wrong."

"'Tis wrong. So wrong," she murmured. "But I canna lie. I do want ye, Ronan."

He growled under his breath, lifted her into the air and carried her to the bed where he laid her out gently on the soft wool coverlet.

Their gazes connected. "There is still time for ye to say no."

Julianna smiled at him wickedly, her eyes dancing with invitation. "But I willna." She opened her plaid, baring her soft, sculpted form to his gaze.

Ronan was already hard, but now his cock pulsed with the urgent need to be inside her. Now. Right now. But first things first. He climbed onto the bed and knelt between her parted thighs. While sliding his hands up her thighs, massaging her hips, he dipped low to tease her puckered nipples.

"Ye are perfection. A sweet escape," he murmured between suckling one nipple and the other.

Julianna writhed on the bed, ran her hands through his hair. "Oh, Ronan, ye make me…"

"Say it, lass."

"Ye make me hot all over."

"'Tis the same for me." While he continued to nuzzle her breasts, he slid his fingers between her thighs, groaning when her slick heat met his fingertips. "Och, lass, ye're so wet."

Julianna answered by bucking her hips upward. She pulled his shirt from inside his plaid and splayed her hands across the expanse of his back. Lord, how he loved when she touched him, explored him.

"Ye said, next time…" She didn't have to finish her sentence, he knew what she was asking, and the thought of her lips wrapped around his cock was almost more than he could handle.

Ronan chuckled. "Next time."

"There will be no excuses then," she said, though her threat was undermined by the sweet breathiness of her voice.

"None. I am yours."

Her fingers skimmed inside his plaid and she gripped his arse. Ronan moaned and reared back. He unhooked his belt and tossed his plaid to the floor. His cock stood out, ready to be sheathed. Julianna leaned up until she was sitting, her legs spread around his thighs. She smiled up at him as she reached out and gripped his cock, her long, slim fingers wrapping around him.

"Your cock amazes me."

Bloody hell, she amazed him!

Ronan was heavy, thick and smooth as velvet in her hand. Her heart skipped a beat, then pounded against her ribs.

"Bar the door," she said, their eyes locked in a heated stare.

Ronan nodded and stepped to do her bidding. The bed creaked as he left it and while Julianna mourned the loss of his heat in her hand, she rejoiced at the sight of his bare arse. An amazing display of hard muscle. Trim hips, a wide corded back and shoulders that spanned the breadth of a doorframe. He was massive, solid and for the next few moments, all hers.

She wasn't naïve enough to realize that inviting him to her bed was not in their best interests. Nor was she fool enough to say for sure they wouldn't get caught. The thing of it was, she didn't care. She never did anything for herself, and Ronan seemed to be the one indulgence she had no willpower to deny.

Julianna craved him. Even when she wasn't thinking about him—she was.

Ronan made quick work of barring the door, then turned back. Her gaze roved from his handsome, sculpted face to his contoured torso and then...the weapon that jutted from between his hips. She licked her lips instinctively, shivered. Her nipples were hard, aching tips, and her sex, wanton and quivering for his entry.

Julianna held out her arms as he neared the bed, but instead of sliding on top of her, Ronan lay down and pulled her astride him.

"I'm guessing the squire didna show ye how to make love like this."

She shook her head, bit her lip as the thick length of his sex pushed against her sensitive folds. Ronan gripped her hips, massaged them, then slid upward until he cupped her breasts, stroking his thumbs over her nipples.

"Ye can be in charge like this," he said, a wicked grin curving his scrumptious lips.

"I like to be in charge," she said, with an answering smile.

"I know it." He took her hand and placed it on his shaft, wrapping her fingers around him. "Guide me inside."

Julianna settled on her knees, her feet tucked beneath his thighs and lifted a little, sliding the tip of his length between her folds, toward her center.

"That's it, lass."

Julianna did as he instructed, the head of his shaft slipping inside. She let go and pushed her pelvis down until he filled her completely, stretching her with decadent pleasure.

"Oh, my," she whispered.

Their gazes locked, an ocean of emotion passing between them. Julianna wanted to ignore it. Wanted to dismiss it as nonsense, simple pleasure making them feel that way, but she knew to do so was false. There was more between them then either of them was willing to admit.

With his hands holding tight to her hips, Ronan showed her how to roll them. "Not unlike riding a horse, sweets," he said. He moved slowly beneath her, pushing up and withdrawing as she rode him. Ronan leaned up on an elbow, capturing one of her nipples in his mouth and suckling gently. The pull of his mouth went straight to her core, her muscles clenched with sweet ecstasy. She gripped his chest, fingers digging into the muscle. He'd said she could be in control, but she felt more out of control than ever before.

Thighs trembling, Julianna clenched tight around Ronan's hips. Her toes curled under his legs.

"Oh, Ronan," she moaned, her body sparking with flames.

Ronan slid his hand over her cheek and into her hair, pulling her lips to his. Their mouths melded in a frenzy of tongue, as though they fought for who could give the other more pleasure.

Julianna gripped the back of his neck, not wanting to let go. She ground her hips into his, feeling blissful tremors ricochet from her center outward, and kissed him like there was no tomorrow.

And there might not be. Not if someone were to catch them. But the added rush of being caught only seemed to fuel her desire. She shuddered and increased her pace, rolling her hips. Her moans echoed around the room and Ronan shushed her, whispering that they'd be heard, but his own growls rivaled her noise. He gripped her buttocks and guided her in moving up and down.

"Och, lass, you're so tight…" He thrust upward rapidly. The muscles of his abdomen tightening, and she couldn't help but stroke over them, touching each ridge with leisure.

They moved in tandem, like they'd made love a thousand times—or as though they were meant for each other. The latter scared Julianna straight to her soul. Her heart skipped a beat and whether that was from fear or from the way her body responded to his she didn't know. Wasn't willing to examine. She shut her mind to all thoughts, absorbed only in the pleasure radiating from their loins. Sweet heaven.

Glorious pressure built inside her. The delicious releases that Ronan had given her before…it was going to happen again. And she wanted it so badly. Rode him harder, wanting that completion.

"That's it, lass, let it come." Ronan didn't cease his thrusts. Stroked the flat of his hand down her belly until his thumb brushed over her curls. Just that subtle touch sent a shockwave through her and she gasped. But it was nothing compared to the flame that struck when he stroked his thumb over her nub. Then it was like the world shattered, the bed rocked and the castle could have fallen down around her for all she knew. She opened her mouth to shout out his name, her body spasming, but Ronan captured her lips with his, seizing her cry. Hungrily, she kissed him back as she rode out the vibrations of crushing bliss.

At the same time, Ronan's fingers dug into her hips and he kissed her all the harder. Between her thighs, she felt him shudder violently, and liquid heat poured inside her. They rocked until their tremors subsided, kissing lazily.

A loud knock shattered the blissful cocoon Julianna found herself in. She spiraled back to reality in a sickening whoosh that left her belly somewhere around her feet. Leaping off of Ronan's lap, she grabbed her plaid that had been tossed to the floor and wrapped it around herself.

"Ye have to go!" she whispered harshly.

"Where? There is someone at your door," he whispered back. He too jumped from the bed and started to don his plaid and shirt.

"Who is it?" Julianna called.

"'Tis Myra."

Julianna shoved her fist in her mouth and bit down on her knuckles. She glanced with fear at Ronan. What had she been thinking? A fantasy, that was all this was and all it could ever be, and she'd tried to bring that fantastical ideal to life. For shame, she was a fool.

"I'm in my bath. I'll come find ye in the great hall when I finish." Julianna glanced at Ronan who raised a brow, and then made mock movements as though he was washing his hair.

She bit her lip to keep from laughing, quickly tiptoed forward and hit him on the shoulder. "Stop that," she hissed.

"I can wait," Myra said through the door.

Julianna exaggerated an eye roll at the door. "Ye know, it's been awhile since I had a bath. I wasn't going to hurry." Julianna knew her words made her sound less than pleasant, and she'd have to make it up to her friend later. For now, she needed Myra to go away so she could get Ronan out of here.

Myra didn't answer, and from the tension seeping through the oak door, Julianna was a little worried her friend might try to break it down. Myra was no weakling. She'd had her own fair share of battles.

"I'll come back. The great hall is full of warriors."

"All right. I will try to hurry." Julianna tiptoed to the door and listened for Myra's footsteps as they faded down the corridor.

Ronan came up behind her, fully dressed and pinned her to the door, his muscular build molding to her back. He kissed her neck and whispered in her ear, "I must speak to the Bruce."

Julianna nodded, turned, wrapped her arms around his neck and kissed him. But after he left, she worried that he meant to tell her brother about them.

And part of her hoped he did. The other part feared it so much she hurried to dress. But by the time she'd tied her boots, common sense kicked in. Ronan wouldn't have the ballocks to tell her brother that the two of them had been rutting like rabbits in spring.

At least she prayed he didn't.

As Ronan descended the stairwell, intent on going to the Bruce's chambers, loud shouts echoed from the great hall. He changed his destination, quickly, prepared to break up a fight between the men. When he entered the great hall, the sounds and sights of men carousing shocked him. Indeed, the room was full of warriors. While they held mugs, it wasn't the drunken revelry Ronan was sure he'd stumbled upon. Instead, the men showed their weapons, their muscles, told battle stories and shouted out their previous victories.

He nodded to several as he passed through the crowd in search of Wallace and his cousins. He found his cousins at the dais.

"What is going on? Where is the Bruce?"

Brandon nodded to the center of the room where Robert the Bruce along with Wallace, engaged in an animated conversation with his men. Ronan couldn't quite make out what their future king was saying, but they all laughed as he threw his arms wide and shouted something.

Ronan turned back to his cousins with a raised brow. "What did I miss?"

The way Julianna had spoken, the Bruce was eagerly awaiting him for a serious conversation, not rehashing old tales with his men.

Daniel shrugged. "The Bruce told them to be prepared for battle soon."

Brandon shook his head as he watched the crowd of warriors. "Next thing we knew, they were popping corks and measuring the thickness of their...swords."

Ronan chuckled. "And how do they plan to fight the battle, with their wicked breath?"

His cousins laughed at that, and Brandon handed him a mug that smelled an awful lot like Cook's spiced whisky. "Shall ye join them?"

Ronan wanted to, but he shook his head. Wallace had assured him they would leave on the morrow for Kinterloch and Ronan needed to be in full capacity of his wits.

"Aye, we didna either," Daniel said, frowning. "'Tis almost like the Bruce toys with the crown."

"Dinna speak against the Bruce," Brandon warned, "else someone overhears."

Ronan nodded. "He's right. Dinna say anything more."

Daniel's frown deepened and he crossed his arms over his chest. "We've all put a lot on the line for Scotland," he murmured.

And Daniel more than Ronan or Brandon. His cousin's lady wife resided with him at the castle until spring made it safe for them to travel back to his home at Blair. Ronan was sure that his cousin was all the more stressed by the presence of his wife here. As would Ronan be if he were to have a wife here... Which he didn't. But Julianna... he cared for her too. If something were to happen...

He turned his gaze on the Bruce and Wallace. Noted that Wallace looked quite reserved and was perhaps feeling a bit of the irritation he and his cousins were. War was not a game. Lives were not so unimportant that they could be lost and chalked up to the price of battle.

As if on cue, Julianna entered the great hall. Back straight, chin thrust forward, hands folded at her waist. She glared at everyone. Full of authority. If he didn't know her better, he would have feared her power.

But seeing her thus only fueled Ronan's desire for her. He recalled the way Julianna's head fell back as they made love, her hair cascading in glorious golden waves, hints of red catching the light from the fire. She looked like Venus rising and falling above him. Her plump breasts swaying, flushed, and tipped with puckered cherries.

His cock hardened instantly and he had to pinch the inside of his elbow as he crossed his arms over his chest to force his mind off of lovemaking.

The men didn't pay so much attention to her beyond a glance.

"Bow, ye fools," Ronan bellowed. "Do ye not know a lady when ye see one?"

The room silenced suddenly. Startled glances were cast his way, including Julianna's. Robert cleared his throat.

"Indeed, may I present Lady Julianna, my sister."

Chapter Twenty-One

There were a few shocked faces at Julianna's identity being revealed, but to her happiness, most nodded, bowed and offered her fealty. She supposed they'd already figured out her level of importance. It was only formality to give her a title.

When she discovered the noise in the great hall, she'd been livid. How could the men go into battle if they weren't prepared? Drinking, sharing war stories, mock fights, this was not how an army of warriors prepared to attack a village full of black hearts and traitors.

Wasting no time, she approached Robert.

"My lord, if I may have a word?"

Robert, looking distracted, nodded and Julianna led the way to one of the darker alcoves. Once they were alone, she fixed him with a penetrating gaze.

"Brother, if I may speak freely?"

"Ye do anyways." Robert frowned, most likely realizing I was about to chastise him.

"Verra well, I do believe 'tis an ill decision to join your men in revelry. They should all be preparing and making plans."

He nodded, his lips pursed almost like a spoiled child, but what more could she expect from her younger brother. Sometimes she wondered if he took the War for Independence seriously or not. And afterwards she always berated herself for harsh thoughts about her flesh and blood.

"As always, your advice is sound," Robert said.

I inclined my head to him. "As is your rule."

The revelry was quickly wrapped up and the men worked out their battle plans. Julianna stood on the side lines. Though her relation to Robert was announced, she didn't want any hard feelings between the men by inserting herself. She fully understood that not everyone was so adaptable all at once. And so she stood and listened, caught Ronan's eye and shook her head or nodded when something was said. At last, the plans were complete and everyone sent to bed to rest, for come the dawn, they'd all be awakened and readied to leave for Kinterloch.

Leaving the great hall, Julianna felt the way she normally did when danger seemed imminent — shoulders heavy, and drawn back into a pinch, pain searing from temple to temple, a permanent frown. She trudged up the stairs, pretty sure she wasn't going to get any sleep. The anticipation was too much. Ross had been a pain in their arse for a while, and at last they were going to put a stop to it.

The minutes, hours, days she'd spent at the Ross camp crowded in her mind like a vicious disease, threatening to weaken her.

A soft touch settled on the small of her back. Ronan.

Julianna stopped before the first stair leading to the upper floors and turned around.

"I wanted to wish ye goodnight," he said. In the darkened shadows of the corridor, she could make out a small smile curving his lips. "May I escort ye to your chamber?"

"You may *escort* me," she said taking his offered arm, the heat of his body seeping into hers. "I fear anything further will deplete us of the much needed energy for the morrow."

Ronan stroked her arm with his other hand, gave her a sly wink and drawled out, "Och, lass, I was under the impression that *anything further* would only energize us."

"Ye're a rogue," she said with a teasing slap to his hand.

Ronan stopped them mid-way up the stairs, pulled both of her hands into his and then glanced about to make sure they were alone. His expression turned grave and Julianna's stomach did a little flip.

"What is it?" she asked. She searched his face, trying to see deep within his startling green eyes. His ginger-colored hair fell wildly over his forehead as though he'd raked his hands through it many times.

Ronan's gaze was locked on hers and, without thinking, she reached up to move his hair, but he caught her hand in mid-air, pulled it to his lips. He closed his eyes, as if savoring her scent and her stomach clenched, her fingers trembled.

"'Tis just that… On the morrow, we will invade Kinterloch. Ye and I at the helm." Again he stopped to glance about, but Julianna had not heard anything that would make him think someone stood by listening.

He was stalling for some reason, and she wondered if it was maybe that whatever it was he wanted to say, he was having trouble forming the words.

"Tell me, Ronan," she urged, her fingers tightening around his.

"I realized something this eve when we were in the great hall. My cousin, Daniel... He was—" He cut himself off, blew out a breath. "I am worried for your safety."

Julianna smiled. "Dinna be scared, Ronan. We've done this together before—well, albeit on a smaller scale."

"A much smaller scale." He shook his head. "This is completely different. Battle is a different beast altogether."

Julianna pulled her hands away, heat colliding with cool in her chest. "I am not naïve. Do ye think I believe we'll just gallop into town and rule the day? Battle is synonymous with death, pain, rage. I am not so green that I dinna realize that. I will do my best to guard your back, just as I've guarded my brother's."

Whirling around, she lifted her skirts and marching two steps before Ronan gripped her elbow, stopping her.

"Julianna, wait."

She didn't resist, but she didn't turn around either. Instead, she gazed down at the hem of her gown. Pretended she didn't notice the way the heat of his fingers seeped through her sleeve, branding her. Her heart pounded, reverberating in her ears, she could hear her blood rushing like a waterfall. Feel the very visceral response his nearness always brought.

"I..." Again he couldn't get the words out.

This time, she did turn around. He was two steps below her, bringing them eye to eye. She put her hands on either side of his face, his whiskers tickling her palms and fingers.

"Just tell me."

Ronan gripped her hands and pulled them to his lips. His breath on her fingers made her shiver, brought back memories of their intimate moments together. How she wished they could just run back to her room right now and relive them. But it wasn't possible. They both knew that. Probably why he was stalling. Also why she turned back around. She had to put some distance between them, and so tugged her hands away.

"My cousin's wife is here," he said.

"Aye, Myra." Why was he talking about Myra? "We're friends."

Ronan nodded, then shook his head. "Daniel is worried about her."

"Why, what's happened?"

"Nothing's happened," he growled.

Julianna took a step back.

Ronan raked both hands through his hair and muttered an oath under his breath. "He loves his wife."

Julianna was thoroughly confused. She put her hands on her hips, only to balance herself. "Is that wrong?"

"Nay, nay, 'tis not that either. He doesna want her to get hurt, and being here, at this castle, in the midst of the future king's warriors, 'tis not a safe place for her."

"She is safer within these walls than she was traipsing the Highlands on her own."

"Aye, I agree, but I think Daniel wishes spring were here already."

"All the better then, that Daniel will be staying behind. That ye and I are going together."

"But ye see, that's just it."

"What?" Julianna tossed her hands up in the air. "Ye are making no sense."

Ronan's jaw clenched, the muscles flexing and he searched her eyes, trying to decipher something, she wasn't sure, then his words came out in a rush. "I am worried about ye, Julianna. My mother…"

Julianna waited patiently for him to finish. He'd not spoken of his parents before.

"When I was but a lad, my mother and father went out on a ride with my older brother, Blane. They never returned. Cut down in the prime of their lives. The world is a dangerous place for women. I couldna bear it if ye were to be injured."

Julianna stroked his cheek, understanding that his fear for her was interlaced with his past. "Dinna worry over me, Ronan. I'm more fit to fight than half the men in your army. I will survive. I promise."

She kissed him swiftly, then turned to run up the stairs, and all the way to her room. By the time she arrived in her room and closed the door, her heart was close to bursting and her feet felt as though they were floating and weighed a hundred stone at the same time.

Had Ronan just admitted to having feelings for her? Was that what he meant with all that mumbled jumble about his cousin loving his wife and being worried over her? She pressed a hand over her heart, hoping to still its rapid beat. After barring the door, she flung herself onto the bed. If she thought before that sleep would not come freely this night, that was even more the case now.

Julianna rolled onto her back and stared wide-eyed at the rafters. After they won the battle, she'd be sure to seek her brother out and discuss the possibility of a union between her and Ronan. She couldn't put it off any longer.

What in bloody hell was he thinking? Ronan watched Julianna disappear around the curving stair, and then leaned back against the cold stone wall. Ballocks, he was an idiot.

He trudged up to his chamber, stripped down and flopped onto his bed. Mind whirling, he was positive he wouldn't be getting any sleep tonight. Their strategy, the risks, Julianna going into battle with him... It was all too much, and he bounced from one to the other, with little rest between.

He didn't want her to go into battle. Didn't understand the Bruce's rationalization for it. So what if she'd been to

Kinterloch. Ronan was plenty capable of leading everyone back there. Wallace would be with him. Julianna should remain behind with Myra. With the Bruce—who was her main charge. He understood her need to seek revenge on Ross. The man had tortured her. Threatened her brother, her country. He'd never begrudge her the need to retaliate against someone who'd put so much evil into her life. But what he didn't want was her to put herself in danger to get that vengeance. Not when he could capture Ross and bring the man back to Eilean Donan. He'd get her the whip and let her take a crack. Turn his back if she chose to poison him with one of her pins or other weapons.

But go into battle? He'd not be able to concentrate on anything save keeping her safe.

Needing a distraction, Ronan went in search of Tad to make sure he'd been fed and bedded down for the night. Lucky for him, Cook had adopted him as one of her own many children. Ronan felt comfortable that the lad was in good hands.

At least that was one person he cared about that he'd not have to worry over for the time being.

The morning did not bring sunshine with it. When Julianna opened her eyes, it was still dark, and if she didn't feel a little rested she would have thought it was the middle of the night. Tossing back her covers, she climbed from bed and opened the wooden shutters. Gloom met her.

The sky was dark grey, wind whipped, pelting stinging, cold rain into her face. She winced, took a step back. The trees in the forest beyond the bridge swayed, their branches bending at dangerous angles, and thunder clapped loudly above followed by a sharp white light searing the sky and smacking into one of the rocking oaks.

This was not good. In the Highlands, weather was unpredictable, and a storm like this could be over within the hour, or turn into a blizzard, covering them in a foot of snow by noon.

Risking another beating to the face, she stepped forward once more and glanced down into the bailey. Not a soul. No one was preparing. Had the Bruce already given the order not to move out today?

Julianna slammed the shutters closed, and hopped on the cold floor toward her wardrobe. She hurriedly dressed, splashed water on her face, whipped her hair into a tight knot, complete with her pins. *Sgian dubh* in her boot, daggers at her waist and more pins up her sleeve, she left the room in search of her brother. The corridor was quiet and dark, all the torches burned out. It felt eerie, and a shudder passed over her. Then panic. Had they left without her?

She quickened her pace, almost running up the circular stair until she came to her brother's chamber. She knocked swiftly three times, sucking in a quick, deep breath. The door was answered almost immediately by Wallace. Her breath came out in a rush of relief.

They'd not left her.

"What is the plan?" she asked, stepping past Wallace into the room.

"With the storm, 'twould be best if we waited," Wallace warned.

Robert lay in his bed and glanced over at Julianna. He was covered up to his chin in blankets and sweat beaded along his brow, making the hair around his temples damp. His skin was pale, nose red. She frowned and took brisk steps to his side.

"Why are ye still abed?" She glanced back at Wallace, wanting answers, but then Robert gave a gut-wrenching cough drawing her attention back. The effort to clear his lungs made his eyes red and bulge.

"Are ye ill, brother?" Julianna's stomach plummeted and she dropped to her knees beside him. He couldn't be sick! Not now!

"Just a small ague," he wheezed.

Julianna put the back of her hand to his forehead. He was not too hot. "Have ye seen the healer?"

"Aye, she's given me a tisane. I will be fine. Dinna worry overmuch." He reached a hand from his blankets and patted her hand. "But dinna rush out in this weather. Ye know our mountains. Snow could trap ye and freeze all of ye to death."

Julianna nodded. "We'll ride out the storm here, but as soon as the sun peeks through the clouds, we are for Kinterloch. What can I do? Do ye need more blankets?" Julianna glanced around the room frantically, wanting, needing something to make her brother better.

He'd never been ill, beyond the common stuffy nose. This sounded awful. And brought to mind images of their father when he was nearly at death's door.

Robert gripped her hand and pulled her down. He glanced wearily at Wallace and then locked eyes with her. "Do ye think 'tis a sign?"

"A sign?" Julianna whispered back, her brow furrowing.

"Aye. That we should leave Ross be?" He searched her eyes, a desperate look coming over him.

Julianna shook her head, squeezed his hand harder. "Nay. Nay, that is not it at all. 'Tis simply affording us more time to prepare. Perhaps even giving us the element of surprise. Ye are doing the right thing. Ross is your enemy. An enemy to Scotland. He will do everything in his power to see that ye do not gain power. He sees Longshanks as his King. He will never give ye fealty and even now he gathers more to his side, more to King Edward's ranks. He must be dealt with. Or forever see Scotland in English hands."

Robert let out another chest rattling cough that made Julianna cringe.

"I know ye are right. But even our own father believes in Longshanks' rule. How can I see this through when the man who gave me life is against me?"

Julianna swallowed past the lump in her throat. "Ye are strong, brother. Stronger than our sire. He is weak and doesna want to have to fight for what he knows is right; he'd rather give in when a chest of coin is presented. He doesna believe in the power of freedom like we do. Everyone here in the castle, this country, they all look to ye for council, as their future king. Ye will rule this country and bring Scotland to greatness. We need ye. Do not waver in your cause. Believe in Scotland."

Robert nodded, his eyes closing and a tear spilling from the corner of one. "I need ye, Julianna. Ye've heart. Conviction."

"I am here. I am with ye always."

"Go prepare. I must rest."

Julianna kissed her brother's hand and then turned to Wallace. "We ride as soon as the storm ends."

Wallace nodded. "I will go and ready the men, so we might be prepared to embark as soon as it's over."

Julianna called in a servant who lurked in the corridor awaiting orders. A young boy. "Get the healer. I want her to sit with the Bruce until he's well."

Then Julianna headed to the castle chapel to do something she'd not done in a long time. She prayed.

Chapter Twenty-Two

Two days later, the rain ebbed. All the rain touched had turned to ice, leaving the world looking glittery and cold. The morning began as though the rain had never visited. The sun shined and the ice started to melt, its water trickling slowly from the trees and buildings. The grass, which had crunched underfoot, became soggy and mud grew prevalent in well walked areas.

Julianna stepped out of the stables, leading Brave, her boots and hem covered in brown muck. If she were more of a lady, she'd be disgusted, offended, perhaps even embarrassed. She eyed Myra who stood on the stairs of the keep. That was where she'd be. Sometimes she wished she was more of a lady, but then... Julianna patted the dagger at her hip, checked for the sword strapped to the side of her horse. If she were more of a lady, she wouldn't be headed into battle with Ronan.

Glancing down at her muddied feet, she smiled. 'Twas just another honor for being a warrior. Being muddy meant she was alive.

She waved to Myra who waved back, then she caught sight of Ronan staring at her. His eyes were crinkled, his brow furrowed. He looked stern. Deep in thought. Julianna smiled, hoping to ease his worry. They'd not spoken since the argument on the stairs. 'Twas better that way for them both. They needed to get through the next few days, and then Julianna was resolute in her decision to speak with Ronan and Bruce.

Her brother was feeling much better. Whatever ailed him appeared to have ebbed. His coloring was back, coughing significantly less. Although it was discourteous, part of her wondered if his illness had anything to do with the confrontation about to take place.

Ronan approached her, his gait steady, smooth. A confident swagger in his step. The way he moved was fluid, sensual in a way that she'd noticed before, but now, having seen him walk without his plaid, all she could think about was the way the muscles of his backside tightened with each step.

Feeling her cheeks heat, Julianna looked toward the heavens hoping to get herself under control.

"Are ye ready?" Ronan asked, his voice low. He stroked a hand over Brave's neck. How she wished it was her own.

"Aye. And ye?"

"Aye." His gaze locked on hers, serious. "I want ye to stay close to me."

"I will. But please," she put her hand over his on the horse's mane, "I dinna want ye to worry for me. I have been trained my whole life."

Ronan took her hand in his beneath the mass of horse mane so no one could see for sure that their fingers were intertwined.

"Honestly, lass, I have every faith in ye. I've seen ye fight. I know ye're good. But there is still the fear that ye might not turn in time to see the axe sink into your back."

"Gruesome image," she said with a teasing smile.

"And to any other lady, I wouldna have planted it, but ye are not an ordinary lady. Ye, Julianna de Brus, are a warrior. Beware to all those who come before your blade. To say I wasn't impressed before now would be to lie. Ye enthrall me."

A shiver laced its way up her spine and Julianna had to clench all of her muscles to keep it from showing.

Before she could respond, Robert stepped from within the keep, looking stronger than he had when she visited him that morning. He was wrapped thick in plaid and furs, and he held up his hand. The courtyard, filled with warriors prepared to leave for battle, went silent as everyone turned to give him their full attention. Daniel and Brandon flanked him.

"Today ye go forth for Scotland. Ye will seize Kinterloch and all those who go against our cause."

The crowd cheered.

"But be sure to show mercy to women, children and those men who have found the truth in our country, in our people. Show mercy to men who wish to fight for us. Who have fallen under the spell of English riches and greed. Let them see a better side." Robert held his fist in the air and once more the men cheered.

Julianna too, raised her fist and shouted, feeling the rush of excitement filling her blood. Soon she'd have Ross at the end of her sword. A few of his bastard soldiers too. There was one in particular, her jailer, that she wanted to see take his last breath.

Ronan leaned close as the cheers died down and whispered, "Dinna let the desire to seek revenge rule ye this day. 'Twill only blind ye. Ross will bleed, but dinna let yourself become a victim because of how hot ye burn with rage."

Julianna swallowed, nodded, and glanced away, pretending those weren't her exact thoughts. She was a skilled warrior, trained. And yet, she had been letting emotion rule her. One of the first rules of battle — and she'd broken it. But wasn't it important to fight with conviction, heart?

"We will return. All of us," she answered. "With his head."

Ronan chuckled. "I like the way ye think. Your confidence is boosting."

"I have faith in ye too, Ronan."

He squeezed her hand and then let it go. "Stay close to me."

"I will." She glanced up at Robert on the stairs, deep in conversation with Daniel and Brandon. Myra hung in the background, watching the crowd, but Julianna guessed, she wasn't really seeing it. Her face was passive and when Julianna waved, she did not return it. Myra had much anxiety when it came to fighting. And Julianna couldn't blame her. She'd been so strong, been through so much, she deserved a bit of peace. Spring could not come soon enough for her, most likely.

When they returned from Kinterloch, there would be much to celebrate.

The Bruce beckoned them; Daniel and Brandon looking stern, flanked him. Myra had slipped down to the bottom stair and when Julianna approached, she gripped her arm and pulled her in for a hug.

"Be well, Julianna. I know ye're brave, and strong. I dinna doubt it, but just be sure to return to us."

Julianna embraced Myra, her heart suddenly full with a good friend and a man she…loved. "I will be sure to return with all those who go with me."

Ronan climbed the steps past her, and Julianna was not about to be left out of whatever Robert was going to say. She gave Myra one last squeeze and then finished climbing to the landing. Her brother looked grave.

"Sinclair will join ye."

"I thought ye were going to stay here and assist Daniel in holding the castle," Ronan said to his cousin Brandon.

"That was my plan, but the Bruce believes it will be better if I were to join ye."

Ronan nodded, and asked Daniel, "Will ye be all right?"

Daniel laughed and punched him in the shoulder. "Ye canna be serious. Of course I will be fine. I'm not only a warrior but a laird. I'll keep Eilean Donan safe until ye return."

"Dinna forget that I, too, am here," Robert said, coughing slightly at the end of his sentence.

"How could we ever forget? Ye are the future king and one of the reasons the castle must be kept safe. We canna risk ye being harmed," Julianna said, studying her brother's color. He'd looked pinker when she'd visited him early this morning. Stepping out of bed must have taken much from him. "Go now and rest. We will do our duty to Scotland and make ye proud this day."

"Ye make me proud every day, lass." Robert reached out to grip her hand. For a moment, she was reminded of their father. They had much the same coloring, the same smile, and her father, too, had once talked of his pride in her.

Julianna's smile faltered. No doubt, she was not the only one in need of praise. "As I am of ye," she answered.

Before tears could threaten, Julianna blinked. Her throat was already tight. She turned away, and came face to face with Ronan. His expression was unreadable, but when their eyes locked, some deep emotion passed between them. Again, she had to look away or face tears. She hoped no one else witnessed their exchange.

Facing the courtyard, she watched Wallace approach. She glanced back at her brother. "We must go, else we willna reach the outside of the village afore nightfall."

"Aye," Wallace proclaimed reaching the base of the stairs. The guards say there's nothing of note beyond the bridge. Best for us to leave now while no one approaches. Provisions, weapons and horses are ready. We'll return within a sennight."

Julianna hoped it would be less time than seven days. The village was only a day's ride away if they ran into no obstacles along the road. They would most likely make camp when they arrived, and take the village in the morning. Another night possibly, and they'd be home within a few days. *If* all went well.

The sun beamed down on them, and the sky was a pretty blue. Spring would be upon them within two months, but the weather made it seem like much sooner. She longed for the time when she'd be able to walk leisurely through a field of wild flowers. Something she'd snuck out often enough to indulge in. The only time she really felt at peace. Besides when she was in Ronan's arms.

She stole a glance at him to find he was watching her. Feeling a blush take her cheeks, she rushed down the stairs toward her horse. The sooner they were off, the sooner she could return. And the closer they were to being together.

The ride back toward Kinterloch was easy. Too easy, for Ronan's peace of mind. Their horses pounded over the road. The few scouts they spotted were easily subdued. The weather held out. Sky was blue, the temperature cold, but the light wind made it so the chill didn't seep into his bones. Julianna's cheeks grew pink and she looked so vibrant, alive. This was in her blood. The chase, the fight, it all exhilarated her and he once again found himself completely fascinated. Couldn't stop looking at her. Watching the way she rode only made the time fly by quicker. Wisps of her hair escaped the tight knot of her hair.

Things just weren't supposed to fall into place this easily. Not when they were embarking on a journey that would change so many things. The country's future hung in the balance. If Ross were to pull more of the Scots to the bastard English king's side, when spring arrived and Longshanks crossed onto Scottish lands, there would only be that many more people they had to fight against.

But if they were to set an example today, that traitors would be punished, it would hopefully discourage others from joining Ross and Longshanks' ranks. Ronan frowned. That shouldn't be what kept people on the side of their own country. They should believe in Scotland. In the future of their country. He certainly did. Wholeheartedly.

Ronan was willing to give up everything for his country. He stole another glance at Julianna. She was one thing he didn't want to have to give up. When he was with her, he felt whole. Alive. Battle used to be the only thing that gave him a rush of excitement, the feeling of immortality. Not anymore. She made him feel that too.

A cold slice of fear gripped his spine. Why did he keep having this feeling that something was about to go wrong. Doom and gloom. Completely negated the beautiful weather and surroundings.

Julianna seemed pleased with how their journey was transpiring as did Wallace, Brandon and the rest of the men. But not Ronan. His skin prickled, his scalp tingled. All signs that his instincts were in a frenzy. Something wasn't right.

For several moments, they continued on, but his stomach tightened, and his blood ran cold. They were too close to Kinterloch for him to not take heed of his gut instincts. Ronan held up his fist in the air for the men to stop. Wallace lifted a brow.

"What is it?" he asked, tone disgruntled.

"I dinna know."

The men hushed and Ronan focused on the sounds in the air. 'Haps his mind and body had noticed something off without him actually taking note of it.

Wind swished and branches brushed on one another. Horses snorted and pawed. Bodies shifted. And then he heard it. A distant rumble. But not that of thunder, 'twas something else entirely.

"Did ye hear that?" he asked Wallace.

His leader's face had tightened, lips pressed together, he nodded. Brandon and Julianna also nodded.

"What was it?" she asked.

"I dinna know. Not thunder," Ronan replied.

"'Tis the sound of buildings collapsing," Wallace answered, his voice flat.

"Buildings?" Brandon asked.

"Dammit!" Ronan shouted. "The village!" What could make the buildings collapse? A trebuchet, if they were slinging boulders, but Ronan couldn't think how any enemy would feel the need to build such weaponry against the small village. Their gate was pitiful at best, and the walls not well manned.

"Ride!" Wallace bellowed.

With swords drawn, they galloped at full force the rest of the last few miles.

The sky ahead was dark grey. At first Ronan believed it to be an impending storm, but the scent of smoke soon filled the air. A storm for sure, but the kind made by a vicious fire.

Good God, he hoped they arrived in time to at least save a few of the villagers—be they traitors or not. The Bruce made it clear he wanted them to show mercy.

"Hold!" Wallace shouted as they crested a hill and looked down on the village below.

Bright orange flames shot angrily from every building in site. Black smoke burst into the air as if escaping the flames and dispersed to form the grey clouds Ronan had seen earlier. There did not appear to be any survivors.

"We're too late," he murmured.

Julianna moved closer to him, her leg brushing his. Instinctively, he reached out to grab her hand. Her long slim fingers were tiny, yet sturdy in his. She held on tight. When he glanced at her, though her face showed no expression, her eyes brimmed with tears. His too stung a little. Just a few days ago, they'd seen this village teaming with people willing to defend it with their lives against two who they thought were their enemies. Today, they were defeated by a blaze that rivaled those he imagined in Hell.

But just how had this fire gotten started? There seemed to be only one answer. Ross. The man had to be responsible. Must have known that Ronan would return with more men to ferret him out, even if he had taken the village.

He'd been a fool to think otherwise.

"We couldna have stopped this," Julianna whispered, as though she'd read his thoughts.

"Nay, ye're right." His throat was tight. "But we can try to help any who may have yet survived." He hoped he gave her as much strength as she gave him.

"Aye."

Wallace cleared his throat, and Ronan and Julianna both yanked away as if finally aware they were not alone. The man had the decency to pretend not to notice, his attention drawn to the fire. "We must see if there is a trace of Ross."

"Should we surround the village?" Brandon asked.

"Aye. Ye take a third of the men to the north side and see if there are any tracks, or people in need. I will take my men straight through the gates—what's left of them. And Ronan, ye and Julianna take your men around to the west side. Looks like a burn cuts into the land there. People may be seeking shelter there, or trying to fill buckets to put out the flames." Wallace gave hand signals to the six dozen retainers behind them.

"Sir, if ye dinna mind me saying so, 'tis too dangerous for ye to go into the village. The flames are out of control. The buildings are collapsing. Ye'll be consumed." Ronan stared at the village inferno with doubt.

Wallace chuckled. "Did ye not hear? There are those in Scotland who believe I am immortal. I will test it today."

He kicked his horse in the flank and took off toward the gate, two dozen warriors behind him. Ronan nodded to Brandon who also took off toward the north with a swell of retainers.

"Let us be of use then," Julianna said, her voice incredibly sober. She too must think Wallace reckless.

They rode around to the west of the village where there was indeed a burn, trickling peacefully beside the raging village. And people. They were covered in soot and lay exhausted by the banks. A couple of men, several women and a small child. Julianna flew from her horse and rushed toward them.

"Are ye all right?" she asked.

The survivors looked up, startled, and jumped to their feet. The men brandished clubs and the women rushed to the sole child.

"We mean ye no harm," Ronan called, trying to keep his voice soft. "We saw the fire and have come to help."

"There is no help for it!" cried one of the women. "They're all dead."

"What happened here?" Julianna asked, giving them some of her flask. Whisky most likely.

The men lowered their clubs, and each took greedy gulps Definitely whisky.

"A visitor. He burned us out." The men didn't look surprised. Which Ronan found in itself surprising.

Had to have been Ross.

Julianna's face tightened and she took back the flask, taking a sip herself.

"Why?" Ronan asked.

"Because. He said ye'd come."

Chapter Twenty-Three

Julianna blanched. 'Twas a trap!

She backed away from the men slowly, one hand on the dagger at her hip, the other raised in a show of surrender.

"What are ye saying?" she asked in a low, non-threatening voice.

Glancing behind her, she watched as Ronan made eye contact with his men, sending some sort of signal. She wished they'd discussed the non-verbal cues. But he let her do the talking, so for now she needed to concentrate on that.

Julianna eyed the women, gave them soft smiles, hoping to ease their fear, in hopes of gaining a couple allies, but also to show them she meant no harm.

Of the three men, one looked contrite, the other two held their ground.

"I meant what I said." He pulled a sword from his back and brandished it toward her. "We've been expecting ye."

"Come now, ye canna think to harm me," she said quietly, holding her hands up in surrender. "I am but a woman. We saw this fire and hoped to help."

The man shook his head, his partner too, but the third looked as though he were waffling in his decision.

"Are we not on the same side?" Julianna asked. "Scotsmen and women?"

That made the leader of this small group bristle. "Dinna try to fool me, lass, I know what ye are."

Julianna smoothed the hair from her brow, hoping that such normal gestures in the face of danger would put the man off his guard. Her pins were in place. Four tightly slipped in her knot. More than enough to take out the two men if she needed. And that might be all she needed to get the third one completely on her side.

"Whoever it is ye think I am, I assure ye, I am not."

"The Ross wants ye alive, lass, dinna fight me."

"Why on earth would he want me?" She scratched her head, slipping a pin from its place up her sleeve, where she held it with her middle finger. "I've no quarrel with Ross." How easy that sour lie slipped off her tongue.

"He told us, ye'd try to trick us," the second man spoke up.

Julianna smiled and gave him a coy look with the tilt of her head. "Oh, come now. There are nearly thirty of us and only five of ye, six if ye count the child. This is silly."

"There are more of us in the woods. The whole lot of us." He moved to raise his hand in the air, a signal she knew would bring a slew of men pouring from the trees. On instinct she whipped the pin straight at the man's arm, catching him in the forearm and sinking deep.

He stared at her wide-eyed, as did the others.

Julianna rushed toward him, shouting to the others, "Dinna move or ye'll get a pin in ye too." She sank to her knees as the leader did, and yanked the pin free. Whispering in his ear, she said, "That burning feeling is poison. I've got a remedy in my satchel, and I will give it to ye, if ye would but let us pass."

He nodded, eyes wide, red and filled with pain. Julianna didn't want to kill the man, but it was imperative he not bring more men to fight than they could handle. And she had to find out where Ross was.

She stood and walked back to her horse, only to hear a shriek and a *thunk*.

Julianna whirled around to see the injured man on the ground, an arrow in his back. The other two men with him looked fearfully backward before diving to the ground. But they were too late. Arrows flew from the trees, also killing them.

"Get down!" Julianna shouted to the women and the child. They dropped, one covering the child from head to toe.

Och! Now, she'd not get the information she sought. She glanced furtively at Ronan who'd drawn his sword, held his targe to cover his face as did his men.

"Get on your horse!" he shouted at her.

Julianna wasted no time in listening and flung herself onto Brave's back.

"To the north!" Ronan gave the order in a bellow.

Julianna rode beside him, leaning low over her horse's mane. They met Brandon on the north side. No signs of the enemy, save for a petite woman he held in his arms. Her hair was as black as the soot on her cheeks, and she studied Julianna with most vibrant blue eyes she'd ever seen.

"Who is this?" Julianna asked Brandon.

But the woman spoke before he could answer, sitting taller in his lap. "I am Lady Mariana." Her voice was silky, French.

Julianna immediately disliked her. "What are ye doing here?"

"I was sent by His Majesty, King Edward."

"Put her down. 'Tis a trick! We just left several others. The fire was a trap to lure us in. There are archers and warriors hidden in the woods to the west—most likely all around us." Julianna pulled her sword from her saddle, prepared to fight should they be ambushed.

Brandon frowned and glanced at Ronan, a brow raised like he couldn't believe Julianna's reaction. She pressed her lips together, trying not to shout at the man. He held an enemy within his arms like they were lovers. She had to give him the benefit of the doubt that he was likely daft.

"Laird Sinclair, on behalf of my brother, your leader and future King of Scotland, I order ye to put the woman down. She is our enemy."

Mariana clutched tighter to Brandon, her cupid lips forming a bow full of fear. Julianna actually felt sorry for her. Either the woman was a great actress, or she was genuinely scared.

Ronan reached out a hand and laid it lightly on Julianna's arm. A frisson of heat shot its way up her limb and into her chest. Why did he have to have that effect on her? Even now when their lives were in danger? She couldn't shrug off the way her body leaned toward him, yearning for more of his touch and the way she suddenly felt safe.

"What is your purpose, Lady Mariana?" Ronan asked, the voice of calm and reason.

"I...I..." And the woman lost consciousness.

Julianna refrained from rolling her eyes. Well played, indeed. An easy out for someone who did not want to answer the question. Her fainting only assured Julianna further that Mariana was the enemy. The woman had herself said that she was sent by Longshanks. Didn't that automatically make her their enemy? Why was she the only one who saw that?

"We'll take her with us. She can give us the information we seek," Ronan said sternly. "Any sign of Wallace?"

Brandon shook his head, his grip tight on the lass. Julianna gritted her teeth. Even if they were able to get away safely, Mariana could be just as skilled as Julianna in taking a life. She'd have to keep a close eye on the woman.

A loud banging coming from the wooden wall at the back of the village interrupted her thoughts. Moments later, Wallace and his men charged through an opening they'd knocked down. Spotting the group to the north, they rode toward them. When Wallace and his men reached the group, he looked weary and covered in soot.

"Any survivors?" Brandon asked.

Wallace shook his head. "Looks to have been torched purposefully as we guessed."

"Aye," Ronan said. "We learned as much from a group by the burn. They were left to capture us. 'Twas a trap. Their group was shot dead, save for a couple of women and a child, by their own men."

"Any sign of Ross?" Wallace asked.

Julianna and Ronan both shook their heads and said, "Nay," at the same time. Ronan held out his hand for her to continue their report.

"The men said they'd been waiting for us. That Ross expected us to come. That he wanted me left alive. But before we could gain more information, arrows flew from the woods hitting the men in their backs." She didn't feel the need to let him know that she'd first injured a man in an attempt to gain more information.

Wallace shook his head. "Traitorous lot."

"Aye," Julianna said. "We've no way of knowing their numbers or if Ross is among them."

"The lady will tell us," Wallace said with certainty.

Brandon watched them all with hard eyes. Why did Julianna get the feeling he was protecting the woman.

"Aye, she will tell us," Julianna chimed in, daring Brandon to nay-say them.

He gave a curt nod.

"Let us get to cover," Ronan said, rubbing the back of his neck. "We are being watched."

Wallace led the way, from whence they'd come. When they were a safe distance away, they stopped and made camp. Lady Mariana had woken and sat huddled on a log Brandon had found for her, wrapped in his plaid—which Julianna found shocking. Would an enemy accept a man's personal belongings to stay warm? If she wanted to keep his guard down she would. Or maybe she was too cold not to accept it.

Julianna approached, but Ronan kept her back. "Let Brandon speak with her. She seems to have formed a bond with him."

"Do ye think the bond too snug?" She watched Brandon sit beside Mariana and offer her a drink and something to eat.

Ronan touched her elbow, then took her chin in his fingers and gently guided her to look at him.

"Julianna, I know ye fear for our safety, but I swear to ye, my cousin is trustworthy. He'd not let his fancy for a woman get in the way of his duty to country and your brother."

Nodding, Julianna felt a prickle of guilt. She'd have to apologize for the way she'd spoken to the man. If Ronan trusted him, then so would she.

"Come, let us have something to eat and drink. I made sure Cook gave us no apples." The teasing glint in his eyes was enough to make her knees go weak. Lord, he was a gorgeous man, and knew just how to improve her mood.

Scouts stood watch in a circle around the camp and a half-dozen more took rounds in the woods beyond. They might be a bit away from the village, but they were still in danger if Ross' new following decided to pursue them.

Julianna was about to sit on the ground when Ronan stopped her.

"Would ye like a log to sit upon?"

She'd not thought of it before, had spurned the idea when she saw Mariana on a log, but Ronan seemed eager to please her, so she nodded. He used his axe to cut a log for her from a downed tree, the patted his handiwork.

"Your chair, my lady."

Julianna laughed. "Thank ye, sir."

Ronan rummaged through his sack and pulled out several wrapped items, then sat down beside her. As he was on the ground, his face was level with her hip. Mouth watering, she watched him unwrap first one linen to reveal left-over smoked venison, and then another revealed a few pastries.

Ronan used his dirk to cut a hunk of meat and handed it to her. "For ye, my lady."

"My thanks." She bit into the fare, sighing at the hints of rosemary and other spices. Venison was her most favorite of meats. "Ronan—" She cut herself off, not sure if she could ask him what was on her mind.

"What is it?"

"Do ye think I compromised our getting information by pinning that man?"

He shook his head. "Not in the least. He was about to pull every Ross follower out of the woods. I wouldn't have offered him life as ye did."

"I believe he would have told me."

"He probably was, and if he didn't, his friend definitely wanted to."

Wallace approached with Brandon by his side and both Ronan and Julianna jumped to their feet. Once again, Wallace studied them together a little too long. Julianna would most definitely have to speak with her brother when they returned, else his most trusted male guardian would.

"She's spoken of Ross," Brandon started, glancing at Wallace who nodded. The four of them moved out of hearing distance from anyone else before he continued. "She reported that Ross has gone. He fled after setting the fire, with instructions for her to remain behind and report back to him, as well as an army in the eastern woods and the bait ye found by the burn."

"And no others?" Ronan asked skeptically.

Brandon looked grim. "There were others, she said. But they perished in the fires. She was trying to help, but eventually ran, and that's when we found her."

"Who is she?"

"I dinna know yet, but I do believe her," Brandon said.

"Did she say why she's gone against Longshanks? Obviously she was close with him, if he sent her with a message."

Brandon's lips thinned and he looked grim. "She did not go into more than to say she could no longer do his bidding in good conscience. I trust that she's turned a new leaf."

"But how can ye trust her? Ye barely know her."

"'Tis a fact, ye are correct, but there is something in her eyes."

Julianna raised a skeptical brow.

"Brandon is one of the best readers of people I've ever come across," said Ronan. He grasped his cousin's shoulder and looked into his eyes. "If ye say we can trust her, then I believe ye."

Brandon nodded, a silent familial nod passing between the two. Not in the mood to argue, and trusting in Ronan's decision, Julianna chose to believe too.

"What of the army? Did she give ye numbers?" Julianna asked.

Brandon nodded. "Aye, she said there are over two-hundred of them."

"Will they disband or join us?" Wallace asked.

Brandon rubbed his hands together and cracked his knuckles. "I dinna know, she didna say."

"Ask her," Wallace ordered.

Brandon left them to go do their leader's bidding.

"I need privacy," Julianna murmured and turned to walk away.

"Wait, ye canna go alone," Ronan said.

She turned around, raised a brow and patted the dagger at her hip. "I'll be fine. I'll scream if I need ye."

With obvious reluctance, Ronan nodded. Julianna marched off into the woods in search of some brambles to relieve herself behind. Her bladder was so full, she could have cried. She'd not noticed until moments ago; probably the rush of danger in her veins made her forget.

The day was not going as planned. There were still over two-hundred traitors itching to slice them into ribbons and one bastard who wanted her taken alive. She'd never go alive; they'd have to kill her to take her away.

Julianna found the perfect spot, checked to make sure she was alone and hiked her skirts.

Sweet relief.

"'Tis a prettier arse than I imagined."

Julianna dropped her skirts, ripped her dagger from its sheath, stood and whirled around to find her enemy standing twenty feet away.

"Ross," she hissed. "Have ye come seeking death?"

How the hell had she not heard him? The man was slyer then she'd given him credit for. And Mariana had said Ross was gone. She shouldn't have believed.

The man had the audacity to chuckle, and crossed his arms over his chest. Living on the run had not been kind to him. He'd been wrinkled and grey before. Now, the top of his head was bald and his face covered in wrinkled and sagging skin. Though his form appeared to be in good shape. She'd not test him until she knew how fit he was.

He took a step closer, and Julianna braced for a fight, fully expecting his men to jump out from all around her. Again, the man laughed and waved his hand as if dismissing her fear.

"I am alone."

"A mistake," she said through gritted teeth and pulled a pin from her hair.

"No, no, no, my lady. Dinna throw one of your poisoned pins at me. I've built up an immunity to mushrooms over the years."

Julianna's stomach knotted, and a cold, hard bubble formed around her heart. She may not be able to poison him, but she could injure him at least. Poising to strike, she stilled her hand when he spoke.

"Ye've killed a good deal of my men, lass. A woman should never do a man's duty." He walked closer and dammit if her feet didn't stay frozen in place. "Ye will be punished for it."

And then he lunged. Julianna side-stepped, but he didn't trip, in fact, seemed to have expected it and lurched to the side with her. He wrapped his arms around her waist and they both went tumbling to the ground. He was heavy and thick on top of her. An old man, but still muscular enough to weigh a ton.

She shoved at his chest, tried to get in a deep breath to scream, but she couldn't. He was crushing her. And then she realized, he was actually doing it on purpose. Pushing himself down on top of her so she could barely catch her breath.

"Ye canna scream now, can ye?" he asked, his breath foul and rotten.

But Julianna was determined, she sucked in as much of a breath as she could and let out a blood-curdling scream. The bastard was not going to get the better of her again.

Ross hit her. Hard. She saw stars when his fist collided with her temple, but still she fought back. Remembering the pin in her sleeve, she worked to pull it free, difficult in the position she lay in, gravity was not on her side. At last, she gripped the pin in her fingers, but Ross must have caught a glimpse of it and rolled away.

Julianna leapt to her feet and lunged for him, but the old man scuttled out of the way. She wouldn't, couldn't let him get away. Fury took hold, and she tried as much as she could to not let her emotions rule her, but they did. Yanking the long dagger from her hip she brandished it toward him. Ross only fended her off with his sword, much longer than her own.

She realized, too late, that using a dagger to fend off a sword was a bad idea. Hopping backward, she flung her pin, tripping over a branch or root at the same time. Her aim was off and the pin only sliced his cheek as it flew past him.

Ross growled, and charged toward her. Julianna scrambled backward, her back hitting a tree, and Ross' sword came within an inch of her throat.

"Say your prayers, my lady. Today ye die."

Chapter Twenty-Four

Red fury blinded Ronan as he burst upon a scene he hoped never to see beyond nightmares.

He let out a battle cry that shook the trees and ran toward Ross at full force. The bastard turned when he heard him shout, giving Julianna a split second to knock the sword away and dive to her left and away from danger.

Ross let out a sheer whistle, that meant God only knew how many were about to descend on them.

Wallace, Brandon and a dozen others surged into view just as a horde of Ross' own men did. The clanging of metal and shouts of pain echoed through the forest air. Two attacked Ronan from behind while Ross hacked at the air in front of him. He cut one down with his claymore but left it in the man's chest, opting for the lighter sword at his hip and an axe. The third man was quickly put down, leaving only Ross who fought like a vicious zealot. When the two had fallen, two more quickly took their place. All eager to protect their lord. The next two fought harder than the first, not wanting to fall victim to Ronan's superior skill, but they soon did, though they got in a few cuts of their own.

Ronan ignored his bleeding wounds and turned back to Ross to find him gone. He searched frantically, cutting down men left and right, but he was gone. Julianna! She too was out of sight.

"Julianna!" he roared, sweat dripping into his eyes.

He whirled in a circle, willing her to appear. More men pounced on him and again he fought with vigor and won. And still no Ross. No Julianna.

"Julianna!"

Ronan ran toward their camp, praying all the while, that she'd run there toward safety, but when he arrived, she wasn't there. Oh, God, no… His mind whirled, every horrid possibility coming to the forefront of his mind. He ran back to the battle scene, which was now just a pile of defeated men, Wallace, Brandon and most of their men still standing.

"Julianna! Have ye seen her?" His voice was hoarse from shouting, his gut tight and aching.

All the men shook their heads, worry furrowing their brows.

"He's taken her!" Ronan shouted, fear gripping his spine in its icy hands. He rushed in the opposite direction, the place he'd seen some of Ross' men come from, followed tracks, though he knew not whether they were coming or going. Panic made his hands shake, fury made him blind.

"Julianna! Ross!"

The sky overhead was turning grey, but not from the smoke. It would soon be nightfall and then his chances of finding her were nil.

A rustling came from behind and he whirled, sword drawn to find a haggard looking Julianna limping toward him.

"Och, lass." He rushed toward her, relief so keen he could have collapsed. Ronan grabbed her and pulled her into a tight hug, kissing her hair and face. "Are ye all right? Are ye hurt?"

She nodded, shook her head.

Ronan didn't want to let go, though he needed to assess her. "Which is it?" he asked.

"I'm all right. Not hurt too badly," she said, her voice tired.

A long slice went down her arm, the fabric of her sleeve open and exposing her wound.

"Ye're bleeding," he said, ripping fabric from his shirt to wrap around her wound.

"So are ye." Her fingers touched his chest and arms where he too had been cut. "We're a mess."

"Mine are just scratches." Ronan wrapped her arm tight enough to staunch the flow. "It doesna look so deep as to need stitching."

Julianna shook her head. "Nay. Was but a nick."

"Ross?"

She nodded. "He grabbed me and threw me over his shoulder. But the man is old and I was not going to let him take me. I stabbed him in the back and he dropped me. My arm caught on a tree branch, which is how I got this." She glanced down at the wound and smiled. "Ye're wrapping me up again."

Ronan let out a shaky breath, his fear finally starting to abate.

"Is he dead?"

Julianna bit her lip and shook her head. "I fear not. When I fell, he ran."

"With a knife in his back."

"Aye. The man is determined to live."

Ronan pulled her back into his arms, her soft body trembling as she pressed against him. Julianna wrapped her arms around his waist and pressed her face against his chest. He could feel her heart pounding against his.

"I thought I'd lost ye," he whispered, pressing his lips onto the top of her head.

"'Twould take a lot more to get rid of me, warrior."

Ronan chuckled. "Even still… I feared never to see ye again."

Julianna squeezed him tighter, pressed her lips to his heart. "I never want to let go."

"I never will." He gently lifted her chin and claimed her lips. Soft, loving, showing how much he cherished her, but when her tongue touched his, his good intentions left him and he kissed her with possessive passion. "Julianna, I love ye," he murmured against her mouth. "I have since the moment I laid eyes on ye."

Julianna slid her arms around his neck, stroked her fingers into his hair. "I love ye, too. And no matter what, we will never part again. I couldna bear it."

Ronan growled low in his throat, kissed her once more with fire. She was his. Always would be.

"I see ye found her." Wallace's voice cut through their desire filled hazes just as his claymore had cut through Ross' men.

But neither of them jerked apart, as they would have done hours before. Still holding onto one another, they turned to face Wallace head on.

"Ye will say nothing of this to the Bruce," Julianna said, authority in her tone. Strong as always, he felt a surge of pride rush through him.

"There is nothing for me to say," Wallace said with a smile, then turned challenging eyes on Ronan. "For I'm certain it is Ronan's intention to beg the Bruce's permission to marry ye."

Ronan glanced down at Julianna, their eyes locked and he smiled. "I've every intention to marry her."

"And I've every intention to marry him."

Wallace coughed uncomfortably. "Well, now that ye've settled it, what of Ross?"

Julianna frowned and this time, she did take her arms from around Ronan, but she kept a tight hold on his hand. "I'm sorry to say, he got away."

"Not without injury?" Wallace asked.

"My knife in his back," Julianna said proudly.

Wallace chuckled. "Rightly so. I'll send the scouts out to look for him. With that injury, he shouldna be able to travel far." He looked them both over with a critical eye. "Ye've both got some wounds that need tending."

"Nothing to fash over," Julianna said.

"All the same, your brother will have my head if ye catch an infection. Go with Brandon and Lady Mariana back to the keep."

Julianna was suddenly exhausted, close to collapsing. She nodded. Was it fear of her brother's reaction, or her own body's attempt to rest from all that had transpired? Probably a combination of everything.

Ronan gripped her elbow, holding her up more than she cared to admit. "I'll carry ye to your horse if ye desire it," he whispered so that no one else could hear.

"Sounds wonderful, but I fear they'd never look at me with respect again."

Ronan chuckled. "My woman deserves to be spoiled." He lifted her easily, sweeping his hand beneath her knees and cradling her against his chest. "Step aside, make room. The lass has lost much blood, we must get her back to Eilean Donan," he said in a voice louder than necessary.

Julianna smiled into his chest, hiding her red cheeks from everyone. "I have not lost *that* much."

He chuckled. "I know it. Ye need not lose face. And I get to hold ye close."

Ronan walked with quick, steady steps back to the makeshift camp and lifted her onto her horse, his hand lingered hotly on her leg. "I would much prefer ye ride with me," he said.

"Aye, but we'll be quicker if we ride separately."

Ronan frowned, and nodded. "True enough. But know this — I dinna intend to sleep alone tonight."

"And I intend to get no sleep at all," she teased back.

Ronan's grin widened and he winked. "A promise I will make sure ye uphold."

"Let us ride then."

'Twas well past nightfall when they arrived on the bridge to Eilean Donan. Ronan sent up a call to the guards to let them know it was no enemy that approached and the gates were swiftly opened.

Half the men returned with them, while Wallace led the other half in a chase for Ross.

They were greeted in the courtyard by nearly everyone, including the Bruce who looked worried over the lack of those returning, and stuttered Wallace's name, until Ronan explained what had happened. He then gave his future king a serious look and asked to speak with him in private.

"I will also attend your private meeting," Julianna stated. Her shoulders were squared, head held high.

"Julianna…" Robert warned, but Ronan shook his head.

"She may, if 'tis all right with ye, my lord." Ronan couldn't take his eyes off her. Despite the bits of dirt smudging her creamy skin, she was still a vision. And nothing had scared the piss out of him more than seeing her quiver at the end of Ross' sword, and then finding her missing.

"All right," Robert drawled, looking between the two.

The man must have started to put two and two together, because his face grew pinched, and if Julianna's earlier projections about her brother not wanting her to marry were true, they might be in for a bit disappointment.

Robert beckoned them into the castle and they followed him up the spiral stair to his chambers. A fire blazed in the hearth and several candles lit the room. Ronan's stomach twisted with hunger, but he ignored it.

"Wine?" Robert asked, holding a jug up.

"Aye, please." Julianna gripped a cup from his table and held it out while her brother poured.

Ronan nodded and lifted his own cup, watching as Robert poured the red liquid with steady hands.

"Sit. Drink. Tell me what this is about."

Ronan and Julianna both took seats while Robert stood, arms crossed and giving them a stare that might have cowed a lesser man. But Ronan was not a lesser man, and he knew what he wanted. Needed. Julianna. He loved her.

"I wish to offer for Julianna's hand in marriage." There, he'd said it.

Robert looked ready to throttle him, but at least no weapons had been drawn. However, Ronan wasn't entirely sure that he wouldn't be cast into the bowels of hell — the Bruce's glower was that staggering.

"I see. Julianna?"

I see? What the hell kind of response was that? Ronan tried not to frown, but couldn't help his jaw muscle flexing with irritation.

"I wish to marry him, brother. With all my heart. I've served ye many years. Since ye were a bairn even. Now I am seven and twenty. 'Tis well past the time I marry." She turned to Ronan and smiled, her eyes twinkling. "And I love him."

Robert let out a disgusted grunt and whined almost like a spoiled child, "Truly?"

"Aye, brother." Julianna turned her attention back to the Bruce, and her voice grew stern. "I've not asked ye for anything afore. I've only lived to serve ye. Give me this one thing."

Robert walked away from them, toward the window. He opened the shutter and gazed out at the cloudless night sky. Ronan could have counted to a thousand in the time it took for Robert to finally turn his attention back to them.

"Ye have my blessing," he said softly. "Though a third born son is well below your station."

Ouch. Ronan felt as though an arrow had slammed into his ego.

"Robert!" Julianna scolded. She gave Ronan's hand a squeeze and then stood, marched over to her brother as though she'd grip him by his ear and drag him outside to the stocks. "His station means naught to me."

The Bruce held up his hand, his face serious. "That is not the way I meant for it to come out. I only mean, that Ronan must be elevated. He has proven his worth to me. To this country. And if he means that much to ye, then I would see him given his rightful due."

Ronan too stood. "My lord..."

"Dinna try to change my mind. I've thought about it. Had been thinking about it afore now. In a few months' time, we will move closer to the Lowlands to prepare for the invasion promised us from the English come spring. When we leave, the castle will be without a laird. Ye, Ronan Sutherland, will be the new Laird of Eilean Donan, in fact all of Kintail. Ross has lost his privileges here, and I hope to see you keep this castle fortified against him."

"Aye, my lord. 'Twould be an honor. And thank ye. I love Julianna with all my heart."

"Good. Because if ye ever hurt her, I will make ye pay. Painfully."

Ronan blinked a few times trying to assess how to react, but the Bruce stepped forward and clapped him hard on the back three times.

"When should ye like to marry?" he asked.

"Now," Julianna and Ronan answered at the same time.

Robert's head fell back and he roared a laugh. "Well, I see ye are both not too eager," he said, his voice dripping sarcasm.

Julianna's face turned a ravishing shade of red, and Ronan felt a little heat creep into his own cheeks.

"Oh, come now. Finish your wine. I will call for the priest."

Less than an hour later, Julianna and Ronan were sequestered in her chamber, a table full of food, a jug full of wine and two hot, steamy bathtubs. Man and wife.

Neither of them was interested in food and drink. And neither of them was interested in the second bath. Indeed, as soon as the door closed, they stripped each other down and Ronan carried her to one tub, settling her on his lap. Lucky for them, the tub was the one Wallace had requested be built for the larger men and so they both fit perfectly.

Between sensual kisses and playful nips, they gently washed each other, careful of the other's injuries. But honestly, Julianna felt nothing but pleasure and elation. Ronan was hers! *Hers!*

Her thighs quivered as she moved to straddle him, feeling the hardness of his shaft press enticingly to the bundle of firing nerves. She gripped his length, stroking over it, loving his groans of pleasure and the way he moved his hips in tune with her hand. More than anything though, she wanted to taste him. To give him the pleasure he'd given her. Julianna moved to kneel between his knees.

"What are ye doing, lass?" he asked, twirling a lock of her hair around his finger.

"I want to taste ye. Ye said next time…"

Ronan's pupils dilated. "Aye, I did."

Gripping the edges of the tub, he stood, and lifted her with him, both of them dripping water. She was covered instantly in goose flesh, but not for long. Ronan placed her on her feet before the hearth and took a linen towel to her limbs, drying her off — while teasing her all over with his mouth.

Then she did the same to him, making sure to stroke and kiss his knees, thighs, stomach, chest and shoulders. He was a gloriously shaped man, making her feel boneless with his touch and light-headed with his good looks.

But even more, her heart soared with the things he said. His devotion, his love. Declarations of how beautiful she was and how much he cherished her.

Julianna knelt before Ronan, his shaft thick and hard, and so close to her mouth. She gripped the base and looked up at him, asking permission with her sultry gaze.

Ronan groaned and threaded his fingers through her hair. She took that as a yes, and bent forward, pressing her lips to the tip. His skin was hot, soft against her lips. Ronan's fingertips massaged gently on her scalp, enticing her to do more.

Julianna flicked her tongue out over the tip, remembering vividly all the moves he'd used on hers. She licked him up and down, all the while stroking with her fingers, and then she had an idea. To suck him. She opened her mouth and took him inside, all the way to the base.

The moan that came from Ronan's mouth rattled the rafters and shook Julianna to the core. Her own sex twitched and sparks spread fire throughout her limbs. She'd not expected that making love to Ronan with her mouth would make her so full of desire, need.

"Och, Julianna," he groaned. "Ye make me feel so good. What would I ever do without ye?"

"Mmm…" she moaned around his flesh, then pulled away, and smiled up at him. "Be a miserable warrior, cold in your bed?"

He laughed, then lifted her from the floor and carried her over his shoulder toward the bed. He slapped her playfully on her bare behind, then tossed her onto the coverlet.

Julianna fell to the soft mattress in a fit of giggles, but her laughter died as Ronan spread her thighs and crawled up her body like a man on a sensual mission. She gasped, bit her lip and trembled all over.

"I love ye," she whispered.

Ronan settled between her hips, his shaft on the edge of her center. "I love ye too," he declared as he thrust home.

Hearing those words said with such conviction as he merged their two bodies made Julianna's heart burst from her chest. Every time she thought she loved him to the moon, he did something else to make her love him more. Every glance, touch, whispered word.

She wrapped her arms around his neck, pulled his lips to hers and gave him all she had with her kiss. His thrusts we slow, deliberate, and he took turns with kissing her mouth and then her neck, breasts, hands. He made slow, sweet, love to her, not leaving a spot untouched, not an inch of her without tingling pleasure, curling her toes.

Making love with Ronan was magical. As though they'd transported Heaven to this very room. And they were married now. Could make love every night. Every morning. And no one could tell them not to.

As their bodies soared to new heights of pleasure, and then whispered words of love in each other's ears, the world around them faded. She was consumed with Ronan, with pleasure.

Ronan gradually increased his pace and she met him, tilting her hips with each thrust until they were both crying out their pleasure as climax devoured them.

Sated and smiling, they laid in each other's arms, gazing into one another's eyes, until their breaths and pounding hearts subsided.

Julianna stroked her hands over Ronan's stubbled cheeks and smiled, her heart full and light. He gripped her hand and kissed her palm, his breath tickling her skin.

"I love ye, warrior bride."

"The End"

If you enjoyed **THE HIGHLANDER'S WARRIOR BRIDE,** *please spread the word by leaving a review on the site where you purchased your copy, or a reader site such as Goodreads or Shelfari! I love to hear from readers too, so drop me a line at* authorelizaknight@gmail.com *OR visit me on Facebook:* https://www.facebook.com/elizaknightauthor. I'm also on Twitter: @ElizaKnight *Many thanks!*

AUTHOR'S NOTE

Robert the Bruce (de Brus) did not have an older sister named Julianna — or that we know of. She is a fictional character I made up for the purposes of this family saga. Robert did have many siblings, including an older sister named Christina.

Eilean Donan was not, that I know of, used as a camp for Robert the Bruce in 1297/98. He did seek shelter there several years later. For the purposes of this story and the castle's mystery and location, I thought it perfect. Additionally, Kinterloch and the issues with Laird Ross are a product of my imagination — although it is known that Ross stirred up a lot of trouble during this time period.

The saga continues! Look for more books in <u>The Stolen Bride Series</u> coming soon!

Book Five– *The Highlander's Triumph* – June 15, 2013

> *He was a warrior fighting for Scottish freedom.*
> *She was his enemy's mistress.*

Laird Brandon Sinclair has given his life to the Scottish cause. Swearing fealty to Robert the Bruce, he will stop at nothing to see oppression end.

Lady Mariana wants nothing more than to break free of the tyrannical hold the English king has on her. When he sends her to Scotland with a message for the rebels, instead of obeying his orders, she finds herself submitting to her desires. After one sizzling, life-altering night, Brandon and Mariana must part ways. But Mariana has no intention of betraying her heart again.

And Brandon is determined to get her back. Stealing Longshank's secrets felt like victory, but taking his woman will be this Highlander's ultimate triumph.

There are six books total in The Stolen Bride Series! If you haven't read the other books, they are available at most e-tailers. Check out my website, for information on future releases <u>www.elizaknight.com</u>.

ABOUT THE AUTHOR

Eliza Knight is the multi-published, award-winning, Amazon best-selling author of sizzling historical romance and erotic romance. While not reading, writing or researching for her latest book, she chases after her three children. In her spare time (if there is such a thing…) she likes daydreaming, wine-tasting, traveling, hiking, staring at the stars, watching movies, shopping and visiting with family and friends. She lives atop a small mountain, and enjoys cold winter nights when she can curl up in front of a roaring fire with her own knight in shining armor. Visit Eliza at www.elizaknight.com or her historical blog History Undressed: www.historyundressed.com

2354911R00157

Made in the USA
San Bernardino, CA
10 April 2013